Mabel Cox is a woman of a certain age who has always written privately whilst raising her three children; however, now they are all grown, she has dared to fulfil her dream to become a published author. When not writing, Mabel can be found walking on the fells in the Lake District or sharing a well-deserved glass with friends.

This book is dedicated firstly to my beautiful partner, who had faith in me when I felt it I lacked it. He also gave me the privilege of time. Also, to my three amazing children. I love you all.

Mabel Cox

FROM SIR

AUSTIN MACAULEY PUBLISHERS™

LONDON • CAMBRIDGE • NEW YORK • SHARJAH

A CIP catalogue record for this title is available from the British Library.

ISBN 9781528934763 (Paperback)
ISBN 9781528968003 (ePub e-book)

www.austinmacauley.com

First Published (2020)
Austin Macauley Publishers Ltd
25 Canada Square
Canary Wharf
London
E14 5LQ

Synopsis

From Sir is the story of an impulsive abduction that throws a confused young man and a middle-aged woman together. The book takes the form of a letter, written to justify and in the man's eyes, explain their three weeks together.

As each day he watches her, his initial anger and resentment towards her starts to change.

As each day she remains, locked in a room and alone, her apparent strength begins to slip away.

They share the same house, but on different floors. They share the same compulsions and eventually they begin to talk.

Set amidst their dialogue are the news reports concerning the missing woman. These provoke a response and he proceeds to use social media in an attempt to rationalise his actions. The fall-out from these postings only serves to create a hysteria which he feels unjustified and superficial. Where he feels misunderstood.

His arrogance is his shield, in contrast with her foul-mouthed rants. Their conversations develop, and disclosures are made. *From Sir* demonstrates the fragility of the human mind, the power or lack of maternal love, the destruction caused by domestic violence and the importance of trust.

This is it…the truth, the whole truth.
To display my integrity, my honesty.
By way of explanation.
The journey of damage reflected and understood.

Thursday, September 14
We Meet

It was a beautiful, sunny day. The last feelings of summer were in the air. People clinging onto that feeling, flip-flops and scarves, fading tans and holidays spent. I was angry. Pent up, an unresolved rage flowing through every part of my being. Any other day and I would not have noticed you. Any other day I would not have reacted to you. Any other day. I was driving. Distracted by my thoughts, I admit, but then you were there, in front of me. Instantly, on autopilot I slammed on the breaks and our eyes met for the first time. I was shaken and cross. You were in my way. I looked at you, small, insignificant, stupid woman. I should have just driven on by. Any other day, I would have, but then you started shouting, angry little bursts in a shrill voice that cut right through every rational part of me.

"Knob jockey, you didn't even indicate, you could have killed me, you twat."

Quite a mouth. An unnecessary outburst of abuse. You were motionless, frozen to the spot. I could see that you were shaking, red-faced, tears coming. I felt nothing apart from anger. You were in my way. I remember staring at you, a middle-aged woman, shopping bag falling from your shoulder, handbag across your chest and you were staring back. You had a look of contempt, like I was beneath you. In just that moment, we both moved. It all happened so quickly, no rational thought, no real thought at all, just reaction. As you hoisted your shopping bag up, I got out of the car and we were next to each other. I towered over you, I had not realised quite how small you were until then and I rather enjoyed the feeling it gave me. Empowerment, strength, superiority. I yelled straight into your face,

"Shut up, you silly bitch."

If only you had walked away quietly. If only you had been quiet, but no, not you.

"How dare you? You fucking piece of shit, I'm going to report you."

Then you were silent and still because I struck you. I do not panic as a rule, I do not need to. I am always in control and know exactly what I am doing, at any given time, day or even month. I have structure and rules which I live by. I am precise. This was not a situation I felt comfortable in. Not, may I add, because I hit you, but just the tedious inconvenience of it all. The messiness. I should have just left you in the gutter, but I did not. I think now I understand my actions. My confused need to fill the void. The anticipated and planned arrival of her in the room, the need for company. A moment of madness. I lifted you up and put you in the back of the car, slumped out across the leather seat. Untidy. There were no witnesses, no cameras on that quiet stretch of road, just the one junction that I had turned at. A few parked cars, a row of splendid Victorian houses and a cat. I drove with you, my roadkill. I continued to shout at you, oh, nothing that really counts for much. Just rants that you had complicated my day, my day that had been planned and was now behind schedule. My day that was supposed to be all mine, a day to adjust, to think, but not to over think. My day to reflect and mourn. Just one day for me.

As I drove through the gates and straight into the integral garage, the reality of your presence struck me. I was beyond angry now, resentment and bitterness consumed me. How dare you affect me? The gates and garage had all closed automatically and neatly. I sat for quite some time, my breathing was shallow and far too quick and unsettled me further. I am always in control and you were destroying my composure, everything in those moments became your fault. A red mist, they, whoever they are, say falls around people when they lose control, when their aggression takes over. Perhaps, indeed, this is what happened to me, because of you. However, the whys and wherefores had to wait, I could not be expected to sit in the car with you all day. Decisions needed to be made. I dragged your dead weight from the back of the car and took you into her room. Annoying as I had not intended to go in there on that day. My day. I dropped you onto the tiled floor. Your face had swollen, I could see exactly where I had landed my punch. I glanced out into the space surrounding you, all so perfect in readiness, all so beautiful and yet now so tainted. It was all just too unfair. My head spun. I do not think that I wanted to hurt you, I just needed to let everything come crashing out of me. Shouting at you, I kicked you repeatedly. As though the pain awoke your unconscious mind, you began to scream. The screaming was beyond my comprehension; hysterical, relentless screaming. You covered your head and screamed, rocking to and fro. I stopped and watched, you appeared unaware that I was even there, just continuing, rocking and screaming, rocking and screaming. This behaviour threw me, it was as close as I could picture to insanity. Not a drop of self-awareness or composure or control. I needed you to stop. I grabbed a knife from the block and started to jab at you, the first spots of blood appeared. I felt nothing. Your screams were relentless and so very loud, I grabbed at your outstretched arm and I cut you, a series of diagonal slashes and your blood flowed out. There was silence. You tried to stand, over-balancing at first then up again, gasping. We stood, briefly in silence, face to face, then the screaming came again. High-pitched, a wail of sound that pierced through the room. Suddenly and with no apparent realisation, you emptied your bladder. Blood and urine all over the newly tiled floor, it was disgusting. You were disgusting, pathetic. I struck you hard and you crumpled just like a puppet whose strings have been cut. Down. You lay there, in your own filth and blood. The room fell into silence, yet in my head the noise continued. I locked the door and walked away.

My Day

My day was finally allowed to continue. Obviously, I had to indulge in a second shower, washing you away. Fresh clothes, the morning's already being cleaned. The car valeted meticulously. Slightly annoying, as I had only recently paid for the executive maintenance service. However, I rather enjoyed the monotony of cleaning and having everything in its correct place. A sense of calm came over me and my thoughts were allowed to flow and to become more effective. Of course, on that day not quite everything was correct, or for that matter, in its place. You were in her room and she was not, but then, there was nothing typical about that day.

Several hours later and I assume curiosity got the better of me. I stared at you in her room. I did not venture back, instead I viewed you through the camera footage, as I sat at my desk upstairs. That was the first time I had used the new screen. All my home security is beautifully accessible through my Mac Pro, this is my world, powerful and professional. This, however, was independent from everything else. A hastily purchased basic piece of equipment. Quite fortunate really that I had installed the cameras after all. There were two and they were discreet, positioned to give full viewing, one in the kitchenette area and one almost above where you lay. Your jeans had absorbed quite a substantial amount of your mess. The diagonal slashes were not clear through the blood, which was coagulated and looked sticky. Your face was mostly hidden under your hair. I felt you to be a disgrace and I was annoyed that you were in there. At least you had had the decency to fall on a wipeable surface, I noted and not on the upholstery or the luxury bedding in the corner. I switched the monitor on to stand-by.

I worked well for the rest of the day. I thought through and adjusted. I e-mailed all necessary work contacts, conference calls and appointments arranged or re-arranged accordingly. Indeed, by early evening, sun just beginning to set and the autumnal chill closing in, I was back within my schedule and I felt happier than I had in months. I am not sure if this was simply due to the release of tension and anger that I had shared with you or was it the feeling of pure strength that was so energising? Whichever, I was feeling good. When I had cleaned the car, I had removed your shopping bag and placed it in the garage without thought. I decided to play a game with myself trying to guess, before looking, what sort of things you would buy. I returned to your purchases and discovered that it was all rather dull. Predictable; wine, wholemeal bread, salads, marmite, yogurts. Nothing important, nothing special. It was then and only then that it occurred to me that you might be important to someone, that they might phone you and where was your phone? It could be tracked and traced. How could I not have thought of this? I am logical, methodical, organised. I am a technical genius. A man of the digital age. You had thrown my natural order into this disorganised chaos. This was your fault. Bitch, I remember thinking, stupid bitch. I went back to my desk and turned on the monitor, your handbag was still across your chest. The frustration at my own lack of consideration was almost overwhelming. How could I have been so incompetent? So reckless? Why had I not just left you? However, this blatant oversight could not be ignored, not now. I had no option, you had left me with no option. I went downstairs and quietly unlocked the door. As I walked in, the stench of ammonia hit me. I had neglected to take into account the underfloor heating that had obviously kicked in to keep the chill at bay. I am not good with odours, I felt a repulsion and disgust for both the smell and the sight of you. As I stared at your handbag, I realised that I would have to actually touch you to remove it. I hastily relocked the door and went back upstairs to my kitchen and returned with gloves. I have many pairs for different jobs, I like the reassurance of a layer between myself and filth. These gloves were for rubbish removal as that seemed the most appropriate at the time. Your head was heavy as I lifted the strap over it. Your hair fell back and revealed your swollen face once again. I emptied the contents, undid the zips, but nothing of any importance. This was a surprise to me. I thought that, in this day and age, everyone carried a phone. Checking and re-checking all social media as though their very existence was measured by the latest trend or twitter feed, but apparently not you. Clearly, you really were nothing, I thought. I kicked your left hand away from your body, ha I smiled, not even a wedding ring. You really were nothing. Feeling a sense of reassurance, I left you again. Relocked the door, this time removing the key, hiding it in the console table drawer. I returned to the calm and sanctuary that is my home. I disposed of the gloves and poured myself a large gin and tonic. It was dark now, clear, a few stars could just be seen, and I felt a sense of peace. All the anger had gone. I suppose, bizarrely, that I thanked you. Maybe it is true I considered, sometimes we all need someone.

In the early hours I awoke, still in my favourite leather armchair, the empty glass just out of reach and I shuddered. Two immediate thoughts screaming in my head.

1. What if you were dead?
2. What if you were alive?

I controlled my breathing and thought each dilemma through. If you were dead, in some ways this was simple. I lived alone, I did not have guests or surprise visitors, I did not even have a cleaner. I employed one once but felt violated and no matter how many times I wrote down my specific requirements, they were not met to my satisfaction. Remote controls moved and not replaced with the correct precision I needed. Cutlery thrown back in drawers, not placed. Toilet rolls put with the tissue falling the wrong way. Oh, the list of annoying faults was too much, I terminated the contract. Therefore, if you were indeed dead, I reasoned that I would simply dispose of you. I would power wash you first, obviously and then bag you up and out you would go, just like the rubbish. If you were alive, this was different. You had seen my face, but would you remember? Would you be able to describe me? I stood and noticed my top was now crumped and distasteful to me. You could wait, after all you could not go anywhere. I changed and freshened up, crisp filtered water on my face, teeth brushed, perfect circular motions for each tooth, then to the kitchen. A double espresso was required, Lavazza Gold Selection, mellow and sweet and yet an intense after taste. I was shaking, this was not a caffeine hit, this was something new. An adrenaline rush, was this excitement? Was this living on the edge? This was intriguing, not even my first million had made me feel this way. That was, after all, always going to happen. This, however, was not in my life-plan. You were disrupting my life-plan. You were effecting change and change was not supposed to happen.

'Stay on the road. Keep clear of the moors. Beware the moon, lads' [1] and all that.

Friday, September 15
Reality

Twenty-four hours had passed since we first met and there we were. I upstairs, you below me in every sense. I knew that I needed to ascertain which state you were in, but I wanted this feeling to continue, to indulge in this new emotion. I was hovering in the anticipation of not knowing my next step. This was an original experience for me and although it was, somewhat, unsettling there was a certain charm. If I could just hold everything perfectly still for a little longer, pause time, enjoy.

I needed a distraction. I glanced around the large, living room. Everything was in perfect order. The large corner sofa with the cushions placed at perfect, equal angles looked inviting and comforting as always. Although I never sat there. My capri, leather, swivel armchair was where I sat. That was my space. The long, glass, coffee table stretched out across the middle of the oak flooring, coasters stacked at the corner. On the wall hung my OLED wall-paper TV, 65 inches, a perfect sheet of pixels. Calm, clean and correct. I clicked the remote and instantly the room was filled with the even sound, the crisp definition lighting up the space and there you were.

You. You were a headline. You were so real. Your face filled the screen. You were smiling, a generous easy smile that made you appear friendly and happy. Quite the contrast between the image and the face I had seen. Angry and swollen, foul-mouthed and pathetic. You looked quite attractive for a woman of your age, but then, I mused, the portrayal had to be made attractive, the public would be induced by that. Everybody wanted sugar-coated, air-brushed perfection. The public's sympathy and attention would be far more easily gained by a pretty face than by an ugly one. They would simply care more.

Words began to swirl through my room, invading my space. I was struggling to listen with the attention required, only catching snippets.

"… has officially been reported missing at 20.00 hours by her partner."

I felt a dizziness that engulfed me and yet somehow, I managed to regain my focus and stared back at the screen. The police spokeswoman continued,

"Her disappearance is completely out of character, she and her partner had arranged to meet friends that evening, a table had been booked at a favourite restaurant, with drinks to follow."

In other words, you had had plans. A contact number was shown for any information, no matter how seemingly trivial. Another reminder that this was not your typical behaviour and your name was repeated. Lillian Brown, known as Lilly, to your friends.

NO. No way. I froze the screen. I was angry. You were not a nice person. A partner? Had friends, likeable? No. I was not falling for this PR-induced, sympathy-yielding, rubbish. You were insignificant, unimportant, I reminded myself. I looked at the image of you, your smiling face was mocking me, and you were in my room, the wrong room. I switched the news off. I knew the truth and I had the power. I returned to my office, pacing ridiculously. Enough, enough. I poured a large gin and tonic. Thankfully, I was well stocked. The Original Gin Company delivered regularly, as were all my essentials and non-essentials come to that. Focused now, I switched the monitor on.

You had moved.

You were alive.

The enormity of the situation crashed around me, you were a missing woman, national news and you were downstairs. I can honestly say that I felt it would have been easier if you had been dead. I was passed angry, but I was not going to fall for this smiley, lovely Lilly image. You were a bitch in my mind. If only you had not provoked me, this was all your doing, all your fault, but the situation was that you were alive and very much a reality, downstairs, in her room, in my private world.

The Awakening

I had an intense need to know how you had reacted when you came too. Meticulously, I went frame to frame and then yes there it was. You had coughed and bought your hand up towards your face and opened your eyes. It appeared to take some time for you to focus, blinking repeatedly, then with a sudden jolt you sat up. Too quickly, you slumped backwards but just caught yourself and then screamed out. I assume you were suffering from concussion and disorientation. The scream a consequence of falling back onto your lacerated arm. A little more cautiously you sat back up, legs crossed. You pushed your hair back, out of your face and smoothed it back several times and then you looked at your arm. It was not fully clear to me if you could appreciate the precise diagonal lines. The subtle mood lighting was not quite sharp enough to allow for total definition and anyway the symmetry was hidden under the clotted blood. I wished I had switched the lamp on earlier. You touched your skin tentatively and winced. Then, as if coming around completely, you began to look across the room, to try to make sense of your surroundings I suppose. You were in the middle of the room and appeared smaller sat that way. You were facing the kitchenette and started to stand but fell again. I noticed your whole body was shaking, uncontrollable, involuntary spasms. You crawled over and pulled yourself up, holding onto the granite surface. You had left a trail behind you, dragging the mess, smudged across the java grey natural stone like an oversized slug. Dehydration and the human instinct to survive led you sensibly to turn on the tap, you had then washed your face over and over again and then went to drink but stopped abruptly. Were you thinking it unsafe? If so a surprising amount of clarity or stupidity, you turned and proceeded to open cupboards looking at everything. To your right you found the integral fridge and took out a bottle of Evian. You turned to face the room and then you drank and drank. I can only imagine you were hit with nausea or dizziness because you then slid down the front of the unit and sat with your back supported, legs pulled up and your head down. You were breathing heavily and slowly, almost measured but not quite, coiled up and shivering. A wreck. I tried to imagine what you were thinking. Were you able to think? Would you just give in? But no, your resilience was a surprise. You lifted your head up again and emptied the bottle and stared out into the space. Your eye movements slow and steady. Across the floor where you had been there was the super-king Benji bed I had chosen from Loaf. The vintage grey velvet off set against the pure white Egyptian cotton bedding. The cashmere throw placed at an exact angle across the end. The simple yet elegant bedside table next to it. Across from here against the far wall, the luxurious corner shaped Bancroft sofa, its defined silver studding looking the picture of sophistication. The floor lamp towering over and yet with its curve hanging at just the right angle, giving a warming glow when in use. Yes, Sweetpea and Willow had added an opulence but not ostentation. The studio, I felt, looked quite beautiful. There were obviously no windows as you were in the basement and there were no personal touches, I do not do nick-nacks or clutter and there was no TV, because she does not like TV, did not like TV.

"Television consumption distorts the brains activity. The higher brain regions shut down."

"Television is an addictive waste of time and reduces personal productivity."

"Television creates stagnant people with no art of conversation or social skills."

"Television creates a lack of interaction with others and becomes a false friend if allowed."

Oh yes, I could hear her voice, on and on, condescending and judgemental. I felt tense again. Angry. I love television, I love the escapism, the way I am willingly drawn in. I love the familiarity found watching and re-watching a favourite film. The repetition of each frame, beautifully predictable, comforting as it remains the same. The indulgence of voyeurism, the company.

Enough, enough. Eleven minutes had passed, and I was beginning to tire of you. Then suddenly as though your consciousness had abruptly returned, you ran to the door. Did you really expect it to be open? Foolish. With your left hand you tried the handle banging your palm against the panels, screaming. Your face appeared distorted,

"Help me, somebody help me, I'm in here. Help, help."

Repeatedly the same plea, as though if you kept going your very persistence would be rewarded. You began to kick the door, hard bursts, left then right, rattling the handle again and again.

"Let me out, let me out, help me."

I watched for a while, you displayed an amazing amount of strength, but I knew it to be of no consequence. The door was reinforced, the studio was sound proof and it is not as if I had any neighbours. Anyway, I was hungry. All these recent events had definitely played havoc with my appetite but now, reassuringly, it had returned with a vengeance. I left the office and ate a late lunch, just light, scrambled eggs and salmon, and went to collect my thoughts in my chair. It occurred to me my usual routine needed to be re-instated. I must not become so distracted that my standards would slip. I would tomorrow wake, run, shower, breakfast etc. as I always did. Clockwork and orderly, efficient and reassuring, organised. Me.

The News

The afternoon hours passed relatively quickly for me, distracted by my own thoughts, lost within my own head. I needed to feel my usual self, regain my levelheadedness. I felt that I was correct that the routine of my day should return tomorrow, and I took a comfort in this decision. I showered, shaved and trimmed. Moisturised and stared at my reflection. My skin looked smooth and bright, but my eyes were tired and a little red. My hair layered and floppy as though naturally falling at that angle and yet was obviously a precision cut. Teeth cleaned and whitened, tongue brushed. Ready. I dressed casually, appropriately, cords, a slim-fitting indigo shirt, moccasin slippers. I poured my usual tipple and positioned myself comfortably. The BBC 6 o'clock evening news. Obviously, you were not the leading headline and I waited patiently and then you were there. The same photo displayed. A press conference had been arranged. The police spokeswoman reminded the public that,

"This is highly unusual behaviour and that your disappearance is deeply concerning. Lilly, a dedicated mother of three has never gone missing before. There were no problems in your personal life, there were no tangible reasons for your disappearance. The police are now treating this disappearance as a possible abduction. Lillian, known as Lilly to all who know her is a petite woman, fifty years of age with light-coloured hair and brown eyes. There had been nothing unusual about that day. Lillian was just going about her usual routine."

Footage was shown from the supermarket CCTV, you could be seen paying for the goods I had found. You had chatted and smiled with the cashier and said goodbye as you left through the automatic doors.

"This was the last known and recorded sighting. If anyone has any information concerning Lillian's location, they should contact the police immediately."

Phone numbers appeared on the screen. A moment's silence followed and then the man to the right of the police spokeswoman looked in to the camera. He was introduced as your partner, he coughed and shuffled, interlocking his fingers.

"Please, Lilly, come home, we love you. If anyone has any information, anything please, please let the police know. Lilly would not just disappear."

He faltered then, your partner. I wondered, who had prepared this brief statement? Had he been instructed to use your name at least twice, trying to reach out, make you more familiar to the public?

"Has Lillian's phone been tracked and traced?" a journalist asked.

"Unfortunately, Lilly had left her phone at home on that Thursday morning. However, this did not give cause for suspicion and was not out of character for Lilly as she forgot her phone regularly."

Your partner began to cry, holding his hands together, knuckles tight and white.

"We all love you, Lilly."

And then the numbers to help with all enquiries were displayed once again and it was over.

I drained my glass and took stock. A mother of three, dedicated mother of three, dedicated? What did that mean? You had pushed three poor lives out? Did this make you more important than a childless woman? Was this supposed to make you special? Missed more? The CCTV footage displaying a friendly customer, how different to the stupid woman I had encountered. I could see your falseness. Your partner, paraded in front of the camera, real-life evidence that someone cared. He looked genuine, he looked kind, anxious though and desperate. I remember thinking how in that room and at homes up and down the country people would be looking at him. Analysis of his body language and his words. He was the prime suspect, even if it was not said, everyone thinks the same thing, it is always the partner. Why did they use a police spokeswoman? Was a female voice employed to create a false warmth? A gentle touch? Woman to women? To mothers? Quite fortunate for me, your disregard for your phone however. My one over-sight, my one moment of thoughtlessness and it did not matter. None of it mattered.

Except it did. You had invaded my day and now my life. Now my home and yes that mattered. I was now left in a situation that was inconvenient, overwhelming and annoying. I was frustrated that although I had complete control with regard as to your location, outside of this lay confusion. No clear-cut conclusions or solutions sprang to mind. This was not how I lived. This was not me. I planned, I thought things through. I behaved in a logical manner. I have the answer prepared before the question is even finished.

I ate, later than I would normally, a simple, pre-prepared stir fry and I tried to accept some disruption could be tolerated. Tomorrow order would be restored.

I was mentally exhausted. After loading the dishwasher and checking everything was correct, my chair left facing the window ready for the morning, surfaces wiped and dried, neat and tidy, I retired to bed.

Saturday, September 16
Explosion

I woke to the first light at 5.35 and had dressed for my run and was out by dawn. As I pounded on, I felt good, my feet were cushioned in my New Balance running shoes, my arms and shoulders relaxed. My breathing was steady. I fall into a hypnotic rhythm. I do not listen to music, I like the quiet, the freshness that this time of day gives me. I feel I am the first to inhale the new day's air, clean, unpolluted, unspoilt. The calm before another day unfolds. When I was a child, I would always relish the bright winter mornings when I knew snow had fallen overnight. I would rush out and make the first dents in the crisp white surface, perfect footprints, clean and precise, leaving my mark for others to follow.

I returned, showered and dressed and drank my morning espresso. I weighed out my 45g of organic muesli and ate, then with my clothes washing and the kitchen cleaned I sat in my chair. It was a beautiful day, the sun reaching in through the triple glazing on to my face and then suddenly, in my mind, your face was all that I could see. You were haunting me, except it was the official face, not the one that I had seen. Immediately you infuriated me and spoilt my mood. My breathing was erratic, the good work undone. I went back to the office and switched on the monitor. I could not see you. I went back to the last frame I had watched and sat down, what had you done? You had continued to hit and kick the door for quite a ridiculous amount of time before slumping down, sobbing, your eyes were red, your nose running, saliva, snot and tears merging. You were dirty and ugly. You appeared to sleep or pass out for some time, I am not sure which, it was of little consequence. When you stood up, you walked slowly across the room, got another Evian and drank. With no warning, you threw the empty bottle across the room and started to shout. The ferocity and the force were quite alarming.

"Who are you? Who the fuck are you? What do you fucking want?"

You were pacing around the island, round and round as you continued.

"You're a sick bastard, look what you have done to me."

You gestured to your arm and continued in your circle.

"You're a fucking monster, you're sick, sick I don't deserve this. I have done nothing wrong. You're a fucking fuckwit, twat."

Then you screamed, continuously, the same note, the same route, just screaming. Not quite the friendly Lilly now I thought. You threw the two Carnaby bar stools across the floor,

"You cannot keep me your fucking prisoner, arsehole, I'm not an animal. Just let me go, just let me go now."

You were hyper-ventilating and hysterical and I remember thinking how badly you must smell. A moment's pause was followed by more out-bursts,

"Fuck you, pervert, fuck you, fuck you…"

Your explosive rants and pointless march went on and on. I froze the frame, your angry and twisted face perfectly trapped and silenced. You little bitch, I thought, who did you think you were? Me, a monster? A pervert? I was shaken and shaking with rage, angry that this could be happening to me, in my home, because of you. Why had I not just left you for some passer-by to find? Allow them the displeasure. Yes, how I wished that someone, anyone else could deal with you. I did not want this enforced responsibility. I had only ever been responsible for myself. It felt as though you were everything that is evil, false, foul mouthed, ill-informed and quite frankly, a stupid little woman. The frozen image of you was clearly the real you. Your true colours, your total disregard for anything or anyone but yourself. Not your fault? Your claim that you had done nothing wrong? This was all your fault. This entire mess was your doing. I resented so intensely, the public perception, the happy mother, the loved partner. You had invaded my world and you were no longer invited. I would show them, oh yes, indeed I would show them all.

Exposed

I was focused, one might even say driven. Obviously, it needed to be clear, the truth exposed simply. I felt the public had a right to know, to see the truth. I felt it to be my duty. I found the image of you lying in the middle of the room, where I had first left you. I had to be careful not to display your surroundings, fortunately this was simplicity itself due to the location of your collapse. I used my Mac Pro to enlarge your pitiful new profile. It is rather brilliant for videos and design and this was my latest version, so this was my maiden use. No links existed. I ensured my IP address could not be located, Tor browser, virtual private networks etc. and then, in what felt like a total moment of euphoria and under the title,

'Looking for Lilly?'

You became an internet meme. You would spread through social media share channels, like a virus, within hours.

No more of this friendly, smiley, clean-cut Lilly images please, spare me. I was incredibly elated with my decision, I felt it to be completely justified and indeed the absolute correct course of action to take.

Synchronised

I was positively glowing as I returned to my viewing. After a considerable amount of time you had stopped pacing and fallen against the sliding double doors on the far wall. I watched you walk through. A beautifully slick mechanism I remember observing, enjoying the way the doors just hideaway into the walls, seamless and quiet. I could not see your face as there are no cameras in this section of the studio. I was a little disappointed, but these doors led into the dressing room, floor to ceiling slide robes, empty of course and a dressing table and finally to the wet room. I had no desire to witness her in either of these rooms. So, this is where you had been when I first returned to you, when I could not see you. I wondered what you had thought? Did you appreciate my continued design flare and high standards of décor? The marble wet room so clean and minimal, elegant quality. The Villeroy and Boch fittings are a delight, the wide rainfall showerhead so refreshing. The underfloor heating obviously continued through and the mood lighting reflects up and through the wall mounted shelving. The fluffy towels and the folded dressing gown from the White Company were neatly placed and a range of products that I had deemed suitable filled the upper shelf. I confess that I had been given a helping hand with these items. My knowledge of female products was a little lacking. However, a lovely lady happily sold me an array of creams, face masks, exfoliating lotions and cleansers from Clarins, Lancôme and Clinique. A manicure set, tweezers, everything one imagined, nothing forgotten. Yes, she had been most helpful. I remembered thinking that I had hoped she worked on commission.

Anyway, you were in that space for ninety-four minutes and when you came out I must admit that I was a little taken aback. You had showered, which could be considered as rude, to simply help oneself, but given the state of you I felt a relief, viewing your filth was rather difficult, the contrast only heightened by your luxurious surroundings. This, however, was not my issue. You were wearing the dressing gown. The gown selected for her and it looked ridiculous. It had been intended for a tall, elegant woman, on you, well, it looked as a child might be dressing up in an older sibling's clothes. You proceeded to make tea. I noticed the herbal teas were pushed to one side of the cupboard, English breakfast was your choice. You opened the fridge and after adding milk to the pretty china cup, you squatted down. The fridge opened and lit up before you. You began placing the contents on to the work surface above. I had only ordered basic items of food, an addition to my usual order from Sebastian and Co. all organic. Skimmed milk, fresh orange, a wholemeal loaf, pitta breads, cheeses, (a black-pepper brie and a vintage cheddar), some smoked ham, a couple of soups, (roast chicken with lemon and thyme, red lentil, apricot and chilli), olives, hummus, salted butter, eggs, peach, mango and natural yogurts, some salad leaves, vine tomatoes and strawberries. Apart from a couple of cereals in a cupboard, (an oat crunch and cornflakes) and some honey, this was it. The selection had only ever been intended for a few light lunches, afternoon snacks or simple suppers. You found the breadknife and cut two slices of the bread and smothered them with butter, chunky as it was still cold, and ate. You replaced everything, neatly in the same precise order, checking each item was sealed and it appeared, rudely reading each best-before date. You made more tea and then, slowly you rolled the gown's right sleeve up, each roll spilling forth tissue and revealing another diagonal gash. There were only four, I had thought there five, however, although clean now they were raw and re-opened from the shower. You filled the sink with warm water and twisted in some sea-salt and then you counted to ten before plunging your arm under the water. You were crying, but you were strangely quiet. You patted it dry and then proceeded to cut the cotton tea-towel lengthways and used this to form a tight bandage. I was surprised by your resilience. Once, I imagined, the pain had eased you looked around the room again. You picked up the Carnaby bar stools and gathered the contents of your handbag that I had thrown out. You placed this on the island and paused, as though suddenly exhausted. Your eyes were drawn to the beautiful bed and you slowly crept across the floor, curling your toes over the tiles, feeling the warmth, and climbed in. Almost immediately you slept. The next twelve hours you slept.

I was now watching your Saturday mid-morning. You had woken, startled and then clearly remembered where you were. After the bathroom, more tea and fresh orange you proceeded to relook through the contents of the fridge. You took a small bowl from the cupboard and a teaspoon and proceeded to count out seven spoonfuls of natural yogurt and then cut three strawberries into halves and placed them neatly around the edge. I was annoyed at this detail. You then cleaned every surface and loaded bits into the mini-dishwasher, only then stopping to sit at the island to eat. Careful, measured chewing and swallowing. After this you wrapped your bandaged arm in cling-film and disappeared for another sixty-seven minutes. This order, this calm was both unexpected and unsettling to me.

Once refreshed you made the bed, positioning the cashmere throw at its base and then you set about cleaning the floor. On your hands and knees, scrubbing your filth away in an oversized dressing gown, tea-towel for a bandage and a blue/black tinge to the side of your face. You looked pathetic yes and yet... No, enough, enough I repeated, enough.

The glossy, grey stone had been restored to its shimmering charm and after some cheddar and hummus with pitta bread, you curled up on the sofa and fell asleep again.

I had by this point become rather agitated by your behaviour. I was already partaking of my second large gin and some of the excitement, in regard to the forthcoming news potential felt slightly tainted. So much had happened in such a short space of time, none of it desired, none of it deserved. By the time you woke again, a further three hours, I had rushed through the frames, more trips through the doors, yet more tea, another slice of bread but with honey until finally it was Saturday evening for both of us. We were together in time scale if in no other way. Together. In my private world.

It was the autumn equinox, the time of year when night and day are exactly equal lengths. This, the beginning of autumn is usually my favourite time of year. The time when dark long nights draw in and it is socially acceptable to remain at home. Safe. Cosy. This was us on that night, alone and yet together in our separate worlds, with our separate thoughts, on our separate floors.

I left you. I freshened myself and enjoyed a rather pleasant chilli stew with brown rice. I cleared and ordered, I was ready.

The News

The ten o'clock news. I had decided to open a bottle of bubbly for the occasion, Albury Estate Classic Cuvee, 2013. I was excited.

"There has been a dramatic development in the case of the missing, middle-aged mother of three, Lillian Brown."

And there it was, my handiwork. The police spokeswoman was reading a statement,

"The shocking picture that has been posted is clearly incredibly distressing for Lilly's family and obviously very concerning. All lines of enquiries are being followed up, house to house enquiries have begun and a full investigation into her disappearance is under-way. At this present moment we have no real evidence to believe Lilly is dead, but obviously this new image is very worrying."

Again, the numbers for any information were shown. It was over.

I felt a little disappointed, the picture was, I thought on screen for such a short time, however, at least it had been aired. I had controlled your publicity shot and felt content.

Sunday, September 17
Creation

I had not watched you after the news, I had finished my bottle but, had not felt the elation I had predicted. I had slept, but not well. I continued with my morning's regime and found some focus for my thoughts. On returning from my run, showered and refreshed I reflected. The image of you was, I supposed, horrible but had I now, unwittingly made you a victim in the public's eyes? A helpless victim with whom they would connect? Whom they might care about? This, of course, had not been my intention in any way. I had wanted them to realise you were there, like that, because it was what you deserved. I went back to the office and proceeded to create a more effective image. Frozen in mid-scream, your features were harsh, angry, twisted. This was much more like it I thought, a clearer picture and so under the title,

"Heeeres Lilly!"

A gesture to the Shining, it was sent, and you were out there.

I felt a little more relaxed once this was done. My morning run had helped me to analyse my disappointment and had led me to these conclusions and now that it was done my day could continue. I had some work to do and briefly thought about her funeral, not that I had to arrange anything, oh no, all that had been organised by her naturally, just so, her way, even in death.

I became quite perturbed, a little flustered even and so decided to watch you. I had intended to do my usual catch up but when I switched the monitor on you drew me in. You were sat at the island with two bowls of water, salt and cotton pads. You had, I noted, cut the sleeve of the gown at the elbow and the homemade bandage had been removed. The four diagonal wounds were angry and red, raised with the thick scabs they had formed. You were counting slowly and breathing heavily, exhaling on each number spoken and then, after the number ten was said, you dabbed around each line in turn. New cotton pads used for all. Breathing, counting, dabbing. You were meticulous and focused and clearly in pain. I am a good person and I resented that you made me feel uncomfortable. The whole procedure took so long, eighteen minutes, I looked around the room. The bed was made, throw positioned, the surfaces clean. What was this? This acceptance, this subservient act? This was not you. This was all false, an illusion that would not fool me. I was angry, I would not accept that you could affect me, you had no right to even be there, you should not have been there, but you were. When you had finished your little ritual, you blew onto each line as though to cool your skin. You threw away the pads and tidied up, cleaning the island's surface with the antibacterial spray from under the sink and then you cried. Sobs that were guttural and loud, you were shaking as if so cold and you seemed small, so very small.

I switched you off. I felt unsteady and walked away, back to my seat, swivelled round and stared out to my unspoilt view. This always calmed me, the fells looming above helped to put my thoughts into perspective. It was raining, heavily and the wind was forcing the moisture across, driving it on. Even in these conditions it was still beautiful, powerful. I must have sat for at least an hour and then as though jolted back to reality I jumped up. I had almost forgotten that it was Sunday. I looked forward to my Sundays, my lunch out and you were not going to be allowed to distract me anymore. My routine would remain, quite rightly, the same. I did not invite change. I had a long-standing reservation for Sunday lunch at a local restaurant at two pm. I dressed. There was no dress code which I like, so a simple Paul Smith shirt, jacket and chinos, finished with jarman boots suitable for the weather conditions and I was ready. I can walk and have on many occasions, but not in the rain. Arriving damp and dishevelled is not my style or for that matter conducive to the enjoyment of dining. I paced in the hallway, aware that I was so close to your door and felt a little anxious, a flutter in my chest. This would be the first time I had left you, not of course that you were aware, not that you even understood the intrusion and disruption your presence was causing. Not that you even knew where you were or that I had been with you anyway.

On time, as always, I was alerted by text that the taxi was outside the gates, waiting. I left you.

The restaurant is situated in the middle of the village and sits next to it's more refined, Michelin starred sister. I have always preferred the more casual dining experience. Inside the thick stone walls, duck egg blue, and under the beamed ceiling I was shown to my usual table. I liked to sit in the window, I can watch both the outside and the inside and feel involved, connected. I am treated with a high level of respect and I enjoy this. I always engaged with the staff, discussing any menu changes, of which there are many, everything being seasonal and locally produced. I feel comfortable and somehow comforted. That Sunday I selected the smoked lamb blade, slow roasted carrot and potato bake, followed by vanilla cheesecake. All to my usual expectations but on that day, there was an undercurrent, a murmur buzzing in the atmosphere. You. I had not anticipated you would be quite so topical and yet I had been complicit in your media creation. As your last known sighting was just over an hour from the village, I suppose it was inevitable that the locals would be consumed and feel a connection. There almost seemed a sense of ownership to the headline. That somehow because it had happened so close they were involved. It was their story too. Before I had enjoyed even two mouthfuls of desert I overheard a snippet,

"Another post, quite shocking…she looks really bad…"

And you were displayed on a gentleman's iPhone for all the table to see. My large glass of Pinot Noir was drained, and I had not even realised. The audible horror that followed was most disagreeable. I placed my money and my usual generous tip carefully on the table and left. I was surprised that I had neglected to think logically, of course you would be talked about here. I, of course, had seen you so much you were neither a mystery nor exciting to me.

The rain had eased but I needed to walk regardless, the freshness of the cold damp air was invigorating and helpful.

On my arrival home, removing my boots quietly I paused just behind your door, I am not sure why. Then speedily ran upstairs, retreating to my space. I needed a shower, I felt unclean.

There are restorative benefits to a long shower, teeth brushed correctly, freshly laundered t-shirt chosen, skinny jeans and moccasins. Reassurance, order and relaxation were all required. I was not sleeping adequately, and my reflection showed this. My eyes were heavy and dull. I decided a gin and tonic or two, then straight to bed, well, once I had watched you both from the office and the evening's news report.

You were cleaning when you appeared on the screen. It seemed you had just eaten the lentil soup with bread, half a slice left on your side plate, saving it for later maybe. The sliding doors were open, and I could see your clothes laid out across the tiles and I realised you had washed them and I was, once again, surprised by your behaviour. You were clearly using the heated floor to dry them. It would seem strange to see you in anything other than her gown now I thought. How quickly I had become accustomed to you lost in that garment. You took a glass from the cupboard and looked at the bottles in the small built-in wine cooler. Quite a slender unit, only holding seven bottles. I had put in a couple of pinot grigio, three of prosecco frizzante, both from the Giol vineyards and a couple of Sancerre. It looks at its best when fully stocked. You selected a pinot, or did you? Perhaps you just took it with no thought, yes, I felt this much more likely, anyway you poured an exceptionally large glass and sat at the island. You were using your right hand so despite appearances I thought maybe it did not hurt quite as much as before. I watched what can only be described as an inhalation rather than a discerning sip and in moments it was gone. I appreciated that these were not exactly vintage bottles, no just everyday drinkers, but really, I thought. You poured a second and then took cigarettes from your bag. I had forgotten I had seen them whilst needlessly searching for your non-existent phone. Then you stood up and switched the extractor fan on and lit up directly underneath, glass in one hand cigarette in the other, carefully blowing the smoke up and away. You resembled a teenager trying to hide their newly found secret. I left you then, enjoying your moment, you appeared content in your five-star accommodation, a luxury that I could not share, I observed, with a slight degree of bitterness. Anyway, the time had come.

The News

I had decided to view a little earlier, partly due to my fatigue and partly my intrigue. I had also made the decision that I would only watch one report a day. I could not afford to allow this situation to dominate my every hour.

"There has been yet another shocking development in the case of the missing mother of three, Lillian Brown."

The police spokeswoman was back along with your partner.

"We now feel there is reasonable evidence to believe Lilly is alive and has been abducted by a person or persons unknown."

The new image of you was on full screen and your features, although ugly and crunched up, seemed now, watching from the comfort of my chair, to reflect distress and pain not the anger I had intended. I was a tad confused. Your partner made a direct appeal to camera, I imagined his words had again been carefully scripted,

"Please let Lilly come home. Please, we all love Lilly and Lilly loves us, please."

Lilly, your name repeated and repeated, I can only assume to personalise you, to humanise you. He was broken and maybe it was not scripted after all. It appeared exposed, raw emotion, genuine. Or I wondered, he could of course be a very good actor. I considered if he was still the prime suspect. Perhaps, by posting the new image of you I had changed that assumption. I had helped him, had I not? Provided an alibi. I felt quite certain he had been under surveillance as soon as he had reported your disappearance. I questioned how many other suspects they could possibly have? Did you have enemies? The police spokeswoman reiterated phone numbers etc. and thanked everyone. The reporter then underlined all the information and they showed your happy image in a surprising contrast to mine. A special debate would be broadcast the following evening to discuss the potential use and misuse of social media in this distressing case.

Aftermath

I moved away, topped up and revisited you. You were eating pitta with humus and staggering. Your now blackened face was less swollen and as you stood you appeared to be holding onto the island for support. You stumbled to the space underneath the extractor fan and lit up again and although clearly drunk, were precise with every exhale upwards. I noticed you had fashioned an ashtray using some tin foil and after running the tab end under the tap, you carefully discarded it. Then, as if only then, remembering that you were drinking, you poured what was the last of the bottle. For a few moments you were perfectly still, frozen, then suddenly you ran to the door, twisting the handle, banging the back. Composure lost.

"Help me, help me, help me, somebody, my name is Lilly, I'm locked in here, help me, somebody help me, let me out, I'm trapped, please."

Relentlessly and persistently banging and repeating yourself. Your voice was strong at first but then began to weaken, almost as though you recognised the futility of your own actions. The wasted energy. You swayed back across the room, back to your glass.

"Fuck you, fuck you whoever you are, you're a bell-end, fuck you."

That mouth. That foul mouth was most disturbing. You had another cigarette in your chosen fashion and drained your glass.

"Fuck you."

Your final protest before you cried. The oversized gown hung around you clumsily, you tightened the belt and wiped your face. You were drunk and dishevelled, distressed and done. You stepped around the island and climbed into the bed, pulling the throw up and over, coiled up in a foetal position and began to rock, you were whispering, but I could hear that you were counting. As the rocking slowed, your counting ceased, and you fell into a drinkers' sleep.

I sat and watched you sleep for a considerable time, I do not think I was unduly concerned, I was just trying to make some logic take shape, trying to formulate what I was going to do. How did I, supremely efficient, controlled, intelligent and ordered, how did I find myself in this predicament? Such confusion, my perfect world and this, my what? My secret, my secret world? I was totally alarmed at the disruption of you and yet I just sat and watched you sleep. I was not responsible for this situation, you were, I knew that, but now I was left with the consequences. I was left with the mess in all its untidy glory, the mess that would have to be cleaned up.

Eventually, I retired to my room, my resolution to sleep must be adhered to. Tomorrow, maybe tomorrow, with a fresh day and a healthier complexion, I would solve the dilemma. I hoped I would find the answer.

Monday, September 18
Order

Monday had arrived, I woke as usual at the first hints of the new week's light and went for my run. The first frost of the season was now audible, under my cushioned feet. I like the sound, light and crisp. The colours of autumn surrounding me, my breath was visible, hanging momentarily in the clean air. I ran well, strong and determined and alone with my thoughts. On my return I felt I had regained a sense of control. I showered and dressed. I looked better, brighter. I measured my muesli and ate slowly. Ready.

Monday morning had an order, a routine that I always looked forward too. Monday was flower day. I had a contract with the local florist for a fresh arrangement to be delivered at ten am. They were always extravagant. I was always ready, by the door with the last weeks, now tired display, a straight swap prepared for. On hearing the car, I move, pleasantries and arrangements are exchanged at the side-gate and the new display can then be positioned. That Monday I had pink roses, hydrangeas, white premium orchids, finished with branches and eucalyptus, all tied with a rhinestone wrap visible through the glass vase. I took my fragrant, visual delight and gently placed it in the centre of my dining table. The structure is reflected in the sleek clear glass of the table top, the frame is made from polished stainless-steel and it shimmered delightfully. The six dining chairs are of a classic Barcelona style, padded velvet grey with buttoned detailing to the backs and steel frames. Hanging majestically above is the quartz chandelier, glistening cut crystals orbiting their steel frame. Opposite the wall of glass, reflecting my view, are three Eichholtz Dior mirrors, art deco inspired, creating the illusion of depth and space. I truly love this room, the way the sun falls through and at different moment's highlights and shadows and shades. It is the perfect room for a dinner party, if ever I had entertained.

So on with the order of the day. I had now decided that I would not concern myself with you long term until Thursday had passed. I had felt a pressure leave me, once this was established in my mind and felt content that this was a sensible course of action. I would have to travel Wednesday evening, no point in leaving anything to chance, one really could not risk the very idea of arriving late. However, this left me with the issue of food for you. I always did my weekly grocery shop on a Monday but now I had the inconvenience of picking extras. Last week that had been fun, but not so now. I did toy with the notion of just not bothering but starvation felt somehow unacceptable and I imagined unsightly. The simple stocks I had provided were running low already. I re-ordered those and added some meals too. They would all arrive tomorrow. My only problem now was how did I get these provisions into the room? Honestly you really were creating dilemma after dilemma. Predicament after predicament.

I had a late lunch, warm chicken and avocado salad, some crusty sourdough bread and a treat. Two dark chocolate and sea-salt cookies, rather good with a peppermint tea.

After all my daily chores were completed I went to see you. I had now decided not to waste my time back tracking your every move and just to see you as and when, live so to speak. You could not be allowed to take all my time as well as most of my thoughts. You had obviously showered and were dressed in your original clothes, a blue, loose fitting jumper, right sleeve rolled up and buttoned at the back, belted jeans and blue Toms slip on shoes. Not stylish but I imagined comfortable and I thought, fine for shopping. Your frame was more obvious in your own clothes and yet, in some way you appeared stronger, rather than lost underneath her gown. You had cleared away from the night before and I noticed the empty wine bottle and milk cartons were washed and placed in a row by the sink. What I thought were you thinking? Were you recycling? I am not sure why this amused me so, but it did. You were in full flow of your arm washing ritual. The lines were dark and strong, but a little less red. On completion you sat quite still just staring and then proceeded to open all the cupboards again, after these were all studied, you moved to the bedside table. In the top drawer I had placed writing paper, a notebook, a parker pen and a Town and Country magazine. Tissues in the second and the third remained empty. You seemed pleased with your finds and made a black tea, all the milk now gone. You curled up on the sofa and proceeded to read from cover to cover the pointless lifestyle guide. I grew impatient and left you. Sustenance was needed, and I wanted everything out of the way in anticipation of the debate. This hurriedly thought up piece of television was scheduled for seven pm.

The Debate

From the start it was made clear that this programme was inspired by your case, or rather by myself, but not about you, as in no way did the producers want to interfere or undermine the on-going police investigation.

However, almost immediately the reporter was asking how could the social media platform, intended for sharing ideas, information and points of view, be allowed to fulfil the impersonal and barbaric behaviour we were all witnessing? Were we all not guilty of feeding this or these monsters? Every time we logged in or shared were we guilty? No platform should be given for the instant gratification of a psychopath. (Indeed, had we all moved beyond the original concepts of communities being connected? The very world? People supported, an inclusive resource?) A place for discussion, interaction and information, forums and networks, education, where distance is no barrier? Indeed, had social media created an emotionless emptiness within our society? Where the only validation now regarded is measured in views or likes or follower numbers. Had, as this distressing case proved, we lost a sense of morality? Of empathy? Exploitation of images so cruelly posted had to raise questions. Were we as a nation following because we cared and supported Lilly or were we complicit? Encouraging even the displays of what must be narcissistic behaviour?

I switched off. This was an unfair portrayal. I have emotions, I am a balanced member of society. I am a good person. You were living within a beautiful room, warm, hot water, food. For goodness' sake, I had just re-ordered. Yes, I appreciated I had been responsible for the diagonals, but that was just a moment.

'We all go a little mad sometimes.' [2]

Fired up, heart pounding I had poured a large gin with very little tonic and tried to think, to focus. How could I change this perception? I sat in my chair and then decided I would post another image, not angry or distressed, but calm and peaceful. I searched through the time line to when you were sleeping and although your bruising was visible, you were clean, you were resting. I wanted to show the completeness, the bed, to demonstrate the luxury, but this would have been foolish, traceability etc., so I created a background of fluffy clouds and sheep, because you loved counting, and under the title,

"Lilly sleeps peacefully."

My work was done.

The News

The news at ten o'clock. You had crept up the story ranks a little I noted.

"The case of the missing woman Lillian Brown has taken yet another disturbing twist today. It would appear that following the broadcast of The Debate into social media, shown earlier on this evening, on this channel, a new picture was put on-line. It appeared to show Lilly sleeping. The police have issued a statement asking members of the public to acknowledge that this was not a game and to refrain from sharing these posts as the investigations continue, fearing this could escalate an already fast-moving incident."

Adding that,

"This is obviously, increasingly distressing for Lilly's family and friends."

All phone numbers displayed as usual.

No comment was actually made of how peaceful you looked or for that matter my attention to detail. Before I went to bed I had checked on-line and you were trending,

#supportingLilly.

No, of course this was not a game, a game has a winner.

Tuesday, September 19
Plans

I had woken several times in the night, yet again annoyed with you. I appreciate that I had other, un-related matters on my mind and that the wind and rain had whipped up, the result of the tail end of a hurricane passing across the country, but ultimately, I felt that you were to blame. As I ran against the forces of nature, I tried to analyse my restlessness. This had been the longest period of time that I had not watched you, was that an issue? Why were you important? How had you managed to entangle me into this unwanted and unfamiliar set of emotions? I was exhausted, both physically and mentally on my return and after my usual mornings ablutions, espresso and breakfast I began to make plans. I was a man with plans to make. The food delivery had arrived, and I placed all in my fridge, dividing the order, yours and mine on separate shelves. How, though was I to deliver yours? I went to my office and switched on the monitor. You were behind the closed sliding doors, I skipped back and then watched, on waking, back in the gown, you had made black tea and eaten what appeared to be the last of the yogurt. You had made the bed neatly and wiped all the surfaces, the granite tops glistened beautifully. I noted another bottle of wine was now lined up, so you had obviously been drinking last night and then you went through the doors, closing them behind you. I timed you, forty-nine minutes until you emerged, now showered, dressed in your clothes. So, I decided that this would be my window of opportunity the following morning. I would wait until you were hidden behind the closed doors and then I would leave your order just inside the room. I would be ready, a cool box could be prepared first thing, simple. Good, I was quite certain that you had just enough provisions and there really was no other logical solution anyway. You would just have to wait. I continued to watch you then, feeling a little calmer, you set about your arm cleaning routine, just as before. The redness was definitely less visible as indeed was any swelling to your face. In fact, the blackness was mutating to green and yellows, almost like an artist's paint palette. Once this task was completed you looked around, as though with purpose, doing laps of the room, counting every step. I found your behaviour to be most peculiar. Then you reversed and continued anti-clockwise, round and round and round. I left you.

I made phone calls with regards to the next day's arrangements. I had obviously received the offer of a driver but had insisted that I would drive myself. No reliance on others was always the best way and the desired reassurance that I would determine my own exit. I would stay at her house, my house, my other family would be arriving too. Reservations had been made for dinner at a hotel that evening. A dinner that I was not looking forward too, the echoes of sympathies, tears and false memories. The pitiful glances punctuating each course. However, I would leave when I chose, I had the right, who could possibly question my actions? I also double checked the funeral arrangements, but predictably, nothing had been forgotten, she had naturally taken care of every detail. I wondered when and for how long these orders had been on stand-by? Had she rewritten her script, depending on her mood, just in case?

I collected all my belongings that were required and packed my overnight bag. I checked my Chester Barrie suit, (a classic charcoal flannel, two button, single breasted), with white basket weave shirt. Black tie, black leather Derby shoes. Simple accessories of onyx inlayed domed cufflinks, a silk pocket square and leather belt. All correct. All prepared. All ready.

I had been so taken with all my planning and thinking that I realised, quite shockingly, I had completely missed lunch so decided to have an early dinner. A light pork stir-fry, nothing too heavy, I really did not think this would sit well. Once satisfied and all tasks accomplished, I returned to you, I had the time then. You were cleaning the bar stools, slowly wiping and shining the smoked Perspex to a glossy sheen. When completed you stood back to admire your handy work. I remembered back to when I had first placed them there and noticed how easily they had marked, each finger or thumb print displayed. They were beautiful, sculptures really, not practical though. Anyway, you then moved across to the sofa and began to write, I could not see the exact words, but the layout suggested you were writing a letter! Did you somehow imagine this would be posted? I had no rational explanation yet again for your behaviour. After what felt like an age you went back to the fridge, you plated up olives and cheese and toasted the pitta bread. You then cut up some of the now tired looking strawberries and placed them in a flute and opened a bottle of the prosecco frizzante, not too badly I was surprised to note, and poured over the fruit. Quite content, nice and settled. What a complete selfish bitch I mused. No obvious thoughts of anything or for anyone else. You sat and ate, well, nibbled truth be told, drank and nibbled. In my mind you appeared not to have a care in the world. You gave the appearance of someone rather enjoying their private suite, all your needs catered for. My resentment was definitely growing, you were safe in her room, you knew nothing of the concern and confusion you were creating. I suppose in all honesty, I was envious, the prospect of escapism was not really a reality for me. You really did not appreciate how lucky you were.

I left you. I sat with my gin and swivelled in my world.

The News

That night the news report concerning you had a new edge. The police spokeswoman, now becoming a familiar face, stated that,

"The growing social media interest and speculation concerning Lillian Brown's disappearance is not helpful to the on-going investigation. House to house enquiries were proceeding in all surrounding areas of Lilly's last known sighting. However, at this present time there were no new leads and no arrests had been made."

"Do the police believe 'Lilly sleeps peacefully' means Lilly is dead?" a BBC journalist asked.

"At this moment in time we do not have any evidence to suggest that to be true and we are very much treating Lilly's disappearance as an abduction case. We are continuing to follow up all possible lines of enquiry and furthermore ask the public, once again, for any information they might have to come forward. We would like to remind everyone that Lilly has never gone missing from home before and that her partner and three children are desperate for any news that could lead to her whereabouts. This case will not be conducted by or led by social media, but by good detective work."

The usual phone numbers. Your original picture.

As I had my nightcap, I was angered and frustrated. My thoughtfulness had been twisted, my point lost to fools. This over-thinking, sanctimonious analysis. I a good man, was the one in distress. I was in an undeserved and unwanted position. I was hurting. You, you were very much alive and blissfully oblivious to the turmoil, ignorant to the trauma you had created. I felt exhausted, exasperated and drained. There were far more important issues for me to contend with and to process. I wanted peace, I needed silence from the outside and from within. I resented everyone, but right then I especially resented you.

Wednesday, September 20
Room Service and Goodbye

I hardly slept that night, anxious about the next two days and anxious that I could miss the moment for delivery. I sacrificed my usual morning run constantly checking and re-checking the monitor. I ate toast to enable myself to be free, to be mobile in and out of the office. Nothing was normal. I had packed the car, suit hung carefully in its protective case. I had packed your things in the cool box and as and when it occurred to me, I had added extras in a basket, toilet rolls, tissues, tea towels, English breakfast tea, fresh towels. What had I become? Your servant? I should only have been thinking about myself and yet there I was, forced in to this absurd roll, thinking about you and your possible needs. You were like some sort of resented pet and I your bitter owner.

I wiped all the surfaces, refreshed the water for the flowers. I was on stand-by, agitated and you just slept. I could see you were wearing her gown as nightwear again, its clumsily cut sleeve was grubby at the frayed edge and quite why I was so disturbed by this I do not know. I added a simple shirt to the basket, just a plain, blue oxford shirt and I waited. I do not enjoy being kept waiting by anyone, indeed I do not usually wait, I do not normally have too. I had calculated my journey time, a second route established just in case, I had a schedule.

Finally, you began to stir, you looked older, your eyes were red, and your skin crumpled, hair in clumps. You drank the last of the orange and made tea. Your face, with its green and yellow shades gave an appearance of jaundice, your arm had smears of dried blood across it, blurring the lines. I assumed you must have caught one of the raised scabs in your sleep. As you sat at the island I watched you stroke your arm and you cried in to the blackness of the china cup. Eventually, after making the bed neatly, throw now folded and placed on the sofa, I noted, you went through the sliding doors and silently they shut behind you.

I rechecked my appearance, smart but casual, comfortable for driving. Fitted white t-shirt, blazer, dark chinos and suede loafers. I do not like to feel too warm or restricted whilst travelling. I glanced over everywhere, all was ordered and correct, I carried the cool box and basket downstairs. I retrieved the key from the stainless steel framed console table, (keys do look so messy just hanging), and swiftly unlocked and opened your door. I placed the goods just inside, briefly looking up and glancing around. I could just hear the shower gently in the background, the room smelt a little bit musty, a slight tinge of cigarette smoke hung in the air but with a hint of something else, lemon perhaps? The antibacterial spray? I closed the door, locked it and put the key safely back in the drawer, gently stroking the glass top, no dust, good. My heart was racing, and I felt clammy, uncomfortable. I went back upstairs, deodorant, fresh cold filtered water splashed on my face. I was shaking. I returned to the monitor and switched on the screen. No, you had not returned to my view, I was torn, part of me wanting to stay, perhaps I wanted to see your reaction? Perhaps to just delay the journey I did not want to take? The other part of me wanted to simply run, to escape. I shut the screen down and took a couple of bottles of mountain valley from the fridge, my mouth was dry. I drank, the sweet flavours rejuvenating. Enough, enough, I could not afford you any more of my time or my thoughts. It was time to say goodbye.

As I passed your door I again paused, touching the wood briefly, this hesitation was fleeting and yet so very vivid. I walked down the hallway and through the door to my car. Out the garage, the doors closing and locking behind me, through the gates, closing and locking behind me. I did not look back. I could only move forwards now.

The Eve of Her Day

The drive was pleasantly uneventful, five and a half hours of time just for me. Finally, a few glorious hours just for me, space where I was allowed time to think. Finally. I did not have the radio on just in case you were mentioned, but in truth, I relished the silence, it created a pure opportunity to let my thoughts flow.

As I approached, the crunch of gravel under the tyres announced my arrival to the now empty house. I felt a little apprehensive, the house, a classic late Victorian, with its commanding elevated position forced me to look up. It is a beautiful property set in formal gardens leading to indigenous woodland. The views and space had always been a draw to me. I entered and walked through to the kitchen, the housekeeper had already been and there was a thoughtful note, bedrooms had been prepared and rooms aired. A fire had been lit in the main room and basic provisions freshly bought. Condolences and sympathies given. I cut a slice of the bloomer loaf and found some cheddar, the kitchen instantly filled with the smell of melting cheese. I strolled through to the main reception room. I suppose one could describe the house as retaining period charm, I would say tired and dated. The charming frame of the window seat is smothered by the dust-absorbing heavy chintz curtains. The clutter of her on the mantel piece and on every surface. The sofas placed opposite one another, their faded florals, tasselled velvet cushions littering the tops. Fabric lampshades, more tassels, lace coasters, more chintz, the rug across the hearth lying on top of the carpeted floor, which although vacuumed and on the surface clean, must be clinging to years of dirt locked up into the very fibres. I felt lightheaded and unable to breathe. I went out to the terrace, the sun was low, the fresh air enjoyable. I sat at the top of the stone steps, knees pulled up close and stared out towards the trees. For the first time in weeks I sat with no agenda rolling through my mind. I faded out from everything but the view, my shoulders relaxed, tensions gone.

I had only moved on hearing a car arriving, my aunt and uncle on my fathers' side and an old family friend, who was also my godfather. We are a tiny family unit, she had no living relatives, an only child from an only child, as am I, my father long gone now. My uncle is a gentleman very much of his generation, very much as my father had been. They had been close, my aunt, who although is not a mother is naturally maternal. A warmth, an instinct to know when a smile or a gentle touch is required. My godfather, a jovial storyteller, would make everyone laugh and feel included and yet had the ability to never really give anything away, a very private man, a confirmed bachelor. Hellos, hugs and handshakes were all exchanged.

When I was younger, I would see them quite regularly and these were good times, but after my father's passing, life changed. I grew up moved away, we all moved in different directions. We gathered back in the main living room, the air a little chilly for my aunt. We sat and talked, superficial comment but kind and then changed for dinner. Perhaps it was good that I was not alone here tonight I thought. I did not really want to reflect, to remember certain situations or conversations in their exact locations.

The evening went pretty much as I had predicted. Her closest friends had already gathered and were staying at the hotel and were to join us for dinner. There was, of course, much talk of shock at the news of her death…Taken too soon… So terribly missed. My tired looks and dull red eyes were accepted, to be expected, my distracted mind, completely understood. Offers of,

"If there is anything we can do?" and, "We are only ever a call away."

Patronising platitudes with every mouthful. I, however, understood, I knew my role in these situations. I smiled and nodded and thanked them for their thoughts and words. Small talk had taken over by the time the cheese and port were served.

"Terrible business about that woman going missing, close to your neck of the woods, hey?"

"Yes, yes I had heard."

"Absolutely awful, so shocking."

Murmurs of agreement echoed around the table.

"Bet she is dead by now though, sad, tragic."

"What do you think?"

"Well, well I, I, I."

My childhood stutter returning. I had coughed and drank my port down, pouring another immediately. It was only a cheap Taylors First Estate.

"I would not like to say, I, I."

My aunt interrupted, gently touching my arm.

"Now, now, come on everyone, let's not be thoughtless, it is a silly subject to raise, this is really not the time or the place for such things."

We left shortly afterwards, back to the house. My godfather took charge and made our drinks. There was a slight atmosphere, a quiet conspiracy. Clearly her friends were hers alone, but this was not spoken out loud. I made my apologies after an hour or so and went, via the snooker room and the bar, a bottle of non-descript gin collected, to my room. The high ceiling and large windows helped with the stuffiness and dark décor. Heavy mahogany bedroom furniture, the olive-green armchairs, the green and brown patterns of the Axminster. I poured a glass and smiled. Silly subject. Yes, I had thought, silly subject indeed. You even being mentioned, had startled me but it had not mattered. I sat and pondered, I tried to guess how you had reacted that morning. I wanted to see you, but I did not feel connecting my internal cameras to my phone a sensible idea. No, you could and would wait.

There was a gentle knock, I opened the door, my aunt,

"Just checking you are alright, well, as all right as could be expected."

She held my hand as she spoke, soft skin and kind eyes. She smiled. I held her, this was, I knew, genuine. I allowed myself to cry and to be comforted. To temporarily be lost in this warmth and contact. As we said goodnight again, I felt calm. Sleep, please. I hoped very much that I would be allowed to sleep.

Thursday, September 21
Funeral

Indeed, I had slept, unbroken and even after a less than invigorating shower, felt better than I had all week. I dressed and went down to the others and together we ate breakfast, pain au chocolat and croissants, fresh orange, a total sugar rush. Sugar to ease the shock, and all washed down with a tasteless instant coffee. I re-brushed my teeth and tongue, my mouth so dry, not just the result of too much gin. My aunt fussed a little, straightening ties, brushing jackets, all quite unnecessary and yet I did not find her actions intrusive just rather endearing. The cars arrived and as we stepped out I appreciated the appropriate weather, grey and cold with a bitter wind. We were seated with no option but to follow her. The coffin was covered in chrysanthemums and pink carnations and there, at the back, staring at me, were dark crimson roses spelling out the word MOTHER. She had out done herself. I, of course, had not arranged or ordered this. I turned away, staring at the people going about their little lives, longing to be anyone of them. Their heads were turned quickly, were they frightened that death was contagious? Were they embarrassed that they were watching another's private moment? Finally, after our long-routed parade, we arrived at the church. Just before we entered my godfather paused,

"Tis but just one day."

Caught off guard I offered no reply, I simply thought yes, but the longest of days.

We were handed the order of service and took our designated places, I read it through,

Hymn There is a green hill far away.
Reading from Isaiah 61. 1-3 (ESV)
Psalm 23 To be read by my uncle.
Eulogy The vicar.
Reading from Matthew 25. 31-46 (ESV)
Psalm 116 To be read by her closest friend.
Hymn Abide with me.
Closing poem God's Garden. *Anon.* To be read by me.
As the service began,

"Blessed are those who mourn for they will be comforted..."

I felt a tidal wave of hatred, it engulfed me, I was shaking uncontrollably, my head dizzy, my vision blurred. I was screaming internally and yet so loudly I felt sure others would hear. Oh, this was her at her very best, every detail dictated. As the acid rose in my throat I had looked up, on either side of her were displays of pink and purple gladioli, their fan sprays at least one metre tall, flamboyant and vulgar and there, a step down, were two even larger displays full of stargazer and Easter Lilies. I felt violated, you had even infiltrated this moment. Lilies are, I know, the most commonly used flowers for such occasions and perhaps, had I thought before, I would not have been so taken aback, but I had not thought through the details. I had had no part in them. Through-out the first hymn I could only stare, the stench of the lilies was unpalatable, choking my already dry throat. I heard little of the first reading,

"To comfort all who mourn…the oil of gladness…"

Oh, like she cared, no this was her vile, arrogant imagining that we needed comfort or that she could even provide it, a saintly gesture to help us. My uncle read the much known and predictable Psalm. He read, I noticed boldly and yet quickly. His tone was flat and completely free of intonation. I desperately tried to find something to concentrate on, to draw me away from it all, a distraction. I needed to regain my self-composure. I was fidgeting like a small child entwining my fingers and crunching up the paper within. I allowed it to fall, I did not care, I did not intend to take a keepsake. The vicar stood,

"We often say that the hour of death cannot be forecast, we imagine the hour to be in the future, but we now face together the truth and have our memories…"

Oh, memories, how I only wished I had none. My thoughts were erratic, the words rushing around me, mocking in their tone,

"Amazing dedication to her charities…a pillar of the community…"

I felt violently sick, the words continued, rebounding from the cold stone walls. Was appearing to be good really all that mattered? A superficial shallowness enough? Her staged and very well documented acts to be celebrated? The second reading, the final judgement. Well, of course I thought.

"Eternal punishment but the righteous into eternal life…"

She could not have spoken any more loudly if she had been stood in the pulpit herself. Oh, so righteous, the gladioli, their fans around her, the roses, spelling out that word, and you, the pure white reminder all appeared merged, as one against me. She was mocking me, and trapped, in that restricted space, I felt you were standing right by her side. I heard little of the next reading, thanksgiving for deliverance, it was so long, too long,

"I will pay my vows to the Lord, now in the presence of all His people…"

Her friend was crying, her voice kept cracking. Head to toe in blacks, apart from a single rose pinned to her jacket. As the final hymn sounded my frustrations were fierce, I wanted to tear each petal from that word staring into me, in front of me, I wanted to rip each Lily from its stem into pieces, to shred them to pieces, to destroy her stage. I did not sing, I had taken my aunts' order of service and was reading through the words she had chosen for me.

God looked around His garden
And found an empty place,
He then looked down upon the earth
And saw your tired face.
He put his arm around you
And lifted you to rest.
God's garden must be beautiful
He always takes the best.
He knew you were suffering

He knew you were in pain,
He knew that you would never
Get well on earth again.
He saw the road was getting rough
And the hills were hard to climb
So, He closed your weary eyelids
And whispered, "Peace be thine."
It broke our hearts to lose you
But you didn't go alone
For part of us went with you
The day God called you home.

Even in death she thought she could control my voice. Revulsion and anger ran through my every vein. I could not pretend, I would not pretend any longer, playing to her audience. She would no longer put words in my mouth, she would not speak for me or over me. I had wanted to speak to her, that had been my intention, that day, my plan, but she had even denied me that.

I stood, but faltered, all eyes were on me. I should have screamed. I should have found my voice and yet I merely shook my head. There was a silence, then a hushed whisper of sympathy, my defiance was completely mis-understood, and the vicar read her poem.

We left, the final step to take, the crematorium. I did not speak. My godfather shared his hipflask with me in the car, a velvet, warming whiskey, not usually my drink of choice, but in that moment, perfect. We did not speak, there were no words. The mourners' prayer was read, another request for His help to comfort us and then at the point of committal Andrea Bocelli and Sarah Brightman broke the silence with a Time to Say Goodbye. Slightly jollied up by the influence of whiskey I smiled, even I could not have predicted that song choice. The excruciatingly slow speed of the curtains closing, eking out every second. The pure self-indulgence of it all and then at vanishing point I almost expected a reverse prepared, an encore, but mercifully no, not even she had ordered that. Her final curtain. Bravo, bravo, I stood and clapped to mark the end of her show. As if fearing they would not look correct or quite mournful enough, her friends joined in. My aunt and uncle led me outside, my godfather already positioned in the car.

The hotel that we had eaten at the previous evening was the venue for the gathering. A light buffet, finger foods, mini sandwiches, (egg and watercress, chicken, smoked salmon, ham and mustard, cheese and pickle and prawn). Crudities and dips, (sour cream and chive, mayonnaise, spicy tomato), mini quiches, sausage rolls and pork pies. A cheese selection, (brie, stilton, cheddar, edam), crackers and grapes. A selection of cakes to follow, (Victoria sponge, chocolate gateaux, fruit cake and a coffee and walnut). Traditional and expected funeral fayre.

Once all were gathered my godfather thanked everyone for coming on behalf of us, the family, and invited them to eat. The woman who had read came over and said, in far too loud a voice,

"Everything had been so beautiful, so terribly fitting a tribute, so worthy...How thoughtful that all her friends had been sent a yellow rose to wear."

I glanced around and shining out from all the blackness, yes, they each wore a single rose.

45

"Apparently," she continued, "the yellow rose symbolises the strong ties amongst friends."

The bile burnt in my throat. Enough, enough. I had to leave. I said goodbye to my family. My aunt became concerned about my long drive, but I reassured her, I would probably be in a worse state tomorrow if I were not allowed to take my leave now. I walked briskly to the house, gathered my belongings and began the journey home, to my ordered private space and to you.

Realisation

The drive was a blur, a constant replay of the sickening display of self-importance, the assumptions made, the contrived programme to encourage maximum impact. Her selfish need to be quite literally the centre of attention. The holy misrepresentation of her.

Home, behind my locked gates, exhausted I showered. The overwhelming need to cleanse myself of that day. It helped, I did feel a lightness, a slight sense of peace. I had also found comfort from seeing my aunt, uncle and godfather and I tried to concentrate my thoughts towards them. I had felt a connection with them that as a child I had enjoyed, yes, but now as an adult it was deeper in some way. I dressed for comfort, dark cords and a checked shirt, moccasins softly encasing my feet. I was ravenous now and selected the beef goulash from the fridge. Re-fuelled, my thoughts turned to you. I had disentangled you from her now. That moment of extreme emotion and unresolved anger, that had felt so real in the church had gone. I am a logical man and I knew you were not connected to her in any way, other than you were both women and had both caused me difficulties. I switched the monitor on. You were sat at the island, dressed in my shirt with the vegetarian pizza I had ordered and delivered the previous morning. It felt so much longer ago now. It was half eaten, and as expected, you had a glass of wine in your hand. I looked around, another empty bottle lined up, nothing else had changed. Everything appeared perfect, immaculate even. You drank and as your arm lifted, the shirt sleeve rose up, I noticed a new tea-towel bandage covered the diagonals. I skipped backwards to your re-entry from behind the doors into the studio. You had immediately seen the cool-box and basket and had frozen, just your eyes flickering around the room, then you ran to the door, banging it repeatedly.

"Hello, hello, help me, I'm in here, let me out, please."

Then, almost as though you knew it would not be opened, you turned to your delivery. The cool-box full of goodies and the freshly folded towels, the shirt,

"What the fuck is this, you can't keep me here, what the fuck is this?"

Your voice was getting louder, you picked up the basket and threw it across the tiles contents spilling out, toilet rolls unravelling. I felt this a little ungrateful I admit, I was a touch annoyed.

"What do you want from me? Can you hear me, fuckwit? What the hell do you want? You cannot keep me locked up like some sort of prisoner, what the fuck is all this shit?"

You were pacing the room and kicking the discarded items.

"What are you? Some kind of pervert?"

Your language, that mouth. You continued to pace round and round, spitting out the word no, no, no, with every footstep. Your face was red, you were trembling and yet you carried on spiralling into hysteria and shouting, you ripped the covers from the bed, tugging and pulling at them, pillows thrown over your shoulder one at a time. You paced round kicking the sofa, tugging at the throw, you knocked down the bar-stools and as they clattered you screamed. This was an uncontrolled destruction, this behaviour was almost child-like, a toddler, a tantrum but with venom. You proceeded to the sink and picked up one of the empty bottles and smashed it.

"What do you want from me?"

Each word was said slowly and separately, your voice so much lower.

"Can you see me? Can you? You fucking piece of shit, what do you want? Do you like this, look, look what you have done."

The idea that you thought I could see you, that you might know, alarmed me, this vicious display, these words, the names, I did not anticipate this reaction. I had, I suppose, imagined you would be happy with my gifts. All around you now mess, it looked as if after a robbery would on some crime show.

"Where are you? Why are you doing this? What the fuck do you want, huh, want to see me cry? Who? What? Ahhhhhhhhhhhhhhhhh."

That long scream, its pitch and its rage made the hairs on the back of my neck stand up, the sound hung in the air. I was appalled and yet transfixed by your behaviour.

"So, you want to hurt me? Is that it? Is that what all this is about, hey fuckwit? Is that it? Push me to the fucking edge, is that how you get your kicks? Is it? Wanna see me hurting? This good enough then?"

You pulled the sleeve of your jumper up and clawed at the diagonal scabs with your left hand, again and again. The wounds re-opening, fresh blood flowing.

"Is this it? Is this what you want? Feel fucking good, does it? Getting off on this, are you, wanker?"

The blood was under your nails, gushing over your hand, little flaps of flesh hanging and yet you continued, hacking through your skin, screaming and lost in a madness of self-harm. Finally, you had sat down in the middle of the devastation. Crying, wiping your face, leaving stripes of smeared blood. This self-destruction, this mutilation, the idea that I would want that, that you could think that I was that evil was chilling. I rose and ran to my bathroom and vomited. I could barely brush my teeth I was shaking so much. I avoided my own reflection. I grabbed the gin and a glass, my usual rule of two doubles only a night abandoned. I sat back at the screen. You lay still, I think you had fainted, you must have just fainted. Half an hour passed and then you began to sit up slowly. You were smothered in blood amidst the decimated room, you breathed heavily and precisely, counting each breath. I breathed with you, thirty-seven breaths. Then you spoke, softly and calmly,

"I am not nothing, my name is Lilly. I have three amazing children whom I love and a partner who is beautiful and kind. I am not nothing. My name is Lilly."

The full and total enormity of the situation crashed in around me. In that moment I became fully aware, a conscious realisation and I was scared. You must believe me when I say that I was truly sorry.

I was numb and yet I continued watching you, watching and drinking slowly, constantly but feeling no tangible effects. You had stood up shakily and walked to the sink, you washed your face and hands and then allowed the water to run over your arm. Quietly, you took out the scissors and cut another tea-towel and proceeded to bandage your arm, as you had before, tucking the top edge in, pulling it tight. You then wrapped cling film round and round, the translucent cover forcing the leaking blood to smudge underneath. You looked at your surroundings, surveying your explosion, as though in contemplation, you lit a cigarette and stared at each section in turn. When you had extinguished and placed the end in your tin foil ashtray, you began to clean. The glass first, each piece so carefully collected and deposited in the bin. You picked up the stools, shook the bedding and remade the bed, smoothing out the sheet, then the duvet cover, precisely placing the pillows. You shook the throw in the same way and folded and neatly placed it on the sofa, the notepad and pen on top. Each discarded item from the basket viewed and replaced, you took them through to the dressing room. You pulled at the cool-box, sliding it across the floor and emptied the contents into the fridge, methodically, taking the time to look at each item, turning each meal or yogurt pot to face the front, bottles of Evian lined up by the orange and the milk. Salad and fruit in the compartment underneath, bread on the top. Teabags away in the correct cupboard, butter, unwrapped in the dish. Wine in the cooler. You were almost robotic, quietly restoring the room. When everything had been organised, you placed the empty bottles and milk cartons in to the cool-box and pushed it back to the door. I was almost as unsettled by you then as I was when you had exploded. I was suddenly cold, I turned up the heating, both upstairs and down, topped up my glass again and continued to watch, strangely drawn in. You had sat on top of the cool-box and were staring across the room, tilting your head for a new angle and then, suddenly, jumped up and you proceeded to clean every surface with the anti-bacterial spray. Big circular movements across the island, smaller swipes on the kettle, gentle rubs around the edges. Then the cupboard fronts, the high gloss finish streak free. The stools were polished up, even the stud detail on the sofa, one by one wiped. On hands and knees, you had cleaned the floor, meticulously working your way backwards from the door. Finally, when all was perfect, you stopped.

I watched you through the early hours, occasionally taking a break, walking away to sit in my chair, to stare at the stars, to try to find a place that felt comfortable, agreeable. There was no comfort, I could not feel it, nor could I find it, not even in the gin.

Eventually, you went through the doors and I assumed showered, when you came back into sight you were wearing the shirt with the gown hanging loosely. You removed the clingfilm and replaced it with new, layers sticking together, bound tightly. You made milky tea and smoked underneath the extractor fan, in your usual way. You looked in the fridge twice but closed it both times taking nothing and then you went to bed. I proceeded to skip through the time-line, you had slept for a remarkably long time then it seemed suddenly to jolt too, as if just remembering. More tea, toast and honey. I was relieved you were eating. The tea-towel removed, salt water and cleaning regime resumed. The diagonals were lost, the wounds were deep, tatty and jagged in places now, all precision removed. The image of you tearing in to them would not leave me, it will never leave me.

I skipped on, you spent that afternoon on the sofa, coiled up under the softness of cashmere, gently rocking. Eventually you left the little corner and had opened a bottle, Sancerre, I noticed and had put the pizza in the oven, freshened up and removed the gown and then there you were, sat at the island in my blue shirt, a half-eaten pizza and a glass of wine in your hand surrounded by immaculate order.

Had I not shared those previous hours with you I would never have guessed or even imagined what you had done. The only evidence now covered, hidden from view.

The sun was almost rising when I left you. I sat outside on the balcony, the crisp new day must have been cold against my skin, but I felt nothing, dumbstruck and empty, devoid of emotion, vacant of thought.

Friday, September 22
The News

I had sat like that for some time, until the cold had finally sunk in to my bones. I had showered, the water so hot it was almost painful, I had brushed my teeth repeatedly, my gums sore. I shaved and moisturised, my skin dull and dry and I dressed. I chose a different blend of coffee for my espresso, from Ethiopia, it's syrupy and leaves an aftertaste of bourbon biscuit, it's usual comfort was gone however. My porridge even topped with sugar crystals tasted somehow bitter. I walked through to the living room, sat in my chair and clicked the television on. The news.

"The case of the missing woman, Lillian Brown, is now in its eighth day and with no new developments there are growing concerns regarding her safety."

The pre-recorded press conference from the previous night's news was then shown. The police spokeswoman was now joined, not only by your partner, but by three young adults. All seated in a line, hands all linked.

"Lilly has now been missing for a week and we are asking the public again to please come forward if they have any information regarding her whereabouts."

"Please, please someone must know something, please."

Your partner looked visibly weaker, exhausted.

"Please just let our mum come home, we love you, Mum."

Oh, I remember thinking, these were your children, they were older than I had expected. They were crying, a row of exposed and raw emotion, a display of pain for all.

"Let us know that she is, that she is, just let her come home."

That she is and then a faltered breath, let us know that she is…I realised alive was the missing word, but they had not been able to say it. By saying that very word implied you could be dead I suppose, and this was clearly too much for them. I did not wait for your picture or the numbers or the questions. I needed the silence.

Anniversary

You had not been a real person to me, I had not seen you, just an object that became a focus for my anger. I had watched you, but up until then I had not seen you. I had despised you, resented your presence, not allowed myself to even consider the effect that my decision could have had on you or those that cared about you. I had thought you irrelevant, a distraction from myself, to myself, disposable. I had picked you up and put you down for my own convenience, for my own amusement, I had used you. I could see that now. In my week of turmoil, I had become a stranger to myself. I was not proud, there was no sense of arrogance now. I knew, at least, that you were clean, warm, had food and drink. At least I could cling to that, I am not a monster. I am kind and gentle, sensitive, the previous week I had not been myself and my actions reflected that. Those actions had a consequence that was over-whelming. In that one transient moment I had changed both our worlds forever. I was in turmoil with no answers or plan to help.

I returned to social media, you were obviously, still trending but were no longer the hot topic. I felt annoyed by this lack of reaction. How very fickle people are, I did not want you to be found for obvious reasons, but I did not want you to be forgotten either. The irony of this feeling was not lost on me, nothing was straight forward, in fact, everything felt confused now.

I used the image of your face when sat at the island, cleaned and calm. I framed you with red paper hearts for two reasons,

1. To obliterate your surroundings.
2. To represent our first week's anniversary.

Under the heading,
"Lilly is safe and loves you too."
I uploaded the image.

Order Again

Despite my complete lack of sleep, I had a new energy. I ate a hearty deli-roll, stuffed with smoked ham, salad and cheese and gathered my thoughts. I decided to reassign all meetings and calls, the art of delegation, under the now ironically useful circumstances this would not appear an unreasonable course of action. I needed time and space. Did I realise that we needed time and space? Several hours later and all was done.

I cleaned, taking pleasure in the detail, cloths absorbing the light-dust highlighted as the afternoon sun came through. It was a beautiful day, quite mild again. The autumn colours were reflected against the brightness, leaves gently falling. I went outside, the winds from Monday night had most certainly left their mark. I swept up and tidied. I do love autumn and am always disappointed when the changes are rushed, stealing away the beauty all too quickly. Organised inside and out I returned to my chair with an afternoon tea and a chocolate pot. I was aware that I was just trying to busy myself, to avoid the situation, to pre-occupy my time with household chores so as not to see you. Procrastination with precision. It was now time for dinner, three bean chilli stew, I had such an appetite and I made a note to myself, to run in the morning. Indulgences are always allowed providing they are acknowledged and equalled out. Calm and full and a little, dare I say excited? I prepared for the news.

The News

"A new and surprising twist to the case of the missing mother of three, Lillian Brown had occurred again. Another photograph of her had been posted and seemed to show her fit and well with a message to say that she was safe, and what appeared to be love to her family."

The police spokeswoman alone had a brief statement to add,

"This disturbing case is an on-going priority and the use of social media again is alarming. The family have taken some hope from this new post, yet it still remains incredibly distressing. Whilst every effort and resource are being undertaken, unfortunately, the person or persons responsible have not yet been traced. We would like to appeal to whoever has taken Lilly to let her go or to inform us of her location."

You were shown, the paper hearts all around and then the CCTV footage was replayed. The phone numbers and your official photo displayed.

I felt a lightness that your family had hope. I felt good that I had let them know that much at least.

I sat perfectly still and considered the events, I did not even care that no mention had been made of my design work even though it had looked rather good.

I checked, you were trending high again, the new image tweeted and re-tweeted, comments growing. It appeared, # supporting Lilly was gathering momentum at an alarming and quite amusing rate. Jumping on a bandwagon of concern, desperately needing to be seen to care, to be involved, albeit with heart emojis and selfies. Fashionable feelings floating through the ether. I left them then, poured a gin and went to you.

Moving Forward

You were sat on the sofa, my shirt on, the throw around your shoulders. I looked around, all neat and tidied, nothing to suggest you had exploded again. I did not look further, there was little point in looking back now. You had a glass of wine and were turning the glass round slowly in your hands. Your arm still bandaged, I could see the cloth was heavily stained. Your face now had just a little trace of bruising. You shivered and stretched your feet on to the tiles and instantly removed them up and under you. You were cold, I turned the heating up. You sipped your wine. I sipped my gin. We sat together in our worlds.

Eventually, you stood and as your feet felt the warmth, you smiled, stroking the floor as you walked across to the cooler. As in the official photograph of you, your smile softened your face. I wondered if you would have chosen that photo? You refilled and stood under the extractor and looked at your cigarettes, you counted them, there were five remaining, you went to walk away but then returned and lit up, so carefully blowing the smoke up and away. I quickly topped up my empty tumbler and returned to you. You were now repositioned and quiet, the crumpled shirt almost like a dress, I assumed your clothes would be drying, I wondered if the blood had come out. I watched you like this until you had drained the pinot and after placing the empty bottle in the cool-box, disappearing behind the sliding doors for a short time, you went to bed.

Despite my lack of sleep, my mind raced. If you were to stay, and really, I reasoned that there was no other option, you needed clothes. I thought about just ordering but ladies fashions were not my usual purchases, sudden deliveries of petite female clothing could arouse suspicion. I considered shopping in town, but again, logically this seemed a risky procedure. Even if all transactions were cash only, I would still be seen, I remembered the CCTV footage of you so clearly. I, much to my own surprise, even considered the local charity shop, feeling this might not be as security conscious, but the idea of touching clothes worn by who? The imagined musty odour ruled even that out as an option. I walked through to my walk-in wardrobe, clothes all neatly hung on rows of identical wooden hangers. Drawers full of ordered compartments. After some deliberation I gathered a couple of sets of Ralph Lauren's loungewear, summer ones, as the full pant would have been ridiculous, a couple of Paul Smith sweatshirts and a pair of Ugg mule slippers which I thought might just stay on. I placed the items to one-side. Your arm was quite concerning, I went to my bathroom cupboards, I found a box of cleansing wipes, some savlon and a couple of bandages, then I paused, I felt anxious, my heart pounding,

1. Could I risk being seen?
2. Perhaps worse, could I risk causing another explosion?

Unsure of myself I placed all the items neatly on the floor and closed the door. I decided to go to bed. Sleep would perhaps provide a much-needed sense of calm. Sleep would restore.

Saturday, September 23
Dialogue

On waking I ran, my steady pace against the crunch of fallen leaves. A fresh and perfect day just beginning. I made a detour from my usual route and went to the newsagents, I had decided to buy you some cigarettes as an indicator that I meant you no harm, a peace offering perhaps, a discouragement against another episode, a gift? I occasionally enjoy the odd smoke myself, but only ever on the balcony, so although not a daily occurrence, a safe purchase. The notice board had a poster of you pinned in the centre. Missing local woman, Lilly. Anyone with information call and a contact number. I must have stared too long or did I even gasp? I am not completely sure, but the newsagent noticed,

"Horrible, isn't it? Some twisted sod behind this one."

I looked at him, twisted? I wanted to explain, I was not, am not, twisted. It was the situation, the timing of our meeting that had created the twisted path. Instead,

"Oh yes, yes, horrible, terrible news, has – has there been any news?"

"No, fingers crossed soon though, it's just not right."

"Yes, mmm absolutely."

I stupidly, almost forgot why I was there, however, other customers were arriving for their morning papers and it drew the attention away from you and to business. I left and ran quickly home. I gathered all the items and placed them in a blue cardboard storage box. I took a piece of notepaper from my study and wrote a simple note,

Do not hurt yourself again Lilly.

I do not want to hurt you.

Lid on, monitor on, you were drinking tea and eating a peach yogurt. I could tell you were, as of yet, un-showered, hair all clumped together, face still puffy. I waited, it had worked once before. After you had re-wrapped the tea towel with layers of clingfilm, you went through the doors. Gosh how I moved, I actually felt happy, excited even. Key retrieved from the elegant console table, I unlocked the door and placed the box on top of the cool-box, just inside then quietly closed, locked and returned. Wow my heart was racing as I made my way upstairs, back to the monitor. I patiently waited and despite my lack of a shower, the obvious body odour, the lack of personal hygiene that would normally appal me, I just waited for you.

Sixty-two minutes passed. You disappointingly, walked to the sink first and shakily unwrapped the clingfilm and removed the tea towel, I flinched, the swollen mess revealed. Tentatively you set about the task of dabbing salty water around the damaged lines, breathing heavily and of course, counting. Your voice was cracking but determined. Eventually you cut the last tea towel and carefully covered your disfigurement, tiny patches of fresh blood instantly appearing, new scabs trying to form. You cleaned away and made more tea and then, finally, you turned and saw. I held my breath, slowly you took the box, not even trying the door, and placed it beside you on the sofa. On removing the lid and placing it by your feet you read my note out-loud, first quickly and then again repeating each word precisely, my words sounding through the room. You unpacked the items, laying them in a row, touching the fabric gently between your finger and thumb, the bandages, the wipes, the savlon and cigarettes, all in a row.

"You can see me then."

You did not know, but as you spoke your face was looking directly towards the camera. I felt you could see me, I felt exposed. I enabled the audio function, simple, push to talk facility,

"Yes, yes, Lilly, I can."

Questions then, oh so many words tumbled out your mouth,

"Where am I? Why have you locked me in here? Why? How do you even know my name? Why am I your prisoner? Who are you?"

All in one breath but spoken, not shouted.

"Why are you keeping me here? Why these things? Why the food, the wine? Where am I? Is this some sort of game to you? A secret big brother experience that you're enjoying? Why? Why?"

You stood then, gesticulating frantically, voice a little louder, a little higher,

"Look my name is Lilly, ha but you already know that, I have three children and a partner, they will be worried. I need to go home. What day is it anyway? How long have I been locked in here? I need to go home now, my place is at home, so, just unlock the door please and let me go, okay? Okay?"

I had not really considered your accent up until then, although you were reported as local your voice, your pronunciation did not reflect that.

"Hello, are you listening to me?"

"Yes, Lilly just shush a moment I need some time to think."

"Shush?! I can't shush, and no you do not need to think you need to open this door and let me out, now."

"I will be back later, just change out of that grubby shirt and tend to your arm."

"No, no don't go, please don't go, just let me out, please, don't leave me in here please."

I could not just open the door, it was not that easy or straightforward. I was astonished by your naïve perception of the situation. How did I know your name? Had it really not occurred to you that you would be on the news, reported missing? Did you think that your partner and children would do nothing, but say be a little worried? #supportingLilly was the trend of the moment. I too had questions, but they also had to wait.

I showered and shaved, dressed, Gap jeans, a green polo shirt and my new olive converse. A relaxed look, a cool look I decided. I made a ham sandwich and took a bottle of water through to my office. You had changed, the shorts were three-quarters of the way down your legs and the t-shirt just above your knee, but they were clean and pressed and your arm was freshly bandaged. You were re-packing the remaining items,

"Hello."

"Hello, are you going to let me out now?"

"No, Lilly, please understand I am not going to hurt you, but I cannot unlock the door."

"But you have to, I'm not your prisoner."

"Well, I think I would prefer the word guest."

"Guest? No, no, no, you cannot keep me here, I must go home now, I need to go home now. For fuck's sake, let me out. I've done what you said, I've changed, ahhhhh," you screamed.

"For fuck's sake."

Then you kicked the cool-box and slumped down on to the floor, leaning against the sofa, knees up to your chest, arms hugging them. A small coil lost inside clothing and cried. Not screams, not hysterical sobs, just tears and whimpers. I watched you. I took no pleasure in your distress I can assure you. We were both trapped now, locked in to the same situation. Somehow, we had to come to terms with this. As your tears dried up you wiped your face, eyes so red and began to re-pack the box you had kicked over.

Explanation

"Lilly, we need to talk."

"Talk? Right, do you watch me all the time, oh my God, do you watch me in the bathroom?"

"No," I shouted.

"No, Lilly, there are no cameras in there, I am not as you suggested a pervert. I am a good man."

"Really, ha right so this is normal is it? This is what good men do?"

"This was never my intention, I did not mean for this to happen, you have to believe me, but it has, and we are here now."

"What do you mean you never meant this to happen, like it's some sort of fucking accident? I mean, what is this place? This was planned, this room, this set up. Oh my God, did you pick me? Or did I just get fucking lucky?"

"No, it is complicated. I did not pick you, you were just in the wrong place at the wrong time and everything just happened."

"Oh right, of course, it's my fault?"

"Well, yes actually."

"Fuck you. No way. You brought me here, I don't actually remember being fucking asked."

"No, but –"

"No buts and ifs, this wasn't planned, what is this place, not everyone has a ready-made prison."

"It is not a prison."

"Well, it fucking feels that way to me."

"Please stop swearing, your language is disgusting."

"Swearing? I will fucking swear, fuck, twat, bastard, I will swear. I have every right to swear for fuck's sake."

"Well, that maybe your opinion but it is really not becoming, however entitled you feel."

"Fuck off, so if this isn't a prison, what is it, where am I?"

"You are in my home."

"You're here too, where?"

"I am upstairs, you are in my basement studio."

"Why though?"

"It is rather complicated, Lilly, the turn of events, trust me this was not intended."

"Complicated, well, explain it to me."

"I am not sure I truly can, it is a little difficult, a little confused."

"Well, fucking try."

"It would take so long."

"Well, I'm apparently not fucking going anywhere."

I was suddenly flustered, your directness, I felt so unsure. You were stood in the middle of the room, waiting, demanding.

"Do you remember when we met?"

"When we met? When you took me?"

"When we met, Lilly, I was driving. You stepped out in front of me."

"That's you, the fucking idiot who nearly ran me over?"

"You stepped out and then your mouth."

"You nearly killed me, so because I swore at your bad driving skills, you did this?"

Your arms were up in the air, you were pacing around again.

"No, well yes."

"For fuck's sake."

"Lilly, if we are going to continue this conversation, will you please stop swearing and try to listen for a change?"

"Right, right."

Your arms were flapping.

"Right."

You made your way to the island, switched the kettle on to make tea, and sat down.

"Right I'm listening."

"Thank you."

I ate some of my sandwich, sipped some water.

"That day I was in a bad place, I was angry, in shock even. I was not in control of my own emotions as I usually am, when you stepped out and started screaming obscenities I just saw red. I reacted in a manner I have never done before. I am not a violent man."

"Really?" You shook your head and lightly held your arm.

"Lilly."

"Right, whatever, go on."

"The rage inside my head just tumbled out, irrational and uncontrolled. It was a moment. I hurt and briefly, ashamedly hurting you helped. It was a release, it felt justified. I panicked, and I bought you here. None of this was premeditated and I most certainly did not pick you."

"Charming, so why were you so angry?"

"My plans had been snatched away from me, everything that I had arranged and thought about for weeks had suddenly gone. I had been working up to that day for weeks, every detail thought through and then there was nothing and it was simply unfair."

"Your plans? What was supposed to happen that day?"

You sat drinking tea and had started to slice some bread, I finished my sandwich. You spread butter and honey and proceeded to pull little sections away and eat them slowly.

"She was coming here, the studio is for her, was for her. I had spent weeks hurriedly preparing, devoting my time and energies to make everything perfect, beyond criticism or reproach."

You looked around again,

"It is lovely, but let me get this straight, you were dumped so you took me instead? Your first intended victim got away, and I was her replacement?"

"No, she was not in any way under any circumstances a victim, trust me. She was powerful and manipulative, all smiles on the surface but underneath, as cold as ice."

"So that's why you were going to lock her up?"

"No. I was not ever going to lock her up, she was just coming to stay."

"Your guest? A guest you didn't even like? So why didn't she come?"

"Because she died."

"Oh, oh I see, well I'm sure she didn't mean to, or did she? Did she commit suicide? Is that why you're so angry with her?"

"No, she did not, she was ill but was expected to make a full recovery with rest and recuperation."

"That she was supposed to undertake here?"

"Yes."

"I'm confused, I get that you were hurt, in shock, sad even, disappointed, but the anger and then taking me, bringing me here, why?"

"Everything happened so fast, you were not planned or thought through, you were suddenly just here."

"Then you hurt me."

"Yes, I know, you were so loud and out of control and I was angry and confused. I just needed you to be quiet. I just lashed out, I think I was scared."

"You were scared? How about me? I did not deserve to be cut and beaten."

"I just wanted quiet, I wanted all of it to go away, I just lashed out, I do not really understand, I needed to unleash and release. My pain and anger melted into one rage and out-pouring, I was in some temporary state of madness. Anger, loss it was all tangled and out of control and I took it out on you."

You finished your lunch and made more tea, you had a cigarette in your way and cleaned. You were surprisingly quiet.

Agreement

I too attended to my chores, attention to detail important. Now no longer working I was at a little bit of a loss, thrown in to unscheduled leisure time. The last few weeks had been so frenzied, suddenly stopping was strange. I went back to you. You were applying savlon all around the deformed diagonals.

"How is your arm, Lilly?"

I had made you jump and you screamed out as your fingers caught the wound.

"It hurts, it really fucking hurts actually. I'm scared it might become infected."

"I doubt it, you have been meticulously cleaning it with salt water, keeping it dry. It is a shame though it was healing neatly."

"Mmm, I hope so. Anyway, I have been thinking, why did you want someone you didn't even like to stay? Why bother yourself? Were you married? Had she left you?"

"No, oh gosh, no. We were linked, yes, but she was not my wife, I am not married. What were you writing the other night?"

You had replaced the bandage and walked over to the sofa, picking up the notepaper,

"I thought you could see me?"

"Not in such detail."

"I was trying to write a letter to tell my family that I loved them, how much I loved them and miss them," your bottom lip trembled, "because I do, and I can't bear the thought they might think I've just left, left them. I wouldn't, I couldn't."

You cried cradling the notepaper and gently rocked. This, so open a display of love was quite difficult, illogical to have written, but the need was almost tangible.

"Please let me go home now, let me be with them."

"Lilly, you know I cannot just let you go."

"You can, yes you can."

"You have seen my face and –"

"I don't remember, I won't remember, it's fine, you let me out and I just won't remember anything, I promise. It's not like I know where I am or anything. I promise, I promise, I –"

"Lilly, enough, enough. We are here and that is the way it is. I will not hurt you and please say you will not hurt yourself again. I will continue to make sure you are warm and have provisions and we shall talk, but for now, we must agree on the situation and deal with it in the best way that we can."

You sat on the sofa shaking, still rocking.

"What if they think I've just left them, abandoned them? I love them so much, so, so very much, what if they are worried or think I'm dead? This isn't about you or me, this is about them."

"We must agree to deal with this situation in the best way we can, calmly and quietly Lilly, do you understand?"

"Not really because it's not fair, I just want to go home, but I don't exactly have any options, do I? I don't have any way out. You just think it's okay to leave me in here with you watching me all the time?"

"I do not watch you all the time."

"Well, how would I know? It's freaky and it's wrong."

"I do not watch you all the time. I am not a freak as you put it Lilly."

"Really?"

"Yes, thank you. In the future I will announce when I am here, does that help?"

"Announce your presence? For fuck's sake, who do you think you are?"

"Lilly, we are in this situation, I am trying my best for you, to make you at ease, calmly and quietly is the way forward, indeed the only way forward, do you agree?"

"Do I really have a choice?"

"Good, good and thank you."

I left you then. I felt awkward with all your emotions swilling around, disturbed by them.

Ashes

Just before dinner my aunt had called, the ashes were ready for collection and what did I want to do? Well, I had almost laughed, I did not want anything to do with them. However, we decided I would travel down on the Monday and we would collect them together. My godfather was still around so perhaps all four of us could spend another evening together? I considered you, obviously, but it had helped being in their company and I rather felt a break would be beneficial. I needed some space. So, I accepted, and the arrangements were made. I felt optimistic, everything was on the up, I enjoy looking forward, to having things to look forward to. It really had been wonderful to be reunited, the four of us, it would be so much happier this time with our own schedule to make. Each other to focus on. I would pack an over-night bag tomorrow before my Sunday lunch at two. My flower order would be fine, I could leave after delivery, I could be on the road by ten thirty. That just left me with the food order to organise and to re-arrange the delivery slot from the morning to the evening. I had done this previously, so not unusual. Yes, everything was pretty good.

The News

The Saturday evening news, gin in hand. I had eaten, tortellini with cured ham and felt quite satisfied, content almost. I had placed some pretzels by my side, a little snack whilst I viewed.

"The case of the missing mother of three, Lillian Brown is in its ninth day now and still there seems to be no answers to her disappearance."

A handover to the press conference, the now predictable line up. Your three children, your partner, the police spokeswoman, all in front of the cameras.

"We would like to take this opportunity to remind the public that we do not believe Lilly would have chosen to leave her family home. The speculation and unfounded theories appearing on social media are not helpful with this on-going investigation and could very well undermine procedure. Lilly had only moved to this area a year ago but had planned for years to do so with her partner. They have a successful business, there are no problems at home or work."

Then your partner, he looked pale and weary,

"Lilly and I love our life together, we love each other. Please just let Lilly come home. Anyone who really knows her, knows that she would not just leave us, Lilly is a happy person."

Suddenly, your son,

"My mum would not just go, this rubbish on social media, it's just not true, that's my mum, this isn't a reality TV show."

He was becoming distressed. Your daughter,

"Our mum would hate this attention, she is a very private person who has no desire to be famous."

Your other son,

"Mum doesn't even use social media."

The police spokeswoman again,

"As I am sure you can appreciate this is an incredibly stressful and upsetting time for Lilly's family. We urge anyone with any information to come forward, let's find Lilly. Thank you."

Phone numbers, original photo. Your families' faces'.

Well, I was surprised and intrigued by the tone and content. I looked through the twitter feeds,

#supportingLilly was still trending, (but infiltrating these increasingly sycophantic statements and comment were a new breed). Not that many but enough to have obviously caused this reaction.

#IsLillylaughing?
#Isthisapublicitystunt?
#SorrymateLillyleftyou!

I was somewhat taken aback. The general feeling from this minority had sparked a discussion that you had thought and planned all this for fame and fortune. I was strangely insulted. I had the knowledge and the control, not these cowards with their stupid theories. You were not that clever anyway. My rather happy demeanour vanished. I poured another gin and tonic and swivelled, annoyed. I returned to the monitor, I did not tell you because I was not actually watching you, I was merely skipping backwards, the image I needed was in there, and then yes, I found it. Your startled face, caught by surprise, your mutilated arm exposed. Perfect. I surrounded you with tears and question marks. A little of the blue loungewear could be seen, but nothing capable of detection. I up-loaded this under the heading,

"Does Lilly look happy?"

I waited but not for long. Outbursts from all over, shock and condemnation. I was amused, everyone thinks their voice should be heard instantly, a race to be the first to comment, but I was leading this, not them. I could see the truth, I was the truth.

Questions

I skipped back to the correct time and to you.

"Good evening, Lilly."

You were sat on the sofa, writing, wine by your feet,

"Hello."

"What did you have for your tea?"

"Moroccan tagine, why?"

"I shall be re-ordering soon, I was merely enquiring to see what you liked. What are you writing?"

"Questions for you."

"How is the wine?"

"The wine is good, it helps with the pain. What did you mean when you said that you were linked to the woman who died?"

"Do you prefer the pinot? It is a very good vineyard."

"I like pinot, I like a crisp dry, white wine. Well?"

"I had noticed."

"Are you going to answer my question?"

"You said that you had questions, plural?"

"That is my first though."

"Ah, well, Lilly, I am tired, we can talk tomorrow, write a list of foods you like too and we can organise anything else you need."

"What like freedom?"

"Oh very droll, Lilly. I am retiring now. I will see you in the morning."

"I guess I'll be here."

You gulped at your drink and walked to your smoking spot. You were crying again.

"Lilly, she was my mother, goodnight."

I left you, click and you were gone.

I am not entirely sure why I told you, maybe I felt that you would appreciate the situation a little better, maybe I just wanted to make you think, to distract you from your tears. I did not want to talk anymore though. I needed sleep.

Sunday, September 24
Questioning Continued

I woke, as always, at first light. I had slept extremely well and felt energised and enthused for my morning run. It was sodden ground, there must have been heavy rain through the night, a splosh underfoot instead of a crunch, but I did not care. The colours and the trees, even in a week, had altered so much, beautiful tones of reds and browns. I ran well, enjoying every wet step. I returned and showered, shaved, trimmed, moisturised. I would change before lunch, so I just popped on a pair of cords and a polo shirt before making breakfast. Poached eggs on wholemeal toast, natural yogurt with blueberries and coffee.

I went to you.

"Good morning, Lilly."

You clearly had not been out of bed long, hair had been brushed, I thought but was still fluffy. You were sat at the island, tea and, I smiled, you were having natural yogurt with blueberries too, the only difference was that you were placing them in a pattern, carefully, one by one. I liked this.

"Is it a good morning?"

"Yes, Lilly, it is. Did you sleep well?"

"Eventually I slept, eventually. So why were you so angry with your mother?"

"She was not a nice person."

"But you wanted her to stay here, to rest and recuperate, you wanted to care for her?"

"I wanted her to stay that had been the plan, yes."

"You said that you had spent weeks preparing, to get everything perfect, why bother if she was not a nice person?"

"Because I am meticulous and organised."

"But why did you bother?"

"Because it was my duty and there was no one else, it had to be me."

"Had she ever stayed here before?"

"No."

"But this room, this studio, you said it was for her?"

"Yes, but only recently, only when I thought she was coming, only when she was ill. I prepared everything, so much of my time, so much effort and thought."

"Were you angry because she didn't see it?"

"She died with no appreciation for all of my work, for all of my time and effort."

"Do you really believe she died just to mess up your plans?"

"Yes, well no but it was typical, her way or no way."

"Do you miss her?"

"No, I just wanted her to be here then."

"Why?"

"I had things I wanted to say, I should have said. I had it all planned, it was my time."

"Whilst she was recovering?"

"Yes."

"Whilst she was weak?"

"Yes Lilly, whilst she was weak, whilst she was dependant, whilst she was in need. Do not judge me, you have no idea."

"I wasn't judging you, I was trying to understand what had made you so angry, so angry that you stole me?"

"Stole you?"

"Well, forgive me if I'm wrong, but I am here against my will, locked in your dead mother's fucking studio, I think it is fair to say that you have stolen me, stolen me from my family."

"I have already explained that I had not intended for you to be here. I am not a thief. I am a good man Lilly. This situation is just upon us both now, we agreed to make it the best we can."

"Have you had the funeral?"

"Yes it was truly awful, completely dictated by her, an egotistic vile display, but, yes, it is done, why?"

I had wanted to explain every detail of that disgusting day to you, but it was too soon then, too soon to re-live the events. Too soon for me to find the words.

"Sometimes that can be a good time to say things, to come to terms with things. When was it?"

"There is no point speaking to a corpse, you are so completely illogical. It was last Thursday."

"What day is it today?"

"It is Sunday."

"It is not illogical by the way, it can be cathartic. You could write your feelings down, that too can be cathartic. Were you scared of your mother?"

"No."

"Why did you need her to be weak before you could speak to her then?"

"I did not need her, I just wanted to ask her things, I had questions. I wanted her to hear me, to listen, to acknowledge me, to explain. In her condition she could not have simply walked away."

"Did she hurt you as a child?"

"Lilly I do not want to talk about her now."

"It might help though, have you ever spoken about her to anyone? You said that you were the only one, it was your duty, so have you no family? No brothers or sisters?"

"No and no siblings. I have an aunt, uncle and a godfather."

"Do they know? Did they hurt you?"

"No they are good people, they were at the funeral, I had not seen them in such a long time."

"Why?"

"Why?"

70

"Why hadn't you seen them, your only family, if they are good people, why would you not see them?"

"When my father died things changed, they were no longer frequent visitors, visitors at all. My godfather travels and lives abroad."

"How old were you were you when your father died?"

"Thirteen."

"Is that when your mother hurt you?"

"No, enough, enough, before you start feeling sorry for an imagined mourning widow. No."

"Were you close to your father? Or did he hurt you too?"

"No, no, my father was gentle and kind and so intelligent, like my uncle, his brother. We were close, I spent all my free time with him."

"So after he died, why didn't your uncle step in, why would he see you less?"

"Enough, enough now. I do not have the answers."

"Well, you should find the answers, ask the questions."

"Oh, should I? Who are you to tell me what I should do? I am going now I need to change, I have a lunch reservation."

"Oh well best hurry then, wouldn't want to disrupt your plans, hey imagine what might happen?"

I went to respond, but I was angered by your intrusive questions and felt no good would come with further comment. I left and prepared myself, a textured blue cotton jumper and Ted Baker jeans, quilted jacket, simple Kurt Geiger Chelsea boots. It was colder now but dry and I intended to walk.

Reflection

I arrived, the cold air and brisk walk invigorating, my appetite encouraged. I was, as always, met with a warm welcome and shown to my usual table. It was naturally fully booked and bustling. I chose not to focus on the other diners this time, not to be distracted. I looked out the window instead. I ordered the braised pork belly, roasted heritage potatoes and carrot smash, a dark chocolate brownie for desert. My large pinot noir was most welcome and as I ate, I thought of our conversation. I thought of my father, my aunt and uncle, my godfather, how we had drifted from one another and how much I had missed them when they no longer came. I remembered myself as a teenager, looking longingly from the window seat, for their cars to arrive, for their happy faces, for the comfort I found in my aunts' arms. It would be good to see them tomorrow. I thought of her too, your questions, your apparent expectation that I could or would just answer you, but also that I had. Why? I reflected, why should I tell you anything? And yet I had told you more than anyone. I was so distracted by my own thoughts I heard nothing around me. Just memories and questions. You were responsible for this, this opening of unopened thought and despite of my usual self I, somehow, felt drawn to its flow. I have never been one to share, not since my father's passing. The culture that now surrounds us is not one I adhere to. A constant need to talk, to analyse, evaluate emotions, support groups scrutinising behaviour types. Self-indulgent me, me, me. Like her. No. I have always been my own counsel, respectful and polite, friendly but quiet, private. Alone.

Tipped and goodbyes, see you next week, thank you so much…all the usual, said on automatic and then back to you.

The cloud was low, the fells becoming hidden, the wind was picking up, leaves falling and swirling around my feet. I hurried back, I still needed to pack, to prepare and I knew I wanted some free time left, some time to talk with you.

Preparation

I organised my clothes, shoes, washbag, coat. Waters ready in the fridge, fresh for the morning's drive. I wiped round and quickly made a note of foods for my part of the order. Then I came to you.

"Good evening, Lilly."

"Is it?"

"Yes, yes it really is. What have you been doing?"

"Ah well, such is my social calendar I have showered and rather enjoyed a new face cream. Dressed in a new set of PJs, da dah."

You were spinning round, I could see you had used the belt from the robe to keep the shorts in place.

"Washed the others, cleaned the stools, cleaned the floor, drank some tea, had a fag. It has just been go, go, go, so how was your lunch reservation?"

"It was lovely thank you for asking. Have you given any thought to foods you would like? I appreciate that you have been busy."

"Ha!"

You looked in the fridge, crouched in front and lit by the light I could see that your face was completely healed now.

"I did like everything really, especially the soups, ooh and the moussaka was good and the couscous pots."

"So if I simply re-fresh everything, nothing else?"

"Well, actually, please may I have some marmite?"

"Marmite, yes."

I remembered there had been a jar in your shopping bag.

"And some more wipes and bandages, just a couple."

"How is your arm?"

"It's pretty horrible, thank you for asking."

"Lilly, I am going away tomorrow, just for one night, so if there is anything else?"

"You're going? So, what about me?"

"That is exactly why I was enquiring."

"Oh for fuck's sake, what am I supposed to do in here all day? I am sick of cleaning, what happens if there is a fire or something?"

"There are sprinklers and I like the way you clean, you do it correctly. You could exercise, write some more…"

"Can't I have something to read, a newspaper, anything?"

"I will see what I can do."

Obviously a newspaper was out of the question I did not want you to read about yourself.

"Where are you going? Is it work?"

"No I work remotely, but not at the moment. I am going to her house to meet with my aunt, uncle and godfather. We are collecting the ashes."

"Oh, what are you going to do with them?"

"I really do not know or care Lilly."

"How did she hurt you?"

"You said you had other questions?"

You picked up the note paper.

"If this room, studio, whatever, wasn't originally for her, who was it for? Or do you rent it out? Don't you need it?"

"Oh the very thought, no I most certainly do not rent it out as you put it. It was the last of the rooms to be furnished, so the contents were cancelled and re-ordered accordingly."

"How should it have been?"

"Well, the kitchen area is as intended, the bed area should really be the space for the snooker table, the aristocrat tournament champion, the best of the Riley range. The sofa I had intended was to be the Terence Conran's beautiful blue leather, a corner of comfort, reclining, electric headrests, perfect for relaxing and enjoying the home cinema, the Bang and Olufsen Beo System 4. The dressing room should contain my gym equipment."

"So this is your party room?"

"Yes, exactly a place for fun, contained and soundproofed, separate yet still my home."

"A space for fun, how ironic."

"Yes, bitterly ironic, it could have been fabulous."

"It could still be fabulous, fabulous fun for you and your friends, just let me go."

"Did you have another question?"

You were pacing around the island again, round you went breathing with deep concentration, counting, as was your way. This strange and almost hypnotic ritual, round and round.

"Well, if that is all, Lilly, I shall go. I will say goodbye before I leave."

Nothing. You continued in your loop, the circumference growing, just a little with each lap.

The News

I settled myself and waited.

"The ongoing investigation in to the disappearance of the middle-aged woman, Lillian Brown, has yet again taken another disturbing turn. Following last night's police statement, a new image was posted, clearly showing Lilly hurt and in pain."

There was no cross over to a press conference, your family were not present. Instead the police spokeswoman was in the studio.

"Given this new and distressing image, what do the police believe to be the motive behind this action?"

"We believe that the public's use of social media has provoked this new response, a reaction. We can only again urge that all online discussions related to this case stop. We are being advised by a police psychologist and it is their professional opinion that these feeds are actually fuelling this horrific situation."

"Do the police now believe this to be the work of one person?"

"Following a detailed process of criminal profiling yes, we now suspect that to be the case."

"Male or female?"

"We believe this is highly likely to be a male, intelligent with possible social phobias. We would like to stress to the public that this escalation in apparent violence is deeply concerning and we formally request that reactions or comments are not put forward online. Our criminal psychologist states that by engaging in this manner it enables and encourages a reaction. We believe we are dealing with a dangerous and highly volatile situation."

"Do you believe that Lilly is alive?"

"We have no reason to think otherwise at this present time, however we do feel that time is of the essence. Any information will be looked in to confidentially and can be given anonymously."

"So, in summary, you are asking the public to close down their social media regarding Lillian Brown?"

"Yes, absolutely. Thank you."

"Thank you."

I could hardly believe it, I am a good man. This was making me sound evil, "criminal psychologist, profiling, social phobias". This was outrageous, hideous. I had not intended for any of this, yes, I admit that I had uploaded the images of you by way of a response but not in a bad way, not to hurt anyone or cause distress. Everything was being twisted, every-time my intentions had been misinterpreted. It was not my fault that they misunderstood and, furthermore, I do socialise and communicate, I just do it in my way, on my terms. I was confused as what to do for the best, what would they understand? I wanted to show that you were not being hurt, I wanted to reassure them that you would not be hurt, but I did not want to provoke the accusations that you were pretending or playing a game. It was so difficult, I felt that whichever course of action I took it would be considered wrong somehow. I decided to do nothing, take time to think things over. I went to bed.

Monday, September 25
A Quick Goodbye

I had had yet another unsettled night, so many recently, really most unhelpful for my complexion. However, slightly later than usual, my run cancelled as the long drive lay ahead and obviously I had to allow some time for you, I rose. After my shower, I dressed and loaded the car. I emailed our food order, I did have a moment's concern that the increase in the amount I was ordering could flag up, but on further consideration, I deemed this a little paranoid. I ate wholemeal toast with a zesty orange marmalade and several lattes. All quite different for me but my stomach felt unsettled, the dark roasted bean worked well with the milk and somehow still had an intensity. After clearing away and preparing the dining room for its new display, I was ready.

"Good morning, Lilly."

You were still in bed asleep. I left you and found your shopping bag. I had hidden it alongside the boot rack in the garage. I unfolded it, the smell of mouldy bread hit me instantly, slimy looking salad clung inside its bag. I returned with gloves and discarded these along with the yogurts and collected your marmite and your cheap pinot. I placed them in a basket ready for tomorrow's delivery. I returned to the screen, I was a little disappointed as you were still asleep. I added my last bandages and wipes. I returned to the screen, still asleep. I chose a couple of autobiographies and I popped them in to the basket too, Stephen Fry and the Rev. Richard Coles, both inspiring, funny men. I returned to the screen,

"Good morning, Lilly."

I spoke a little louder now, I had a schedule, I needed to be on the road immediately after the display had been received and safely positioned.

"Good morning, Lilly."

I raised my voice and much to my relief this caused the intended consequence. Startled, you sat up, the soft blue of the mood lighting gives a silver glow and so is not unpleasant to adjust to, I knew. You stood up and were muttering as you went behind the doors. A few minutes later and the kettle was on.

"Good morning, Lilly," I yet again said.

"Is it?"

"Yes, yes it really is. I shall be going quite soon Lilly, as promised I wanted to see you before my departure."

"Great, well, here I am."

"Yes indeed Lilly, along with the empty bottles place any washing that you have, towels, robe etc. inside the cool box. It also occurred to me that the bin must be full, there will be a new liner ready, so leave that with the box and basket, by the door."

"When for?"

"I will be back tomorrow."

You were drinking tea and cutting the last of the strawberries, carefully placing them on to the yogurt, precisely spooned out. Apart from the un-made bed everything was perfectly in order.

"How long did you circle the room?"

"Until I couldn't, until I started drinking."

"Why?"

"Why not? I'm trapped, I need to keep calm, but I'm frightened, walking is my way to calm, even if it is round and round, road to nowhere."

"Lilly, I said that I would not hurt you. I will be back tomorrow."

"You are hurting me though can you not see that? Locking me up, keeping me in here, that hurts, that is hurting me."

"Look we will talk tomorrow night, I am too busy for this right now."

"Yeah, yeah, fuck off then. Ashes to ashes, have fun."

"Well, I am hardly going to find that fun."

"Why? You hated her, throw them out where you like and tell her what you think. Laugh and let it go, just watch out for the wind direction."

I paused, these words had caught me off-guard. I had only allowed myself to think of that day as time with my family, her connection carefully edited out.

"Goodbye, Lilly."

"Goodbye, what is your name by the way?"

I obviously did not reply. You cleared away the breakfast things, another tea brewed, the bed carefully made, clingfilm wrapped around your arm, drank your tea. I knew this routine, slowly and steadily, next the surfaces, then the floors, then a shower... I had to go.

I exchanged the old for the new at ten, perfectly punctual. They were, as usual, stunning. Magnificent pink garden roses and antique hydrangea wrapped and bound with silver thread sparkling through the large glass vase.

I took the waters from the fridge and left on time, ten-thirty exactly.

Ashes to Ashes
Dust upon Dust

The weather was blustery but clear and bright. I had obviously missed commuter chaos and my drive was as uneventful as one can hope for. As I crunched my way around the drive, my aunt was already waiting in the doorway. Your words had filled my head throughout the journey, your demanding tone re-heard and re-played. Find answers, ask questions, tell her what I felt, laugh. It was a relief to arrive and to escape. The previous feelings I had had of apprehension were taken over by the sheer joy at seeing my aunt's smiling face, arms outstretched to greet me. I was hugged and ushered in, the smell of wood burning and the cheery tones of my uncle and godfather could be heard. How very different it all now seemed. I took my things up whilst my aunt prepared afternoon tea. We gathered in the main room, relaxed, eating scones with too much clotted cream and jam, my aunt fussing wonderfully. She had arranged for us to collect the urn before six and then the four of us to have dinner at the hotel for eight. Reasoning I would need time to freshen up after such a drive.

The men had chosen to remain, loading up the fire and re-settling. I drove the short distance, my aunt by my side. I did not speak, and I felt my lack of social grace completely understood. As we walked towards the funeral director my aunt held my arm, gently patting my hand. We were met with what I can only say felt like a ridiculous presentation as we were handed an over-sized, gilt covered gold and blue urn. Apparently, we were informed, "An excellent choice for display purposes."

"A real keepsake."

We left in silence. We drove in silence. I almost swore, and I briefly thought of you. We arrived back at the house and placed the offensive object in the hallway and re-joined the others. My godfather was preparing pre-dinner drinks and I drank thirstily and gratefully. I left them, showered, changed, when I returned, a hush came over the room. My aunt looked to me, concerned,

"Was I holding up? Did I have an appetite?"

"Yes, yes," I replied.

I was fine and yet I was shaking, not in shock but with that inner rage again. As we walked passed the ornate pot, I resisted the urge to kick it over, the thought of the contents covering my suede boots just enough to dissuade me.

The hotel was warm and just busy enough to create a welcoming atmosphere, a low level of noise and some laughter. We were seated in a corner in front of a large bay window, perfect. The restaurant is called the Oak Room with panelled walls and an open fire. The chairs are high backed with dark grey upholstery, it is elegant and traditional. We ate, I had the quail scotch egg to start followed by a dry aged sirloin with blue cheese sauce. We shared a couple of bottles of Chateauneuf-du-Pape, (2003) and began to relax. Small talk of work and travellers' tales from my godfather which were delightful. We opted out of desserts and even coffees as my uncle informed us that he had a rather good vintage port already decanted and warming by the fire. My aunt had prepared a cheese board, crackers and fruit. So out in to the cold we went, chattering on, our breath blowing out against the late evening air. The fire was loaded up, the drinks were poured. My godfather took out a box of Montecristo No. 4 cigars and offered them, my aunt looked at me anxiously, my uncle smiled. She would not have allowed this. I took the Cuban treat and lit up, enjoying the gentle flavour. Suddenly we were all laughing, ridiculously silly outbursts, almost forgetting why we had even begun, a contagious conspiracy of pure joy. How much, how so very much I had missed them, we were cosy, the four of us, together. I raised my glass,

"To us, it has been too long."

"Here, here."

Clink, clink. My aunt then seemed teary, explaining they were all so pleased to see me looking so well and coping, how they had worried over the years, how they hoped we would, could remain in contact now.

"Of–of course," I had stammered slightly, "of course."

Then guard down maybe, port-induced confidence perhaps, I asked the question,

"Why had they not visited after father's passing?"

I could not have anticipated the fallout from my question. My aunt was aghast,

"Oh, how we had wanted to see you, to take me out, have me to stay with them, holiday with them, but when the letters remained unanswered they felt I had made my decision."

"Le–letters?" I had stammered, "What letters?"

My uncle shook his head,

"We all wrote. We even, in the beginning, came in the evenings to talk to her, to allow us to be part of your life, she told us that you no longer wanted to see us."

He had thought that his incredible likeness to my father unsettled me so. He had felt guilty. My aunt then,

"We called so often, we came but you were always with your friends. We thought that you had come out of your shell, we were pleased for you, but how we missed you."

In the end they had reluctantly agreed to stay away and to simply write. My godfather recounted how they had been told to,

"Let the boy decide."

"So, obviously when no response came…"

He had been humiliated and cursed in front of her friends on an accidental meeting, for encouraging my obvious disposition. My stomach literally turned.

"I was never out, apart from school, I was always there. She never told me," I faltered.

I explained how after tea I had always been sent to my room at the back of the house, my window overlooking nothing but the landscape. I would sit with my headphones on, computer games and software, the internet my world. I never came out of my room,

"She-she, she would lock me in," my childhood stutter.

"I–I–I–I did, did not know, I m-m-missed you."

My uncle topped our glasses, my aunt held my hand. The realisation of her true evil, her destructive and hideous nature was finally unfolding, and it felt oppressive, filling the room, smothering me. I drank in silence, trying to logically process this new-found information, my heart was racing, my head spinning. How I hated her. Spurred on by this intense sense of injustice I leapt to my feet and frantically ran up the twisting staircase, down her hallway and flung open her door. The smell of Estee Lauder lingering in the room, I never went in to her room, it was forbidden. The floral fabrics and wallpaper were oppressive, the padded headboard was slightly tinged from where her head must have once rested. The dressing-table and upholstered stool covered in her untidiness, her derangement clearly displayed. I swept my arm over the surface scattering the contents, sending them in to disarray. The two mahogany wardrobes stood across the far wall, I marched to them, flinging open the doors, revealing a jumble of the must-have labels swinging on hangers, I pulled at them, some falling, some tearing. I did not care. There were stacks of footwear squeezed at the bottom in a jumbled assortment, some boxed others just left entangled. They smelt of old sweat and my stomach lurched again, I slammed the doors shut. On the top were old suitcases I pulled them down over my shoulders, crashing to the floor. Clouds of dust and clumps of fluff, years of matter clinging to their surface. I could feel it in my eyes, my nose, my mouth. I desperately rubbed my clothing, shook my head. I felt as though my skin was on fire. I wanted to run, to breathe fresh air. I do not know exactly what was driving me, an unconscious knowledge? A need to disrespect her rules? To intrude or to quite simply destroy? I kicked at the old leather cases in turn, the rusty locks clicked open, mildewed lining exposed in the first, I threw it to one side, I continued kicking the second and the smell of damp, musty paper hit me. Inside and unopened were piles of envelopes all addressed to me. Some had faded Sellotape on the backs, these I remembered, had always excited me as a boy, these had always contained money. I had not noticed but they had been watching me from the doorway, my aunt ran to me, my uncle, such a stoic strong man, was crying, looking towards the ceiling, apologising to his brother, asking him to forgive him. My godfather lit another of his cigars, in her room, and quite simply said, "Bitch."

They had written until I was eighteen and had then decided, as I had moved away, to cease. In front of us lay five years of unfulfilled hopes and plans, my lonely ignorance and her depraved and nefarious practice.

We talked and drank long in to the night. We played snooker, laughing at out our own inaccuracies, we smoked our cigars. We were together. If only my father could have been with us too. When I was a boy I had such happy memories of watching the three of them in the snooker room, becoming louder as the night drew on and the drinks went down. My godfather was always the barman, new drinks would be lined up and much back-slapping and silliness would prevail. I was always with my father and on these nights, when the four of us were together, I felt so proud to be included in their private men's club.

Eventually when, quite frankly, standing had become difficult, my aunt called time. I do remember clinging to the bannisters, dragging myself up and to bed. I removed my boots collapsed and I slept.

With a thick head, a mouth that tasted of the night before and a furry tongue I awoke. Normally I would have been disgusted, my clothes still on, teeth unbrushed and the state of my suede boots, splashed with brandy residue and falling bits of ash. Normally, but not this morning, I smiled in-spite of and because of it all. My godfather, aunt and uncle were having morning coffee and my aunt took pity on me, fussing, plumping up my cushion, making me toast, pouring me a large black filter. It was just after nine, I knew I had to leave no later than eleven thirty to ensure I arrived home for the food delivery at six. I gratefully accepted another coffee, rehydration required, and we decided to do the deed. Although a little hazy in my mind I recalled our plan. We had decided to take her and throw her in the woods. She had never appreciated the views or the beauty of the trees. Coats on and with an excitement almost, we left the house. My uncle carried the garish urn and we strode purposefully, how funny we must have looked. We reached a suitable spot, the red and gold leaves, a canopy around us, the smell of damp mosses and the sun shining down on us.

There was a little discussion on how we were actually going to undertake the procedure but as none of us wanted to touch the contents we agreed to merely tip them out. I smiled and remembered your quip about wind direction and pointed this out. My godfather licked his finger and placed it in the air,

"Ah all was fine if we turned to the left," so unceremoniously, we let the dark grey ashes spew out, the bone fragments resembling grains of sand. That was it, she was deposited. My aunt held my hand and asked if I wanted to say anything, I still had so much to ask, to question, but just knowing that they loved me, that she had kept them from me and it was not a reflection on me, was comfort. The truth was unfolding and in that moment that was all I needed. I was reminded of a line,

'If only your mother hadn't been such a bitch we could've shared something important.' [3]

I surveyed the fallen mound,

"I am relieved and happy that you are dead."

Enough, enough, that truly was all that was required. My hand was gently squeezed, such kindness in my aunt's eyes. My godfather hugged me, my uncle smiled and requested a moment for himself, so in a connected line we three began to walk back. There was talk of lunch, the dampness in the air and the beauty of the woodlands at that time of year. I glanced back briefly and caught a glimpse of my uncle stamping on the ground. He caught us up, no comment was made, no comment was needed.

I felt secure, linked and content. My hangover had lifted, I had a peace within me that was calming and gentle and warm. Naturally there was much encouragement for me to stay longer but I insisted, due to my commitments, that I would have to leave.

There were obviously some legalities regarding the house, probate, the will, but all were to be dealt with by the family solicitor, however, it was decided that they should remain at the house and I would travel back down at the weekend.

As I drove home I thought of you. It seemed so right to be coming back to you, having enjoyed the company of others I was reassured not to be returning to an empty house. I was excited, eager to tell you, the revelations. To share my joy. To share with you.

Tuesday, September 26
Home

Five thirty pm and I was safely back, enclosed behind the gates. I removed my boots and smiled at the memories that they displayed. Upstairs I unpacked quickly and selected a change of outfit. My phone rang, and the delivery arrived. Two trips up and down the stairs and it surrounded me, I put my things away and left yours in the cool box. Your wines in their case. I did so want to rush to see you, but I needed to shower. When the washing was on and I was refreshed, evening meal decided, a simple lasagne with a spinach salad after the excesses of the evening before, I came to you.

"Good evening, Lilly."

You were positioned at the sink, clearing away your dinner things I assumed, I glanced around, all perfect with the boxes and the bin bag all stacked behind the door.

"You're back then."

"Evidently, have you just eaten?"

"Yes, my last meal, spinach and ricotta pasta before you ask."

This again made me smile, you had indeed anticipated correctly. I noted how much I was smiling.

"I have your food, the order has arrived, I added extra treats."

"Gee thanks so how was your trip?"

"Oh Lilly, it was amazing!"

I joyfully recounted the events. As I spoke you poured a glass of wine and listened intensively, occasionally interjecting, clearly startled by the letters. You laughed when I revealed my uncle's actions.

"You sound different, less acidic, softer."

"Do I? I do not think acidic a fair description, however. So, Lilly, what do you think?"

Your opinion mattered, strangely, this new experience of sharing and wanting to share was surprising but you encouraged me, supported me. I liked this.

"About your mother? I think she was cruel and quite possibly jealous of your relationships, with the others and with your father. Tell me though, why didn't you just try and contact them?"

"I was thirteen Lilly, in shock, deep, deep grief and I was told by her they had no interest in me. I was told and teased repeatedly, no-one wanted me. As a child I did not understand, I did not question. I could not comprehend how everything had suddenly changed. I just retreated."

"Did you have school friends?"

"I muddled along with them, no one was particularly close to me."

"Did you enjoy school?"

"Yes, well the academic side."

"Not a sports fan then?"

"I am fit, I have always run well, I just never found team sports appealing, football, rugby, cricket, no not my thing."

"You say you retreated, what do you mean?"

"Just that, I would go to school, return, eat my tea with our housekeeper and then I would go to my room."

"How did it feel to be locked in your room?"

"It was my world Lilly and the world was with me."

"Where was she?"

"Oh, she was always busy, one social occasion after another, evening dinners, charity events, fundraising balls, she would be there."

"Did you ever try to talk to her?"

"Yes, but she had no time for me. I was not good enough, I was not what she wanted in a son."

"Why do you say that you were not good enough?"

"Oh, I know, she told me."

"That does not make it true, maybe she wasn't good enough."

"But you see everyone loved her, every organisation wanted her as a figure head. They would fluster around her, at dinner parties they would gather, gift bearing, hanging on her every word."

"That does not make her right and it most certainly does not prove anything, she was not good enough, especially to be a mum."

"It was me, I was a disappointment, not the strutting confident son."

"No stop it. Think, think. Any woman who could hurt a grieving child is sick, let alone one who is supposed to be their mother."

You sounded angry, you poured another glass of wine and lit a cigarette.

"It makes me so cross, so fucking cross, you know, what is your fucking name by the way?" You gestured up with your hand.

"So cross, if you are lucky enough to have children you should treasure them."

Your lip was trembling, you were starting to cry. I was touched. I poured a gin and tonic, back to my usual tipple tonight, I put some lentil and sea-salt crisps in a bowl and returned. You had finished your cigarette and were already topping up your glass. The speed you drank with sometimes was astounding.

"Lilly, do you have a drink problem?"

"What? Oh, listen to you, high and almighty, no I don't, I just like it quite a lot."

"Well, you might just try and sip it, enjoy it then."

"Mmmm, well yes, it's just sometimes I just want it to take away my emotions, to dull them down, it's what I do and anyway, you gave it to me."

"Yes that is perfectly true and for your information I am enjoying a G and T, even after all that brandy, so I was not being high and almighty."

"Whatever."

"How is your arm, Lilly?"

"I think it is a little better today, I might dare to leave it uncovered soon, looks a mess though."

"If only you had left it alone, it would be healed by now."

"Oh my fucking, you've got a nerve, you self-righteous twat, you did this."

"Language and no, no, Lilly, I did not do that. Why do you swear so much? It is so vulgar."

"Vulgar, huh, but you, slicing my arm, what's that? Keeping me locked in here, that's socially acceptable is it? But a few fucking shitty words oh my that's wrong! Wow!"

"I just feel swearing displays a lack of control, a lack of language skills."

"No, it doesn't, it emphasises, it's powerful, saved for special occasions. Anyway, it's my go to cross, upset, whatever I swear, it just happens."

"You allow it to happen."

"Yes, okay, I do unintentionally. It's just a way to cope, no big deal."

"Like walking?"

"Yes."

"Is that why you count?"

"Yes, yes and the counting helps my breathing to slow down, to give me back the feeling of control, to stop the panic taking over."

From the way that you spoke it was apparent that this coping, as you put it, these responses were not new, they had been learnt, they were habits, established habits. I needed a break from you, I took another drink and went to my seat. The night was catching up with me, the events all starting to sink in. Your reaction to her had moved me "you should treasure your children" kept ringing in my ears, I returned,

"Lilly, I forgot to ask, what did you do yesterday?"

"Ha, well I had a party, in my party room, it was fantastic, dancing, drinking, laughing. Shame you couldn't make it!"

"Really?"

"Oh yes and I saw my children too."

"Really? How are they?"

"Amazing and beautiful."

"And your partner, Lilly, how is he?"

"Oh gorgeous as ever, we danced, all of us, like we do."

"Do you?"

"Oh yes."

"It sounds fun, they sound like fun. They know you love them, Lilly."

You were pouring the last drops of wine in to your glass and opening another, the last in the cooler, luckily provisions were lined up I thought. Your hands were shaking as you filled the glass to the very rim and returned the bottle. You lowered your whole body to take the first sip or gulp I should say, then lit another cigarette.

"I don't just love them, I love them to the moon and back."

You were swaying and not long from your sleep, I could tell.

"Moon and back, moon and back," you were whispering.

"Goodnight, Lilly, sleep well."

"Goodnight, yes, you too."

I clicked the screen off and I remember how it pleased me that you had bid me goodnight too. I had not seen the news, I did not want to view that night, possibly tomorrow, possibly. Something about you had unravelled me, I saw you for the first time as a vulnerable soul? A crazy woman? Or was I just over emotional myself? Over-thinking was not my thing, but I really could not stop, not now, all my compartments of thought and memory were unlocked along with that case. I felt an exposure and a depth of pain, of regret. I was raw, quite possibly still in shock and exhausted. Sleep. I needed to sleep.

Wednesday, September 27
Sir

As soon as I woke I thought of you, who were you? As much as I did not want to admit to myself that you had been right about finding answers. Your words about her "not being good enough to be a mum, of being jealous" had put a twist to my thoughts in regard to myself. I am a good man, maybe I had been a good son, good enough. I could not focus my thinking and was uncomfortable with all of this. I felt too drained to run and was relieved to see the rain lashing down. No beautiful autumn day, just relentless rain, darkness, the trees being stripped prematurely. I showered, shaved, moisturised and dressed. I made porridge and went to you. You were still sleeping. I took the cool box, basket and wine to just outside your door. I momentarily thought to deliver and retrieve right then, but no logical thought won through. I returned upstairs but could not settle, although lethargic and the weather against me, I decided a brisk walk might help. I found myself at the newsagents, your poster was still there, looking a little tatty now. I bought your cigarettes, the shop was busy so, thankfully, no time for conversation. I came home, dried my hair and had made tea, lemon and ginger and yet I could still not settle. I concluded that maybe I was coming down with something, understandably when I considered all that I had been going through.

Monitor on and you were finally awake, drinking your English breakfast, emptying the yogurt pot, spoon by spoon,

"Good morning, Lilly."

"Is it?"

"Well, actually, no, it is raining."

"Who would have thought you could miss the rain?"

"Did you sleep well? You were rather drunk."

"Mmmm, yes, do you have a garden?"

"Why?"

"Could I go in the garden? Feel the rain, the fresh air?"

Although not over looked directly, my courtyard was not covered, I could not take the risk and for you to access the space would create so many potential difficulties, it was just not feasible.

"The rain would not be good for your arm Lilly and you do not have a coat."

"I could borrow one and I cling film my arm when I shower."

"I have been reflecting on your observations regarding her by the way. Do you really think she was jealous?"

"That's a no then is it?" You paused, "Yes, yes I do, she clearly resented you, do you think she even wanted to be a mother? Did she physically hurt you?"

"I had not thought, I had just assumed, that to have a child would be a natural desire."

"Not necessarily and just because you can does not mean you always should, did she hurt you?"

"When I stammered she would beat the backs of my legs or as I grew my arms, in time with every syllable she snapped."

"Did you ever hit back?"

"No, gosh no. I just stopped speaking and she stopped beating. It was simple. I always felt that if only I were stronger, my speech bold and clear that she would be happy, not so disappointed."

"Her behaviour had nothing to do with disappointment and everything to do with bullying, can't you see that?"

"I was very shy as a boy, young man even. I could not cope with all those social functions."

"You were intimidated and bullied, were you ever involved? Surely if people were at your house?"

"I would be briefly introduced or acknowledged on occasion, but I could not be the social charmer for her to display proudly. I was just the boy and then I would retreat politely."

"A mother is proud of her child, it is unconditional love in its purest form, a mother should encourage and create a platform of support and help build confidence, not belittle and undermine."

"If I had been different though?"

"Oh for goodness' sake, this is hard I appreciate, but no, let's face it your mother was a bitch. I totally agree with your godfather. If she had come here what were you going to say?"

"I thought somehow, if we could speak, now I am in control of my stammer, that she might like me."

"Honestly? Listen, for whatever her reasons, she was not right, had no right to do what she did. You were a little boy, lost without his father, this was not your fault. Your family all love you and always have so it is not logical for you to think you are unlikable, unlovable, is it?"

These words were quite overwhelming, not my fault, not logical, but emotions are never logical that is why I am not an emotional person. You poured a glass of orange and cleared away.

"You don't need her to like you, you need to understand, as difficult as this might be, that she was a bad person, not you and no amount of time would have changed her. You do not have the power to change a bad person, only they can do that. You were not responsible or indeed the cause of her behaviour, you were her outlet, her victim. You have to accept that you would never have made her the mother that you needed, the mother that you deserved. You need to speak to your family."

Your voice was gentle and yet serious, your words floated in my head, they were thoughtful and kind.

"Thank you."

"You're welcome. I need to shower now."

You were wrapping your arm.

"Are you okay?"

"Yes, yes actually, I think that I am, Lilly."

And you went behind the doors.

I ran down the stairs, took the cigarettes from my pocket and placed them on top of the basket. I felt so happy that I had made that purchase. I took the key from the drawer, lightly dusting the top of the table as I walked past and unlocked your door. So very, very quickly. I exchanged the old for the new. My heart was racing, the wine clanked slightly and made me jump but you remained enclosed. I shut and locked the door, returned the key and took everything upstairs. I put my cleaning gloves on and took out your washing, your original clothes, towels and one set of lounge wear, the beltless robe. Washing on, I threw out your rubbish and recycled. I cleaned the cool box and stacked it with the basket back in the garage. All ready for the next time. Organised. Eagerly then, I rushed back to you. I was excited, not worried this time, just simply excited. Eventually you returned in view, you instantly saw everything. Your arm was on display, uncovered, I recoiled slightly, it's appearance was quite disturbing, large raised scabs, protruding edges of flesh, jagged and uneven. You smiled, a full smile, like the one in your official photo and cuddled the books to you.

"Thank you," you said.

"You're welcome," I replied.

You proceeded to unpack, everything studied and carefully put away.

"I hope you like my choices Lilly, the lemon possets are one of my favourites."

You began your ritual, salt water and savlon, focused breathing and gently wrapped the new bandage around the disfigurement. You were visibly in pain and sat for some time counting. I watched and waited. I was a little annoyed that you had not seen fit to acknowledge me. Slowly you began to move, to clear away.

"Lilly, I am still here."

"And so am I, the food, the wine, books, cigarettes."

You were gesturing but without the vigour from before,

"What does this mean? How long are you going to keep me? Please I just want to go home."

You were crying but feebly, I was uncomfortable again, this was really rather annoying, and I admit I did feel it to be a little ungrateful.

"Please, please, Sir, let me go home."

Sir. This rather startled me and pleased me in equal measure.

"You called me Sir."

"Well, you won't tell me your name, I am exhausted and drained. I think the pain and the fear have drained me. You Sir have drained me, but don't be flattered, I considered fuckwit or twat, but the constant use diminishes their impact, so a nondescript Sir is who you are. And I think you're a bit of an arrogant tit."

"Nondescript? Arrogant?"

"Yes, Sir, exactly."

I was not expecting this. I felt deflated and disappointed even but mostly I was infuriated. I left you then.

Truths

I spent the rest of the day with an inner rage, not quite as before, not in quite the same way, but I was disappointed by the turn of our conversation. I mean really who did you think you were? I sorted your washing, I even ironed your jeans, it was like doing a child's laundry. I am not arrogant, I just have standards, high standards. By the early evening I had an overwhelming sense of resentment, I felt that I had been insulted.

I returned to you. You were eating one of the meals that I had given to you.

"I am not arrogant, Lilly."

"Oh really? Well, you could have fooled me, Sir, maybe it's a façade then, your way to face the world."

"A façade?"

"Yes, a mask, a shield even."

I considered your words. A shield, did I carry myself with pretence? A false front? No this was incorrect, I merely did not feel the need to wear my heart upon my sleeve. You were wrong I was sure.

"What did you choose for your dinner?"

"Pumpkin casserole with lentils and spinach."

"Oh yes, I enjoy that, a lovely autumnal dish."

"Do you eat these meals too? Can't you cook?"

"Yes naturally I can, the housekeeper taught me, I am rather a good chef actually with a refined palate."

"But you don't cook?"

"It is just the mess, the effort for just myself, it simply does not feel worth the time and anyway, this meal company are so good."

"You said this room was the last to furnished, does that mean you have recently moved here?"

"Well, a little over a year ago now."

"But by yourself. You work remotely, so tell me Sir do you live your life remotely too?"

"I manage my life perfectly well, thank you."

"Manage your life, that is not the same as living your life."

"And who, may I ask, are you Lilly to pass judgement? Are you perfect? Look at you."

"Yes look at me because that is what you like to do isn't? Just look, that's weird.

I'm not perfect and I wasn't making a judgement, more of an observation."

"You know nothing of my life."

"Well, that's not fucking true is it? You obviously grew up with financial privilege, you're rich."

"You're jealous."

"No, well yes I suppose, but only because money allows choice and removes so much worry. My point was that you have that, you probably had a great education. I assume your work is successful? If this room is anything to go by, your house must be gorgeous. I mean, you said that this was intended just to be a fucking party room and yet you buy these meals and are by yourself, don't you want to share your life?"

"Of course I am successful and yes, my home is perfect thank you. I have a good life."

"But are you happy Sir? Why have all this and not share it? Where are your friends? Don't you want a partner?"

"I am perfectly organised, I do not need others to complicate my life. I do not rely on anyone. I do speak to people, I know people, you are misguided."

"So why build a party room?"

"I do not believe that I ever gave it that title."

"Right, fine, snooker for one, films for one. You build a perfect set but then leave it empty."

"It is not empty though you are there."

"Oh my Sir, for fuck's sake, I shouldn't be here, I'm not a fucking mother substitute. I am not her."

"I am more than aware of that thank you and may I remind you that it was never my intention for you to be here. I was merely making an observation."

"Sir, I appreciate she was a bitch, she hurt you, but you have to deal with it and move on, live your life. You have everything, let me go and get on with it."

"How very naïve you are, Lilly, my life is good. I manage everything perfectly."

"And remotely. For crying out loud everyone has shit to deal with, it's how you deal with it that affects everything. You're young are you not? How old are you?"

"Almost twenty-five, but I see no relevance."

"Twenty-five, I am old enough to be your mother for fuck's sake. Twenty-five is so young, you have your whole life in front of you to enjoy, to live. Don't let her hold you back, deal with it, be free. When bad shit happens it's how you cope that defines you. Fear is debilitating. Happiness, true happiness, rather than managed existence is the best revenge in the world."

"Fear? You are yet again, misguided. Your simplistic reasonings and assumptions are ridiculous."

"Are they? So, are you happy all alone?"

"I have a good life."

"But could it be better? You have not answered, by the way, are you happy?"

"I am perfectly content, just because you need to be surrounded in your smug life, your children, your partner, how arrogant to assume that I need the same. I am stronger than you are Lilly."

"My life is not, smug you fucking idiot, it is full. My gorgeous children have all grown up now and moved away but they are still in my life. I share my life with my partner and it is warm and funny, that is not smug, that is appreciating life and sharing it. You're the fucking naïve one and I want my life back."

"Well, we do not always get what we want, do we Lilly?"

91

"But we could Sir, if only you would allow it, we both could."

I left you then, this analysis, this conversation had run its course for me. Enough, enough. Anyway, I was aware that I needed to catch up with the evening news.

The News

I had deliberately avoided this situation for the previous two days, but I was curious, if not a little agitated at the prospect of further character assassinations. I was beginning to feel a little victimised.

'Somebody up there has got it in for me, I bet it's my mother.' [4]

That aside and a generous gin in hand I watched.

"On the thirteenth day of Lilly Brown's disappearance the police seem no closer to finding the mother of three or, indeed, any answers."

The CCTV footage was again shown, the familiar photograph, the phone numbers, help with enquiries, any information, etc. No press conference, no family. They had scaled back their investigation rather quickly, I felt. You were old news. I looked through social media, you were trending,

#supportingLillylovenotwords

My posts had been taken down, as had all the original negative comments. Interesting to try to have some control over the internet. It is a world with so many layers, so many freedoms it can never be controlled. It is both beauty and the beast. Obviously, many people were still reacting, the new tag line being re-tweeted habitually. The need to share and over share, to be seen to be the first, the last to have an involvement. The unconscious social need.

I sat in silence and swivelled.

Reflections

Our conversation was playing heavily on my mind, you were annoying. So much unnecessary comment, causing me discomfort. I did not appreciate your questions, they made me question myself, this was a new experience and not a pleasant one, most certainly not invited. Was I happy? I was content, organised, effective. A stage, an empty stage? Really quite dramatic, so typical of you, but was that true? I walked from one perfect room to another. The unused dining room, the sofas, cushions at undisturbed angles, the guest bedrooms. I remembered my excitement when you had described the studio as my party room. I had replied exactly, so immediately, as I was excited that you could visualise my intention, but also and perhaps most importantly, because you had thought of me as a man who holds parties, who entertains. The Host with the Most. Had I created an empty stage? The perfectly dressed set? Was I too afraid to allow the curtains to open? The stage to be filled? The people in? I picked up each correctly placed cushion and tossed them back on the sofa, free to land and remain, casually scattered and walked away.

I was angered by your ability to see me. You had been correct about answers needing to be found, were you correct that I should share my life? The risk, the intrusion, the disruption, the potential for mess on so many levels? Why did I need that? Why would anyone? Did I enjoy my life remotely? Did I enjoy just looking? Watching? I was not unhappy, but could my life be better? Oh Lilly, before I met you none of these thoughts would have been allowed. What had you done to me? My order of thought, that I prided myself on, was unravelling.

A nightcap to calm my mind and a quick realignment of the cushions, their precision pleasing, I went to my bed.

Thursday, September 28
Anniversary

A new day. I had yet another disturbed night, jumbled thoughts that you had created. I ran, fresh air and the discipline, the hypnotic rhythm of each foot pounding on the earth, helping my mind to calm, to focus. I was a little disgruntled that they could so quickly remove you from the headline news. I was not allowed this luxury of forgetfulness. You were ever present physically and mentally. As I showered and undertook my usual routines I reasoned to post a new picture of you. I concluded that even they could not misunderstand, misinterpret, again. I could not be wrongly accused of being provoked or feeding off feeds, thank you. I did not really care for the last image, still so fresh in my mind anyway. Fuelled by espresso and the knowledge that I was correct in my chosen action I skipped through time with you. There was a familiar frame, you sat at the island, talking, one hand slightly raised, your head slightly tilted. I uploaded this snapshot, surrounding you with speech bubbles and a delicate border of cotton plants, the downy fibre cotton bolls fresh and white. I did this for three reasons,

1. To mask your surroundings.
2. The cotton to represent our second week together.
3. To encourage conversation.

Under the new title,
"Lilly loves to talk."
You were out there.
I was very pleased with the result and my continued thoughtfulness. "Happy anniversary Lilly," I spoke out loud and my words almost seemed to hang in time, echoing through me.

Potential

I switched the monitor on, you had already showered, and the studio was immaculate. Your arm still covered. The loungewear and one of the Paul Smith sweatshirts on. You looked so lost inside these garments. The marmite was out, and you were cutting a slice of bread, tea by your side.

"Hello, Lilly."

"Hello, Sir."

You emphasised the word Sir with a sarcasm I found unnecessary, but I ignored this.

"Are you enjoying your marmite?"

"Yes, thank you."

"Lilly, nothing is quite as simplistic as you seem to think, maybe in your small world, maybe for you, but for me your ideas are not conducive."

"I don't think I ever said things were simplistic, just possible."

"Possible?"

"Yes. If you're logical, Sir, and I think that you may be, what's the worst thing that can happen?"

"My life could be disrupted."

"And would that be so bad really?"

You had taken out some blueberries and yogurt and proceeded to carefully arrange the fruit.

"I do like the way you decorate the yogurt."

"Like the way that you like the way I clean?"

"Yes, it is precise, considered and respectful."

"Order. There is a reassurance found in order, I understand that, but too much order can be disruptive too."

"That is illogical, Lilly."

"No, it's not, not really. If you hide behind your order and the order becomes the most important factor, then it is that very order that disrupts the possibilities that you have."

" Order is important. You just said that a reassurance was found within it, that is good, can only be good."

"Yes, if it does not consume you, hold you back. Look around me, order, perfectly clean, why Sir?"

"Because that is correct."

"Ha, yes, but it is something I do, it is a way to cope, to feel secure. When I have no control, when things upset me or scare me I clean, I order. The happier I am, although never messy, the more relaxed I can allow things to be."

"Creating order is not bad, by your own admission."

"No, not bad, but it is a reaction to understand, not to be ruled by."

"I am not ruled by anything Lilly."

"Okay, so by avoiding any disruption to your life, is that not holding you back?"

"I am not comfortable with all this analysis."

"Because it disrupts what?"

"My thoughts and anyway, holding me back? As you have already correctly observed, I am rich and successful."

"And happy?"

"What do you care anyway? Why so many questions?"

"Well, forgive me Sir, but I am trapped in here with nothing to do."

"You have books now."

"Yes, but nothing else, nothing to focus on apart from the cleaning, my arm and you. I am terrified at the very idea that I might never see my family again, hear their voices, see their faces, to know that they are alright. I am so fucking scared. It hurts so much to think about, so it makes sense that I think about you, focus on you and ask questions."

"As a distraction, well, thank you."

" What do you expect, fucking gratitude? Well, fine, I am grateful that I have food, food that is lovely too, that I have juices, wine. The most beautiful bathroom products that I could only dream of. I am grateful for these clothes and the warmth under my feet, but I am still your prisoner."

"I am pleased that you appreciate your surroundings and my efforts."

"Does that make you happy?"

"You, Lilly, seem to have an obsession with that word."

"And you Sir, seem to have an obsession with ignoring it. Rich and successful and all at almost twenty-five. I guess you must have worked really hard to be where you are today?"

"Yes, I have been focused and driven."

"And so focused, so enveloped in your work that you made sure that there was no room for anything else, anyone else?"

"You do not get to be as successful as I am without focus Lilly."

"Professionally and financially successful fine but what about personally? Have you fulfilled your potential there too? Money is great, but it is not the be all, money is not the most important thing in life. It is not a replacement for happiness."

"Why did you tell me about your reasons for cleaning, the order?"

"Because I thought you would understand."

"You understand, you accept, that this is the way you behave. You have clearly thought about the rationale behind your actions, so why do you doubt mine?"

"Just because I have accepted myself, understood myself does not make it right. I try not to allow my fears to destroy my potential, but I have limits. You're so young, you don't have to cap your life, you need to live it."

"I need to go now Lilly. I will return. What are you having for dinner?"

Your eyes rolled, your hands held high.

"Well, I'm not sure, hang on."

You walked to the fridge and began looking,

"Mmm, I think I will have the smoked ham and pepper pizza, what are you having?"

"Well, I was not sure either, however, I will join you with pizza, I have a rather good red onion and chorizo one."

"Join me?"

"Figuratively speaking, Lilly."

I left you then. Potential, personal potential, happy, these words repeating in my head. I went through to the living-room, the sun was low and so strong and although beautiful was a curse. Every shiny surface reflecting a layer of speckled dust. I cleaned.

Dinner

At seven, pizza sliced in to tempting triangles, gin poured, napkin ready, I returned to you.

"Good evening, Lilly."

"Good evening, Sir."

There was no sign of your pizza, just you and a glass of wine on top of the island.

"Where is your pizza?"

"I was not sure what time dinner was, I thought five would be tea, so dinner at six or seven? I have the oven ready, I will pop it in now."

You had waited for me and I felt strangely touched by this.

"Have you eaten?"

"Just about to start. I should have said what time, that was a little amiss of me."

"It's okay, but I am hungry. I've lost the concept of days in here, but the oven clock is my guide for the hours and I have been eating at six. Anyway, I'll just have to pour another glass, how is your pizza?"

"It is really good, crispy base."

"What day is it, Sir?"

"It is Thursday."

"Thursday, how long have I been here?"

"Two weeks today."

"Two weeks. Have I been reported missing? Am I on the news?"

"I have not watched the news, but I am sure your family have reported you gone."

"What if they think I have just abandoned them? What if they think I just don't care? Sir, will you watch the news for me?"

I had responded so quickly to your question and yes, I lied to you. I did not want to discuss the news reports in all their detail. I did not want to explain my involvement. I could not explain my involvement. You moved to the oven and slid the pizza on to the chopping board and sliced through, precise triangles formed and placed on a plate that I noticed you had warmed. You returned to the island and sat.

"Sir."

"Yes, Lilly."

"Will you watch the news for me?"

"I will see what I can do."

"Thank you."

I ate and watched you eat. I drank and watched you drink. The silence was disagreeable to me.

"What would you normally do on a Thursday evening?"

"Oh nothing much, after dinner we cosy up and watch TV in front of the fire, glass of wine."

"What do you watch?"

"Thursday, mmm – I have a rather guilty pleasure, I do love EastEnders and then maybe catch up with something on the planner, a Grand Designs or a Goggle box."

"I too watch Grand Designs."

"Did you build this house?"

"No, but it was designed by a local firm of architects who specialise in the creation of one-off bespoke houses. I bought it whilst it was still under construction."

"That must have been exciting, watching your home come to life?"

"Yes it was, what is your home like?"

"Ah, it is a work in progress. We moved just over a year ago, it's a four bedroomed old farmhouse, open fires and slate floors but it does need some updating."

"And yet you have been there over a year?"

"Yes, but we have spent this year doing up the separate out-building which we rent out as a holiday cottage."

"So that is was why you thought I could possibly rent out the studio?"

"Yes, it's great now, all up and running. I handle the bookings and the maintenance, cleaning etc. We are fully booked."

"Does it not bother you, having strangers in your home?"

"They are not in my home, they are across the courtyard."

"Close though."

"Yes, Sir, close but separate. You know, most people are lovely, you need to trust more."

"Do you enjoy it?"

"Oh yes, this has been our dream, loads more to do in the future, so many plans, just got to do one piece at a time."

"Why?"

"Why what?"

"Why one piece at a time?"

"Finances. I love the way that doesn't occur to you. First stage is complete now, so using the money from the rental we can finish our home. It is going to be beautiful."

"How will it be?"

"I love the charm and the solid stone of an old house, but we are creating a modern interior. The kitchen is already ordered. We talked for so long about this, our dream, once the children no longer needed us in the same way. It is everything. We are not rich, but we have enough, we are comfortable and happy, so very happy."

"Happy, your favourite word. Happy being a servant to strangers?"

"I am not a servant, I enjoy preparing the cottage, making it perfect, knowing our guests enjoy their stay. Don't take the piss out of my life, it's a good life and I miss it."

You stood up and poured another glass of wine and lit up, blowing the smoke defiantly up in to the extractor fan. Your half-eaten pizza left. I poured another drink.

"How do you cope cleaning up after them though?" Just the very thought of it was making my skin crawl.

"Most people are respectful, you really do need to have more faith, and anyway, I am not silly, I furnished it with up-keep in mind."

"Oh and how may I ask?"

"No carpets, leather sofas, wipeable surfaces."

"I do like a wipeable surface. Do you not like your pizza?"

"I have lost my appetite."

I cleared away my plate and tidied the kitchen. I had mocked you and I knew that I had upset you. This apparent ease that you felt with other people unsettled me, so far beyond my comprehension. I returned. You too had cleared away and were seated on the sofa, snuggled up in the throw, reading. Your wine by your feet.

"How is the book?"

"It is really good, brutally honest and funny, have you read it?"

"Of course, the Reverend Richard Coles is an interesting man."

You placed the almost completed book by your side and retrieved your glass.

"Are you cold? I could turn the heating up?"

"Yes, I am, that would be lovely."

"Lilly I am going to watch the news now."

"Sir please will you come back and let me know, let me know if I'm mentioned, if they are looking for me?"

The tone in your voice had a fragility to it.

"Yes, yes I will."

"Thank you."

The News

Another drink poured, my discipline seemingly a thing of the past, and I viewed.

"Two weeks to the day and another twist in the unique case of the missing mother of three, Lillian Brown. This morning another image was posted online. We cross now to the press conference."

The police spokeswoman returned, your partner and children. The row reformed.

"We are now confident that Lilly is alive, and we are directly asking that whoever has Lilly to please allow her to return to her family."

"Do you believe the quote of 'Lilly loves to talk' is in a direct response to the minimal press coverage that the police enforced?"

"Yes, we do. Our highly professional team believe that whoever is holding Lilly is seeking media attention."

"Are you any closer to locating Lilly?"

"At this moment we are proceeding with all possible lines of enquiry and the investigation team has been expanded."

Your partner spoke, he looked distraught and grey,

"Please, whoever you are, let Lilly come home. You're right, she does love to talk, and we miss her. Lilly's place is at home with us."

"Please, we need our mum back, we want her back." Your youngest son.

"We miss talking to her." Your daughter.

"Just let our mum go." Your eldest.

"Please. Please." Your daughter.

The four of them side by side, holding hands, all holding back tears to one degree or another. A line of pain, joined, a united front for all to see. A very public display of desperation and how that camera lingered.

"Are the police now intending to actively use social media directly, despite their initial stance?"

"We now feel, as this case unfolds, that it may be the link to finding Lilly. We would ask anyone using social media to be aware of any unusual postings or comment and to report them immediately."

The usual phone numbers, your original photo.

I was shocked, the sheer audacity of their behaviour. They had scaled back their investigation and just could not admit it. Not now, not with my intervention, not with my new image out there. I did not want their attention. I had merely uploaded and updated to remind them of you. I had obviously been correct as it had clearly worked. No mention was made of my care and attention to detail. No gratitude given for the reassurance displayed. My thoughtfulness overlooked. Yet again, my actions were simply not understood.

Messenger

I was somewhat anxious returning to you. I regretted my decision, I should have said no, pure and simple, but one cannot change the past, sadly.

"Good evening, Lilly."

"Sir, did you watch, was I mentioned?"

"Yes, Lilly, I did and yes you were. Now Lilly, you must promise me that you will not become hysterical."

You had jumped up from the sofa, the throw discarded and stood in the middle of the room.

"Just tell me, please."

"Your family are looking for you, they have reported you missing, does that help?"

"Oh my lord, yes, tell me everything."

"There is not much else to say, they do appear to love you."

"You saw them? Were they okay? Did they look okay?"

"Everyone is fine given the circumstances."

"Oh Sir, you must let me go now, surely. I told you, I have an amazing, beautiful family, I miss them, I need them."

You were physically shaking, I noted and so was I. The Lilly on the news and the Lilly in front of me had been separate, removed from one another and yet now it was all confused, tainted. Your tears, their tears with myself in the middle. The balance had been lost. You poured another glass and stood in your favourite spot.

"Sir, please, please."

And then you cried. I knew you would, I so wished that I had been quiet.

"What did they say?"

"No. Enough, enough now, they love you, they miss you, they showed your photo. That is all."

"My photo? I never thought, oh fuck, I don't want to be famous."

"Really? Imagine fame and fortune?" I laughed.

"No. Imagine found and fortunate," you replied.

"I thought everyone sought fame these days."

"No fucking way! I wouldn't even want fifteen seconds, let alone fifteen minutes, let alone fucking national news. Oh, for fuck's sake I don't want this. They won't either, the intrusion, the worry. You have seen them, they are good people. They do not deserve this and neither do I."

Your tears were flowing, your face red. You paced round the room, deliberate breaths in time with your steps.

"You need to let me out. I need to go."

Your voice was louder, pacing quicker. You went to the door and began to hit and kick.

"Let me out, for fuck's sake, let me out. This cannot be happening, you can't do this anymore! This is not fair, are you fucking listening to me? Let me the fuck out now!"

You were shouting, your face angry.

"You have no right to keep me here, can't you see that?! Are you listening? Are you?!"

"Yes, Lilly, please calm down."

"Calm? Calm? Are you stupid? Are you fucking crazy? Calm? My family is out there looking for me, upset, worried and you expect me to be fucking calm?! You saw them, you said, didn't you feel anything? Don't you feel guilty?"

"As you know, Lilly, I did not mean for this situation."

"Situation? Let's not fucking dress it up, you have stolen me and are keeping me against my will, as a prisoner and why, huh? Because I swore at you? For fuck's sake I will swear you twat, you complete fucked up piece of shit."

"Lilly there is no need, you will accomplish nothing."

"Really? Well, I'll piss you off though and that might help, just let me fucking go."

You returned to your wine and took a long drink, draining the glass, lit a cigarette and cried again.

I found your behaviour distressing, the venom in your voice upsetting. Your apparent desire to hurt me felt like an insult. I had been trying to help.

"Lilly, I did not have to tell you about your family, I thought it would help, you said you wanted to know."

"Ha, yes but now I do know it is even worse. It's not just me you're hurting, you're messing with my family, their lives, their minds, don't you feel anything?"

"Unlike you, Lilly, I do not allow emotion to rule my behaviour."

"Ah right, of course not, Sir, and this fucking inability to face emotions is really going well, isn't it? If you hadn't been so fucking repressed none of this would have happened."

"Repressed?"

"Yes, repressed, all that anger that came out, that fucking explosion. If you had only dealt with your shit, then I wouldn't be here. You know what, your mother was obviously a bitch. She hurt you, I get it, but you're a man now, practically twenty-five years old. Shit happens, but you have to deal with it, understand it, accept it even and move on."

"I am moving on, as you put it."

"But you're not, are you? Self-assured arrogant twat. Thinking that you can control everything with no emotion? You're a human being not a robot."

"Emotions cannot be allowed to control."

"Oh my lord and look what happens when you try to pretend that you don't have them, they spill out."

"I do not pretend that I lack emotion, I just have a resolve that you could do well to learn from."

"Learn from? For fuck's sake. I would hate to be a cold, unemotional person like you. You uptight, judgemental, self-important prick. Hiding away because what? You might get hurt? Someone might not be very nice to you? Oh, poor you, get over it."

The sarcastic sneer was both cutting and offensive and yet I knew your description was true, even then. Although self-importance was a step too far. I poured another gin, your alcohol habits clearly rubbing off. I watched you pour another glass and I considered that you should really be quite inebriated and yet, despite your frame, you appeared stone cold sober. I disliked your words, they felt almost physical. I was still shaking and despite myself I cried, quietly, but uncontrolled, I cried into my gin.

Friday, September 29
The Morning After

I had moved away from the screen, I had closed the office door. Shut you away and I had continued to drink, sat in my chair. Crying and drinking until I had clumsily collapsed. When I came to my morning's schedule had been destroyed. The quiet, uninhabited slot in which I scheduled my run had long gone. My head was pounding, my eyes were red, and I was still shaking. I showered, the maximum pressure of water spilling over me, flooding my every pore and yet I still felt unclean. I cleansed, moisturised, trimmed and tidied. I selected crisp, clean chinos and a cotton poplin shirt, soft suede desert boots, but nothing felt comfortable. I tried to drink my usual espresso but was met with nausea. I poured some fresh orange and sipped tentatively. Eventually I ate some toast, the crisp crumbs helping to remove the taste from my mouth. I brushed my teeth and tongue and I packed my overnight bag. I was tempted to just leave. I loaded the car, blazer hung in the back, waters chilled and ready. I wiped round, refreshed my flowers. I stripped and re-made my bed. A pure white, satin striped cover against crisp, white, linen sheets. I made peppermint tea. I sat.

Eventually, I reopened the office door and returned to you. You were seated, your arm exposed. The wound was still inflamed, red, flaps of tissue over-hanging above open flesh, not bleeding but almost marbled, white patches entwined with dark. The skin appeared thick around the edges. You had almost completed your task judging by the number of discarded cotton pads. I watched and waited patiently until you moved to make your tea,

"Good morning, Lilly."

Your head moved, but you said nothing.

"Good morning, Lilly," I repeated.

You continued with your tea, then proceeded to take some strawberries out of the fridge, cutting them in half, placing them in a bowl.

"Good morning, Lilly."

You continued, six spoonfuls of yogurt in to a separate dish, blueberries perfectly patterned on the top. You cleared away, sprayed the surfaces, then, placing everything on top of the shining granite you sat down.

"I am leaving soon Lilly, so I just wanted to say goodbye. Why are you not speaking today?"

"I have decided there is little point as you are not listening."

"Obviously I am listening, Lilly."

"No, Sir, you are not. There is a great deal of difference between hearing and listening."

"Oh, Lilly, I do not feel myself today, so I will stop this conversation. I only wanted to see you to say goodbye."

"You don't feel yourself? Is that because you are incapable of feeling?"

"You contradict yourself. I am not a robot."

"Oh clever, are you capable of empathy?"

"Your arm is a little improved I feel."

"I have been thinking, what if this is the last food I eat? How long do you think I will live? Three days? Five days? You can watch as starvation mode kicks in, as my muscles waste away, as I drift in and out of consciousness, as my stomach bloats and I guess eventually as I breathe my last, eyes looking at you, Sir, mouth open and quite probably in my own shit. It will be messy."

"Lilly, stop. You would not do that."

"Why? Why wouldn't I? Would you continue to watch as rigor mortis sets in? Then what will you do? Leave me here? Decomposing every day on your lovely tiled floor?"

"Stop it. I am not sick, and I know you could not do such a thing because of your children, your partner, you would think of them."

"I would think of them? Do you not realise I think of them constantly, their faces, their beautiful smiles? The conversations and laughter, the way we are. When I get into that bed do you not think I miss him? His arms around me? Do you really not understand that you are killing me anyway?"

"I have to leave now, I have a long journey ahead and the forecast is set for rain."

"Yeah you go. Go to your family because family is important, isn't it, Sir?"

I had no words. I watched as you threw the remaining food in front of you away. I watched as you cleaned the surfaces again, as you carefully washed and dried up, everything put neatly away. I watched as you curled up on the sofa, gently placing the throw around you, leaving just your arm exposed. I watched as you cried. I still found no words and I left you.

The Drive

My thoughts were chaotic as I drove, crashing threw me with no order, just a constant noise. I found myself shouting to try to drown them out, but all my abilities to dismiss unwanted thought had gone. I wished that I was robotic. This exposure to emotion was deeply disturbing. I did feel a responsibility to you, your family. I had spent my life hiding, in a sense you were right. Although I had always seen this as driven and sensible. I had a career to concentrate on, a focus. As I drove, I reflected yet again, trying desperately to restore my composure, my mind. I had studied hard and succeeded at school, locked away with the world at my finger-tips. I had found my calling. Four years at university and naturally a first under my belt, I had transitioned easily from studies to work. I was sought after and highly regarded, working in app development, the speed of change, the passion and dedication understood. Expected, assumed even. There is an acceptance that I am professionally brilliant without the social interactions other jobs may well require. Everything had fitted so well and in such a short space of time. I had not drifted from or doubted my path. Not ever. Then established and safe, I had made the move from the city and purchased my house. My energies were focused on creating perfection. There had been no time, no space for anything, no interruption. Until now.

The rains came for the final hour of my drive, slowing the traffic frustratingly. How I wanted that journey to end. You had told me to talk to my family and I felt that this time was so important for me. You had filled my head with questions and a desire for answers.

Finally, the familiar sound under the tyres, I had arrived.

Secrets

My aunt's ever-welcoming arms were as open as the door and I practically fell in to them both. She led me through to the sitting room, the fire was roaring, my uncle and godfather stood, hugs and handshakes flowed. Drinks were poured, traffic discussed and the obligatory, "How are yous?" all exchanged. I glanced around the room, it appeared brighter, lighter somehow. My aunt followed my gaze,

"We have cleared away some things, do you mind? We have kept them."

"Mind? No, it looks so much better."

"We thought in preparation for the sale."

"Absolutely, clear out the clutter."

"Here, here!" My godfather.

We all laughed, any potential tensions evaporated. A table had been reserved back again in the Oak Room. I was pleased, refreshed and changed we made the short walk. We ordered, although I was drawn back to the steak I opted for a change, slow cooked pheasant and a warming mushroom soup to start. We drank a rather lovely Bavarian pinot noir and slipped back in to our comfortable conversations. My godfather paid for our meal and ushered us out in to the cold. He said he had a surprise in store. Although now seventy-eight he has never lost his enthusiasm and mischievous twinkle. We hurried along, my aunt calling for less haste as I held her arm. The fire loaded for the evening, my godfather opened a box beside his chair, he withdrew a light wooden container, burgundy lettering on the front, my uncle looked,

"Well, well, the Glenfarclas."

"Indeed, I thought tonight we could enjoy the christening tipple."

"I do not understand, what is the significance?"

"Ah, my wonderful Godson, this whiskey was your father's choice, in your honour, on the evening of your christening. This fine, fine single malt has been maturing since 1993 until now. It was bottled and ten out of the five hundred and thirty-six were reserved for your father. His intention had always been to toast to you on your twenty-fifth, but I feel he would deem this to be a good time, no need to wait any longer."

The drinks were poured,

"It is strong, take it easy."

We toasted to my father. My uncle and godfather became engaged with happy memories, single words sparking another smile or an outburst of laughter. Now whiskey, despite the beautiful sentiment, is not really my choice and I felt it was rather wasted on my palate. I exchanged for a bottle of Hendricks that my aunt had thoughtfully purchased, the cigars re-appeared, a cheese board and crackers. Feeling an opportunity whilst nostalgia was running high, I shuffled and then breathed precisely, like you, until I felt calm, until I felt ready.

"Tell me about her."

"Why, my darling? What do you want to know?"

"I feel I need answers to who she was and why."

"She was a bitch."

"Yes, we know that now, but she was not always that way. We must be fair and honest, there have been more than enough lies told in this house."

I smiled with gratitude, my aunt settled herself back, choosing her position with care, ready for the story to be told.

"Your mother, darling, was, as you know, a stunning, elegant woman. When your father first introduced us to her we all knew that she was the one. He had had relationships, but the pressures of his work had always caused conflicts in the past. She was content to be at his side. The corporate events, the endless functions, dinners, she was perfect in her role. Difficult deals were smoothed by her charms and your father was incredibly proud. She, in turn, wanted for nothing and their partnership really was the envy of all who met them. However, there was a sadness, an emptiness for your father and that, of course, was his desire to have children. The years passed, their lives were hectic, but your father became more determined, doctors were to be consulted. We all felt for them both, I understood their pain."

My uncle held my aunt's hand so gently, I witnessed the love held between them. A private acknowledgement of their shared past, their unfulfilled longing. I realised then why they had no children of their own.

"I'm fine, I'm fine. It was then, when your father returned home unexpectedly, a forgotten folder I seem to remember, he went to find her and discovered contraceptive pills on her bedside table. Obviously, he confronted her, and the truth came out, as it always does."

My uncle spoke about how his beloved brother had told him, his anger violent almost, his hatred that turned to hurt.

"We all felt betrayed, it was a most horrible time."

"So why did he not throw her out? Find someone else?"

"Oh, darling, you forget that he loved her."

"And you do not realise the hold she had on him. She explained, justified her actions, claiming to be terrified, of not being able to support him enough. She begged him for forgiveness and my misguided wonderful brother accepted."

My uncle was shaking his head. My godfather silent.

"And then I was born?"

"Yes darling. When she was pregnant her every whim was catered for. Diets and dresses, nursery designs, baby clothes, everyone helped. Everything was done."

"She was the centre of everything and had the best of care continuously. Obviously a first-time mother at forty had the potential for concern, but she was fit and if she was uncertain or unhappy, we never saw it."

"And so the new year bought you."

"Did she love me?"

"Oh, darling, we all loved you instantly, obsessively. It was hard for your mother in the beginning, your birth had been traumatic. An unplanned emergency section, there were complications, she was quite, quite ill."

"So who looked after me?"

"We did and, of course your father. He took early retirement, he had always planned to, but your birth made the decision so easy for him. He was totally besotted by you."

"Just me and my boy." My uncle smiled.

"So, when she recovered, were they happy then? I do not remember doing things with her, or her being there when other boys' mothers were. I remember she would be with us when we holidayed, but she was distant or sun bathing or resting."

"Did you mind?"

"I did not question anything, I just knew that he was always there, until he," I shrugged, "until he was gone."

"She found the bonding process difficult darling, but it was not your fault, you must understand that."

My godfather replenished our now empty glasses and cut in to the mature cheddar, selected a couple of crackers.

"You were a delight of a baby, a toddler and a young boy. She missed everything, and I do not hold with this not bonding theory. She did not even try. Suddenly and correctly you were everything to your father and their lives had changed forever and quite frankly, I think she was jealous of you. Selfish bitch could not cope that the world no longer revolved around her and her hospitality."

My aunt held my hand,

"Darling, I am sure that she loved you."

"Are you?" My godfather scoffed.

"Yes. Yes, I am. She just did not know how to and maybe, I am a little to blame. I was always here, the months turned to years and the pattern was established. Your father did not mind, he was simply content and happy. He would be the proudest parent at any school show or gathering. Your weekends were full, and it was simply accepted that she was busy."

"Was she never with us?"

"Yes, sometimes."

"To keep him happy, to keep her lifestyle."

"Stop it, that is not fair, it just seemed to be how it worked, worked for us all. Families can be complicated, even a tiny one like ours."

"So, after he passed, why did you go?"

"Oh my darling, as we said, we thought that you were growing up and not wanting to smother you, we trusted her."

"If we had realised the truth, we would have done so much more. We should have done so much more."

"I genuinely thought that she had changed. With your father gone, I believed that she would find you and, if we were removed, become your mother fully. I am truly sorry."

"We are all sorry."

My uncle stood and threw some logs on to the fire.

"The truth is that she lied to everyone in some way. My brother never forgave her, but she was your mother and he accepted that she should stay. You must remember and never doubt how much he wanted you, how much he loved you. He was a truly good man."

"Here, here."

For several moments I absorbed all that had been said. I thought of you, your instincts had indeed been proved correct. I had merely been a sticking plaster to her, to keep her world. She had resented my arrival and the subsequent change it bought.

"Tell us, have you settled in now, made friends?"

I told them about every detail of the house, the morning runs I enjoyed, the local restaurant I loved.

"Please may we visit?"

I was a little thrown, how I so wanted to say yes, return with me tomorrow, but I obviously held back.

"Don't worry darling, whenever you're ready, it would be lovely."

"Yes soon, very soon."

"So as a young man, are you out all of the time? We will not stand in your way or cramp your style for too long." My godfather chuckled.

"No, I am not."

"Well, you should be, make the most of your youth."

I smiled.

"Yes, I do need to get out a little more, someone else also said that to me recently. I need to live my life."

"Well, whoever they are, listen to them."

There were little looks exchanged, my aunt smiled. Clearly, they had all jumped to the same conclusion, that this someone was significant, special, my special friend. Little did they know that the someone was you, a secret hidden in my studio.

'If you want to keep a secret you must also hide it from yourself.' [5]

I shivered, remembering your words just before I had left. I drained my glass and my head was spinning, I was exhausted. My aunt stoked my hair and suggested that I should rest, there would be time for snooker tomorrow. Goodnights were exchanged, and I quickly took my leave.

Social Hysteria

Alone in the bedroom I could only think of you. I checked social media on my phone and my, oh my, Lilly, you were the user generated content.

#SupportingLilly was joined now, not only with words but thoughts, opinions, theories from everywhere and it appeared from everyone.

#LetsfindLilly was encouraging "all the nerds to find the perve!"

#LiliesforLilly suggesting everyone to buy the flowers, to display them as a gesture of support.

#WeloveLilly was a sickening stream of outpourings from people who knew you. Facebook and snapchat displaying images of you and yet more opinion or some hurriedly remembered memory. It appeared that the police had activated a virtual world to communicate and connect, to co-ordinate and comment. This online interaction, this saturation of site upon site was intense. From the lady in your late-night store, people claiming to have attended the same school as you, to neighbours, both past and present, an ex-boss, to complete strangers who "just cared". Like levelled against like. It was a twitter competition and you were the prize to be seen with. This sharing, this social stand stimulating action and reaction was spiralling out of control. My head was spinning. I closed everything down. I splashed my face with cold water and simply stared in to the mirror, the intensity of your image was so vivid inside my head. I needed to calm. You were safely locked away, but you were locked inside of me too. I could not escape. We were bound together in this bizarre situation that had to end. This had never been my intention, this was out of control. I knew then that a solution had to be found, but, in that moment, I was at a loss as to how. More water, teeth cleaned and undressed, I went to bed.

Saturday, September 30
Home

On waking, I knew that I had to return to you. Originally, I had intended to stay another night. The drive so long and time with my newly found family was so precious, but I needed to see you. I was troubled, unnerved, anxious as to what I might discover. You had been so unpredictable on occasion and yet by contrast so calculable. My aunt fussed over me, morning coffee and insisted I ate more than toast when I explained I would have to return home, work commitments looming. Sausages and scrambled egg lay heavy on my stomach as I re-loaded the car. My godfather was sitting out on the terrace, the beautiful view reflecting the bright sun's rays.

"Last day of September. Autumn will soon turn to winter. It all passes so quickly, promise me that you will only look forward, not back. Embrace your life and enjoy every moment."

"I will try."

"No my beautiful boy, you will succeed. Spread your wings and soar, live everyday with purpose and vigour and joy. Promise me."

"I promise."

We stood, his arm around my shoulders and watched as a huge number of geese flocked above us. A spectacle of migrating birds returning home. Goodbyes and promises of invitations spoken, I began my journey, homeward bound and bound to you.

Butterflies

It was already dark when I arrived, how quickly the evenings draw in. The moon not quite full, but bright, illuminating the sky. I entered the hallway, glancing at your door briefly and moving upstairs. I freshened up and unpacked and decided on the braised beef goulash for my dinner. It was now six-thirty. I hoped that you had already eaten, I so hoped so. I felt agitated as I switched the monitor on, food by my side. I looked around. I could not see you, only the signs of your presence, the throw crumpled across the corner of the sofa, the book opened, face down. The notepaper, pen and scissors were on the floor, the island was clean and clear. It was then that I noticed a paper butterfly hanging from the lamp. Intricately patterned and cut with perfect symmetry. You appeared then from behind the doors. You looked so pale and lost in the dark fabric as you walked across the floor.

"Good evening, Lilly."

I had startled you, a gasp and a jolt stopped you in your tracks.

"You're home then?"

"Yes, Lilly, I am home, have you eaten?"

"Worried, are you?"

"Well, actually, yes."

"Of the mess? Or me dying?"

"Lilly, stop it, please do not mock me. I have returned early, have you eaten?"

"Gee thanks and yes, yes I have eaten. Feel better?"

"I feel relieved Lilly, so relieved. What did you have?"

"Red Thai chicken curry, I have only just finished it actually, it was a little hot."

"Are you alright?"

"Yes, I just poured loads of natural yogurt over it."

"Very wise but I actually meant, how are you feeling?"

"Trapped."

I was silent, you had, yet again, thrown me slightly.

"I noticed the butterfly, you have been busy."

"Mmm, it took me ages, but hey I have the time."

"Indeed, why a butterfly?"

"It doesn't matter, you wouldn't understand."

"I might."

"I am drawn to them and I believe they are symbolic."

"Really? How?" I smiled.

"They are signs of joy, of transformation."

"Explain, I am intrigued."

"Don't laugh at me."

"I am not, Lilly, I am listening." I sat and quietly ate my dinner.

"When I see a butterfly, it makes me happy and they always seem to appear when I need something or when I am sad or sometimes when things are changing. I can't really explain the connection, but it is true, and it helps me. I love the way they dance, the colour, the peace they create when I watch them."

"Symbolic of what though?"

"They represent change as a positive, hope and life."

"Go on."

"No, you will think it just illogical."

"I would expect nothing else, Lilly."

"Well, if I see a white butterfly, I feel protected, like I have an angel just reassuring me. If I see a blue one I feel that it is a sign that things might go my way, a yellow one is happiness and fun and possibility, an orange one is a reminder to be positive, purple is like a message to carry on, to have faith that things will change, transform. Whenever I see a butterfly I just feel a connection and a comfort and protected. They are beautiful."

"Well, yes, I suppose they are, I cannot say that I understand your connection, but it is rather sweet."

"Don't patronise me, I don't care if you understand, I know it's true. Butterflies are beautiful and strong, they survive the darkness and emerge into beauty and are free to fly."

"Ah. So, Lilly, do you see butterflies frequently?"

"Yes, I do, and I take the time to acknowledge them and to appreciate them. I know you're laughing at me, Sir."

"Lilly I am not laughing, I am trying to understand your peculiar fascination. Perhaps you could help me?"

"When my daughter rode her bike for the first time without stabilisers, a yellow butterfly sat on the basket in between her hands. The sun was shining, she was smiling, her horizons just beginning to grow."

You hesitated, I watched your bottom lip as it began to tremble, clearly the mere thought of your daughter was upsetting.

"Breathe, Lilly, please breathe and continue."

You took a little time, I waited.

"Once, when I was in a really bad place, I was suddenly surrounded by a kaleidoscope of butterflies and they gave me hope and a lightness. When I lost my job, I sat in the garden a lot and every day in that first week, I saw a butterfly. I could go on, it is all true but there is no point, is there?"

You poured a glass of wine and rested your arms across the top of the island, your head flat against the surface. How strange you looked, all flattened out, resting in this curious way. I finished my meal and I also poured a drink. After some time, you moved and continued to sip away.

"Are you there?"

"I am here, Lilly."

"So how was your family visit?"

I re-told the events to you, slowly, every detail disclosed. I appreciated the way that you sat and listened quietly. It was good to talk, to say everything out loud, it ordered my mind. I felt a sense of calm as I continued this sharing, a peace almost.

"Your aunt sounds kind." You said.

"She is, gentle and giving."

"And she clearly loves you, a mother's love, her misplaced guilt."

"Guilt?"

"Well, she sounds like she blames herself for your mother's lack because she did too much. Pushed her out, maybe she made your mother feel inadequate. Her love for you came so naturally."

"Well, I do not think that she should feel guilty, my mother, as is now so obvious, just did not want me and my aunt did. Anyway, forward looking, I made a promise."

"Do you feel better now that you understand?"

"Yes, Lilly, I do. Why did you decide to eat? Or did you never really intend to starve yourself?"

"I did consider quite seriously to give up, Sir. I even imagined in detail, the distress it would cause you, but I couldn't do it. There is always hope."

"So you made your butterfly?"

"Yes, I made my butterfly."

Moving Forward

"Sir, I was thinking about things that you could do."

"In what way?"

"You say that you like cooking, why don't you enrol in a cookery school? Meet other like-minded people and do something you enjoy at the same time."

"I can already cook."

"Yes you said, but you don't. Anyway, as good as you think that you are a good restaurant, high end, would run a cookery school that would challenge you and teach you new skills."

"I am not comfortable with the idea of publicly being tested."

"Everyone would be in the same position though and I don't think the idea is to make you feel uncomfortable, more to encourage and teach."

"And what if I fail?"

"Ah, you are so negative, what if you don't? You could be the star baker! Imagine when your family come, you could astound them with your newfound skills."

"Star baker, like in The Great British Bake Off? You are ridiculous, Lilly."

"Yes like in The Bake Off, but just on a smaller scale. It's not ridiculous, you would have fun."

"Would I?"

"Yes. What have you got to lose?"

"My dignity?"

"Oh for goodness' sake. Right. Right, if you won't consider that, which is silly by the way, how about joining a supper club?"

"A what?"

"You know, a group meet, eats at different places, shares the experiences, enjoys the food, the wines."

"With total strangers?"

"Who could become friends?"

"Or enemies."

"Do you have to be so bloody negative? It is quite exhausting you know."

You poured another drink and so did I.

"Cheers," I said.

"Cheers. Just think, right now, you could be face to face with new friends, clinking your glasses, socialising, laughing."

"You really do go on."

"Because I am right."

"Oh, are you? Do you always think you're right?"

"No, not at all, but with regard to people I usually am."

"I thought I was the arrogant one?"

"I am not arrogant, just quite good at people and I am quite old, so I have had more time to learn."

"You're not that old. Why do you love people so much? Do you always surround yourself? Do you have hundreds of friends?"

I was suddenly reminded of the outpourings on social media that I had read the night before.

"I love people, Sir, because most people are lovely and it's fun to chat and find out a little about other peoples' lives. As for hundreds of friends, no absolutely not. I have a small but amazing group of close friends and I care about them deeply. Then there are a lot of people I know and like, pleasant chats in the pub, but that's about as far as it goes."

"Do you wish that you had more friends?"

"No, you don't need hundreds, just a few real friends. Anyway, to have genuine friendships takes time. Plus, I don't think that closeness can be so easily spread."

I considered your words. I wondered how you would react if you knew that so many thousands of people were talking about you, had befriended you.

"Have you always found making friends easy?"

"Acquaintances? Yes. Idle chit chat passes the time of day, that type of thing. Real friends are different. I am a very private person Sir, but when you click with someone then it is natural, it flows and as you learn more and share more together it grows. Baby steps.

I am not for one minute, suggesting that you fill your house with strangers and expect instant bonds."

"I am not a baby, thank you."

"I didn't say you were. By baby steps, I simply meant small steps, gentle small steps."

"You say that you are a private person and yet you can so easily mix. The two do not make sense together. Yet again, you are illogical."

"I am private with regard to my inner thoughts and feelings. I am protective, but that does not mean I have to be isolated. To proceed with a little caution, I feel, is sensible as long as you do proceed."

"Proceed with caution? It sounds like a traffic report in the fog, not like fun."

"I just mean that you don't have to wear your heart on your sleeve. Reveal all your inner thoughts, let your guard down completely."

"Let my guard down? Is this a fight we are discussing?"

"Oh stop being so literal! I am just trying to relieve your social anxiety."

"I know how to behave socially, Lilly."

"Do you know how to misbehave though? To really let your hair down? To just be silly?"

"May I remind you proceed with caution?"

"For fuck's sake, you are being deliberately annoying. A little anxiety is understandable, that is what I meant. Take everything at a pace that suits you, then the rest will follow."

We paused. I watched as you walked through the doors, I watched as you returned, I watched as you smoked. I watched you as I waited for our conversation to continue. I knew you would not be quiet for long.

"Are you there?"

"I am here, Lilly."

"You could join a running club, share your runs. Or if people really are too much, you could get a dog. You would meet so many others, puppy training, walking but with the dog as the focus and not you."

"Enough, enough. I enjoy my runs alone. It is my time and as for a dog, I really could not cope with the mess. The smell of wet dog, muddy paws and there is absolutely no way I would ever wish to clear up after the animal."

"For goodness' sake, I am trying to help here."

I sensed you were becoming a little exasperated with me and I did not want our time to end or, quite strangely, for you to be quiet. I was listening, I was trying.

"I do understand. It is not as though I have never thought about the way that I am. I have been too busy, too focused to allow the privilege of time."

"Well, you're not too busy now, are you? It is time you went out in to the world rather than just letting the world come to you."

"Travel?"

"Well, yes, why the hell not? Would you like to? Where would you like to go?"

"Thailand, Vietnam, India, Iceland, Australia. Everywhere."

"Wow that's amazing. So, do it. Book your ticket."

"Just like that?"

"Absolutely! Why not?"

I paused and poured. I did so long to travel. I had secretly fantasised, watching programmes, imagining myself. Absorbed in other's cultures, their cuisine and then I had dismissed these flights of fancy, so focused on my path of success.

Your suggestions, although I could see were meant with good intention, felt rather boring to me. I would probably be sat with people twice my age, like you. All very pleasant and polite, but I am young and the person I wanted to be had a party room and adventures. I laughed at my own thoughts.

"Well, are you there?"

You were pouring another drink and staring up, one arm gesturing.

"Yes, Lilly, I am here. I have just poured another G and T myself."

"Cheers."

"Cheers."

"Well?"

"I am thinking, Lilly."

"Of ways not to proceed?"

"Actually no, I am questioning whether I could?"

"Realistically or emotionally?"

"Well, both I suppose."

"Break it down then. You said that you worked remotely. I don't really understand what that means, but I'm guessing the internet allows this, right?"

"Put ever so simply, yes."

"Whatever. So, I believe that there are internet cafes everywhere?"

"Obviously, Lilly."

Your casual dismissal of whatever, regarding, my work was shocking. You clearly had no insight into the digital age. I remembered your son saying that you did not even use social media. I thought again, if only you knew. You might not know it, but it certainly knew you.

"So, what difference does it make where in the world you are?"

"It would not."

"So, work is not a problem."

"I am busy though. I have an ordered, structured life. I do not know that I could be so care free."

"Is your ordered, structured life fulfilling and happy though?"

"You and that word. It is a comfortable life."

"And lonely. You have surprised and amazed me with your thoughts of travel, I had assumed you just needed friends, but your ambitions and ideas are far more exciting."

"Amazed you?" I smiled.

"Yes, for someone who seems frightened…"

"I am not frightened," I interrupted.

"Really? If you'd let me finish my sentence, I was going to say that you seem frightened to let people in. I had not expected you to want to travel, to leave your comfort zone."

"Well, that is what I have just explained, Structure and order are important to me. Are you not listening to me?"

"Of course I am, but you, Sir, were the one who suggested travel and then listed all these places, so you must want to do it. I had limited you with my own assumptions."

"I would like to travel, but to just go, to change everything would be unsettling and I am not sure that I could."

"When you picture these places, do you feel excited?"

"Yes, who would not?"

"So concentrate on the excitement. Change can be scary, but you could still create order. Plan your travels, have an itinerary."

"Yes, I know that I could."

"Money is not an issue is it?"

"No."

"How lucky you are. You could pick all the best places to stay, they would be clean, and you would be taken care of. I'm guessing that you were never thinking to back-pack and stay in hostels?"

"Gosh no, that would be a step too far." I laughed.

"Thought so." And you laughed too.

We sat this way for a little while. You fiddled with your glass and then prepared some pitta bread and hummus, neatly cutting the toasted bread, carefully dipping it in to the tub, slowly chewing. I watched you. The calm you, was rather pleasant, almost logical at times even, if not a little annoying. The extreme you was totally disturbing.

"What was the job that you lost?"

"I was a waitress. It was a couple of years ago now, before we moved, before we could pursue our dream."

"A waitress? Did you enjoy it?"

"Yes, very much, regular customers would come and go, it was fun, little snippets of their lives, their families, the weather.

I would have left anyway, when we moved. It just happened a little earlier than planned, that's all."

"Why? If you liked it?"

"There was a clash of opinion."

"With whom?"

"Me and my bosses. I didn't agree with their beliefs and that didn't go down well."

"I thought that you were good with people?"

"Ha, well, yes. I still think that I am, but that does not mean that I don't make mistakes or, on occasion, misjudge a situation. Anyway, sometimes you just have to stand by your principles and not allow others to bring you down, even if they are paying your wages."

"What was the clash of opinion about?"

"They were prejudiced and narrow minded, I am not. I spoke up, against their offensive words and hey ho, lost my job."

"Was your partner not cross with you? Your actions were a little rash given the consequences."

"No, absolutely not. He was my biggest supporter. We had our own plans and so we concentrated on their development."

"What other plans do you have? I remember that you said you had so many?"

"Ah, we do, we do indeed. We really want to buy a property with more land, a couple of acres or so and build a couple of Mongolian yurts. Each completely hidden, with fire pits outside and seating all around them. Beautiful fabrics and cushions; luxury but in the outside setting. Wood-fired hot tubs underneath the stars. We either want to rent them out or sometimes just have our friends to stay and party."

"Why?"

"Because it could be, will be amazing and so much fun. Camping but with style. Sitting or dancing around a fire, gazing at the night's sky, it's just us. We are going to host big party nights too, live music playing, marquees, fairy lights, hog roasts. Start small, but they will grow. Not too big, not out of control. We will get a licence for a couple of times in the year, charge a little for entrance, just to cover the costs. It is not about making money, it is all about having fun. People will be able to stay and bring their own tents or book a room nearby. Anyway, that's the long-term plans."

"You have thought about this, I can see."

Your eyes had come to life, your face was happy, smiling, your body language relaxed.

"It lacks a little on the business side of things. Clearly you are not an accountant. But I imagine that it would be popular."

"Why thank you, of course it would. It will be, one day."

I left you momentarily, to prepare some supper. Watching you eat had given me an appetite. I re-filled and set out my hummus, some olives and sea salt crisps. I relaxed back, you were smoking neatly, full glass in hand.

"Are you imagining your yurts, Lilly?"

"I am, are you imagining your travels?"

"I am."

"It will be good for you, to venture out, to be immersed in other cultures. Travel broadens the mind, I guess. You might find it quite humbling though."

"Why do you say that?"

"Well, some of the countries that you listed are so very poor in comparison."

"I am aware, Lilly. Have you travelled?"

"No, Sir. All my children have and do. I have listened, seen photos, watched programmes."

"If money was not a consideration, where would you choose to go, Lilly?"

"Home, Sir. Home every time."

That sentence. So genuine and so heart felt ended, my feelings of fantasy, my imaginings. That sentence hurt.

I wanted to call you Dorothy,

'There's no place like home.' [6]

But I knew that I would regret it instantly. I did not really want to mock, nor did I want to halt our conversation.

"Why do you encourage me, Lilly, to find answers? To travel? Why do you care if I am happy?"

You paused,

"Because Sir, if you move forward I think that you will allow me to do the same."

"What if I just booked my ticket and left?"

"But you wouldn't. You said that you would not hurt me again. You couldn't, knowing I was here, just left to rot. You couldn't do that, could you?"

Your face was distressed, tears were coming, I knew the signs.

"No, Lilly, I could not."

You swallowed,

"So, to move forward, to go on your voyage of discovery you have to let me go."

"A voyage of discovery. Indeed, I rather like that phrase."

"Good because that is what you can have and as you discover the world you will find yourself and maybe even allow your wall to tumble and maybe just maybe, allow others in. Now imagine that!"

Yes, I did imagine that. Although it seemed a daunting prospect it suddenly no longer felt impossible. Indeed, it seemed the only logical way to go. To move forward, to keep my promise. Dare I even say I wanted to find happiness?

I was somewhat alarmed at my own admissions, of these new feelings.

"Lilly, I am retiring now. We can breakfast together in the morning."

"What time?"

"Shall we say eight-thirty am?"

"Okay, have good dreams."

"Indeed, you too, Lilly."

I had to leave. I needed some time on my own.

I sat in my chair. The sky was so clear, the stars so bright. I swivelled, dizzy with my own thoughts. I felt empowered, I felt that I could achieve my dreams. I knew that I wanted to. There was just the small problem of you.

Sunday, October 1
Beginning Anew

I had slept surprisingly well that night. I awoke and felt energised as I headed out for my morning run. The first day of October, change was all around me. The leaves were just holding on, a few more weeks and I knew that they would be gone. The air was crisp, frosts would come soon, winter snows would follow. The seasons coming and going in their reassuring cycle. I did enjoy the beauty of it all and perhaps because I was considering leaving, I appreciated it all the more.

I returned and showered and dressed casually. I would change for lunch later. As I toasted some sourdough, I spooned yogurt in to a bowl and carefully arranged blueberries the way that you did. Marmalade loaded onto the bread, espresso hot and ready, fresh orange poured, yes. With everything completed and fitted neatly in the wooden tray, I went through to my office and switched on the screen. It was eight-fifteen am. You were waiting by the kettle and appeared not long out of bed. Your hair was clumped up on one side, the bed still unmade.

"Good morning, Lilly."

"Good morning. You're early."

"Just a fraction, how are you?"

"I will feel better when I have had my tea. My arm really hurts, I think that I laid on it in my sleep."

"I am sorry to hear that."

"Are you? Sorry? Sorry that I am in pain? That I feel awful? That I miss my family? My life? That I'm here?"

"Well, you are really not a morning person, are you?"

"No I'm not. Every day I wake up and realise I'm still fucking here and it hurts. That door looking at me, these clothes, the smell."

"The smell?"

"Stale smoke."

You made your tea and began to set out your water bowls and cotton pads.

"You choose to smoke, Lilly."

"Ah, I know, it doesn't mean that I like the smell."

"Oh, how so very illogical you are."

"Fuck off."

"Lilly, please, I awoke in such a good mood."

"Good for you."

You started the cleaning process. The wounds were still quite swollen. You were understandably hesitant, but focused, breathing controlled. The irregular flaps and edges demanding precision. On completion of your task, my breakfast eaten, I watched as you cleared away. Surfaces sprayed, hands washed meticulously. You made a fresh cup of tea and I noted that your hands were shaking.

"Are you cold, Lilly?"

"You're still here?"

"Yes. Lilly, are you cold? You're shaking."

"No, it's the shock, the pain, it eases soon."

You counted out your yogurt and dressed it with the blueberries, just as I had done and re-positioned yourself at the island. To say that you looked pitiful is an understatement. I felt strong. Stronger than I had in so long and you, in contrast, seemed so very weak.

"You look unwell."

"I feel like shit. It's always worse in the morning."

"What is? The pain?"

"The pain, the oppression, the realisation that I am still here. The fear, everything. It's fucking shit."

"So early for your language, Lilly."

"I don't give a flying fuck, I just want to go home."

Your demeanour did not reflect the strength of the words you spoke, your eyes were filling up. You pushed your breakfast to one side.

"Lilly, you must eat. I will re-order tomorrow, is there anything new that you would like?"

"Sir, please. This can't go on, I cannot go on. I know that I will shower soon, clean the wet-room, clean around here, exercise, read another chapter, pull myself out of my thoughts, but every day it is getting harder. The walls are closing in."

"I did not realise that you were exercising. That is good, good for your well-being."

"It's a time filler, but you are deliberately missing the point."

Obviously, that was true.

"Lilly, I do not know what you expect me to say."

"That I can leave."

"Perhaps you should shower now, begin your day. I think we would be better served to share brunch, not breakfast. Give you time to come around."

"Time. Time is all I have, time to think, time to fill."

"I appreciate that this is a difficult situation,"

"Difficult?! For fuck's sake, Sir, come on. It's not difficult to unlock that fucking door, turn the key and let me go."

"And yet it is, Lilly, is it even possible?"

"What is the alternative? You said that you wouldn't hurt me, that you couldn't just leave me here."

"I know."

"You could book your ticket and get on with your life and allow me to do the same."

"How simplistic you make everything sound."

"Because it is."

You washed your breakfast things up and proceeded to make the bed, then through the doors, you disappeared.

You were right, what was the alternative? But, how? How indeed I thought. Your fragile appearance, walls closing in, you could not go on. I wanted to help you, to make you feel better, but obviously I could not just unlock the door.

I went downstairs and picked up the basket that held your laundry. I retrieved the key and quietly slid my offering into your room. The door locked quickly, the key safely returned to the console table drawer. I returned with some haste and cleaned and ordered. I selected a crisp white shirt, navy detail and a cashmere V-neck in dark blue. Slim fitting wool trousers, Chelsea boots to finish. The sharp style of Ted Baker's suits me. A simple funnel neck coat completed the look and would keep the cold at bay. I made a peppermint tea and sat in my chair. I was contemplating my next course of action when I received a text message. My florist, reassuring me that as a valued customer, some lilies had been kept to one side for my display. Owing to the high demand and knowing how I would want to show my respect for the missing woman. No additional costs would be incurred.

Well, I assumed that I was supposed to feel a sense of gratitude. I could hardly respond with a no thank you, I see quite enough of Lilly, I do not need a symbolic reminder, could I? I simply replied that the assumption was indeed correct, and that I appreciated their thoughtfulness. I drank my tea. At least someone was benefitting from all of this.

I returned to you. You had found the laundry and were dressed in your own clothes, it made you seem unfamiliar. You had placed the clean loungewear on your bed. In the basket, new towels had been swapped for old, the robe removed, washing folded on top.

"Hello, Lilly."

"Hello, thank you for my clothes."

You sounded brighter now, less exhausted and looked a little healthier.

"You're welcome. What are you having for lunch?"

"Some bread, cheese, maybe some ham. And you?"

"I have a reservation for lunch, I go every Sunday."

"Of course you do."

"Excuse me?"

"Your ordered, structured, comfortable life. Well, why don't you make this your last visit for a while?"

"Lilly, I will see you this evening. I am pleased to say that you look better."

"Cancel your reservation, tell them of your intention to travel."

"I will reflect over lunch."

"No reflecting. Just make the decision, book the ticket, begin the journey."

"We will speak later. Goodbye, Lilly."

You looked up but said nothing. I paused but you had turned towards the fridge. Clearly not in the mood to respond. At least I knew that you were preparing lunch, that made the thought of mine even more enjoyable. I changed and left.

The autumn sun was so low that it blurred my vision but felt good against my face. As always, I was met with warmth and shown to my window table. I ordered the beef, roast cauliflower, slow roasted carrot and potato bake. Traditional Sunday fayre, done to perfection and matched with a Penfolds 707. Roast beef and Bordeaux, a rather classic combination. I gazed out. It was beautiful here. The gentle conversations around me, the charming street, old stone buildings, the flickering flames from the open fire so warming. I could conceivably continue to frequent, every Sunday. My ordered structure was comfortable and not unpleasant, but the pace of my work had been allowed to slow, the house practically complete, was it really enough? I again toyed with your ideas in that, oh, so cosy, a setting. The supper club had made me think of middle age. I could do that then, in another twenty-five years. This restaurant would no doubt still exist or another in its place. The months would turn to years and what would I do? Safe, yes. But would I be fulfilled? Would I simply be filling time for the very sake of it? Would that not be a waste? I could allow myself to be happy, I did indeed have choices. I did not need to cap my life, as you had once said.

As I ate the chocolate torte with honeycomb, I looked slowly around. My fellow diners were glowing, the afternoon's wine and good food taking their effect. The stone walls and beams were solid and familiar. The staff were politely engaging, table to table. I imagined you and how you would be, the idle chit chat, your ease with people. I thought of you and your words from the morning. Oppression, the walls closing in, pulling yourself out of your thoughts. I shuddered. I suddenly felt an unease, a desperate need to escape. I needed to leave immediately. I paid and found myself explaining that I was going away for some time and that my table would no longer be required. There were statements that I would be missed, questions of business or pleasure and promises that they would look forward to my safe return. I placed a ridiculously large tip in the bowl on the bar which was sat next to a vase full of lilies and I left.

The crisp freshness helped to clear my head. I had said that I was leaving. I think I had surprised myself and yet, I had made my decision. This would be the beginning. I smiled. Yes, this could, no this would, happen.

There are many tourist shops in the village. Little gifts, keepsakes of the area, physical memories for people to purchase. I occasionally browsed, and that afternoon felt drawn to do so. Halloween themed window displays would soon turn from orange and blacks to the reds and greens of Christmas. As a hint of what was to come, on a cabinet in the back of one of these shops, was a display of candles. All shapes and sizes, glass holders and pintail candles in tins. Scents for the season. I found one, fireside. I purchased and walked home. Taking my time, enjoying the sights and sounds as the night drew in. I think I had already started to say goodbye.

Key

On my return, I felt inspired. I sat in my chair and began to explore. Obviously, I had a current passport, I was in good physical health, I had the finances. I could start in Australia, no language barriers or vast cultural change to begin with. I could develop my itinerary from there. Any necessary vaccinations, malaria tablets, rabies shots could be obtained here. Sufficient clothes would be packed and again could be purchased to suit my needs and destinations. This, I realised really could work. You were right. It was quite straightforward, bar the one complication which was you.

Time had slipped by unnoticed and forgotten in my excitement. I prepared a light supper, poured a gin and came to you.

"Good evening, Lilly."

"Is it?"

You were sat on the sofa, curled up. You looked pale. You had redressed your arm with the clean bandage.

"Yes, it is a beautiful evening. How are you?"

"I am not well, and I don't feel like talking."

"My lunch was good. Traditional roast beef, wholesome and correct for a Sunday."

"Is it Sunday?"

"Indeed it is."

You shuffled, repositioning yourself and closed your eyes.

"Are you tired, Lilly?"

"I'm exhausted and drained. I thought that I was stronger than this, but I think I've reached the end."

"The end?"

"I have no fight left. It's too much. And it's not fair or right. Not like this, not in this way."

"Lilly, you are a positive person, you told me so."

"Well, I don't feel positive anymore. You've won, congratulations."

"I have not won. This is not a competition, or a game, neither is it a fight."

"It is though, a fight to get up, a fight to hope, a fight to be free."

You again adjusted your position but appeared to find no comfort. You got up and poured a glass of wine.

"I never thought that this would be how I would end up. You have no idea how wrong it is, how unfair. I don't deserve this, it's not right. It's just not fucking right. I need my family, my man. They are me, my strength. I am weak without them."

"I appreciate that the situation is far from ideal,"

"Far from ideal? Fuck you and fuck off, Sir."

You sneered as you said Sir, but your voice was quiet. You stood shaking your head, tears falling. I had wanted to tell you about my decision, but you had taken away the optimism that I felt. I wanted to talk about the destinations, the hotels, the adventures I would have. I was disappointed with your lack of energy and it unsettled me. You could not give up.

"Lilly, we are in this together."

"Together? Like we are equal, really? When you, Sir, hold the key? The key to the door, the key to my life."

"I do not have all the answers yet."

"Just let me go. I can't die here, locked in. I can't do this anymore, I'm scared I'm losing it. Everything is closing in. I am not as strong as I used to be, my reserves are spent."

"You are not a reserved person, Lilly."

"Funny. Yeah you laugh. I am a good person but there is only so much that I can take, I deserve my life. I want my life returned, I haven't got the strength to just keep on fighting, one too many battles."

This deflated and defeated you was alarming. I was gaining in strength and confidence and your energies appeared to be ebbing away. Surely you could not seriously give up, could you? And leave me with your carcass? This was not fair on me. I had made my decision. I agreed with you. I had a future to enjoy. We had our futures to enjoy. Those had been your words and I needed to believe that somehow, they were possible, that they were true.

I so wished that you were gone but not dead, I did not want that, not ever. I just did not want you in there. Although, I confess, it did fleetingly occur to me that if you did give up and die it would be a death by natural causes. No one's fault, not my fault, not my responsibility. Your body simply found somewhere. You would, at least, be gone.

I watched you, slumped against the island, small and still, sniffling and sipping, then occasionally shaking. Your little frame hidden under your clothes and you hidden in your surroundings. You looked frail and pathetic, feeble and weak. This was not the Lilly I knew, this was not the Lilly I had expected to see. This was not the Lilly I wanted.

It was unacceptable to me. I left you in what I considered at the time to be your indulgent display of selfish self-pity.

The News

I sat in my chair, irritated and disturbed by your behaviour. I had not followed social media since the hysteria began and I had avoided the news, but as I sat, I automatically switched on the TV. Some Sunday night drama was just ending, moody scenes and I dare say a cliff hanging moment for those who viewed. Then the news. After another Trump twitter headline and more Brexit concern, you.

"The case of the missing mother of three, Lillian Brown, is now nearing the end of the seventeenth day since her last known sighting. We now return to the press conference held earlier this evening."

The usual line up filled the screen.

"Do the police still feel the same degree of confidence that Lilly is alive?"

"Yes, we do."

"Despite there being no new posts?"

"Absolutely, we have no evidence to suggest anything to the contrary. We would like to thank all the members of the public for their support and diligence with regard to potential suspects online."

"Can you give us any further information regarding the man detained for questioning yesterday?"

"We have released a member of the public following detailed investigation. No arrest or charge was made."

"Does this mean that you no longer have a suspect?"

"We have followed up several lines of enquiry given to us and are continuing with others."

"Do you still feel optimistic that whoever has Lilly can be found?"

"Yes, we do. As a professional team working alongside computer experts and using our combined skills in conjunction with all information given to us by members of the public, we have every confidence that Lilly will be found."

Your partner looked haggard. He looked directly at the camera,

"Please, we don't care who you are or even why you took Lilly. Just let her go now. It has been seventeen days, we have never been apart this long. Please, just let Lilly come home."

He came across as genuine, as desperate. Your daughter took his hand.

"We need our mum back, we need to know she is safe…"

Tears poured, your partner held your daughter, your youngest son in turn held her too. Suddenly your eldest son stood.

"Whoever you are, let our mum go."

He was shouting and there was an anger that visibly shook the room. The police spokeswoman quickly rose to her feet.

"Obviously, emotions are running high. Lilly is a much-loved mother and partner and we again appeal for her release. Thank you."

Your photo. The usual phone numbers.

I switched off.

The strength of emotion. The unscripted outburst from an angry young man. The tears. Your tears. The unity of your family was clear and strong. You had obviously been happy. Your words of one too many battles did not sit sensibly with in this idyllic family picture, but then I reasoned there was nothing logical about you anyway.

But who was the man? I looked at the latest coverage. He had been named publicly, a local man. A Mr Johnathon Bradshaw, aged fifty-two. He had been taken in to police custody following information which led the police to believe that he could help with their investigation. He had fitted their profile; middle aged, single, and removed and his online activity had aroused concern. However, he was later released with no charge. His picture was shown.

He had fit their profile. I took some comfort from this, the age bracket clearly wrong. This man's life would never be the same, people would always regard him with suspicion. A neighbour had been interviewed saying,

"He was a little odd, kept himself to himself, but I'd never thought him dangerous."

How many others would be exposed in this way? Their secret habits laid bare for the hungry audience to devour. Their lives put on show and judged by all. This was trial by social media. I knew the mistake of the police was not my fault, yet I felt awkward and unnerved. The net was closing in.

Monday, October 2
Delivery

I had slept badly. Fits of wakefulness, sudden flashes of holiday destinations, followed by images of you, images of your family. A nightmare in which I discovered that you were dead. Your angry face, your tears. A beach and sunshine. Thoughts of you being discovered, of my exposure. All this overthinking heightened my desire to leave. Despite my exhaustion, I maintained my discipline of the morning run. The weather was gloomy, low cloud blocking out any outlines or views. The ground was sodden, and slippery under foot. The dampness seemed to fill my lungs. I ran badly.

On my return, I called at the newsagents. Your poster, now a little yellow around the edges, was still there. I bought your cigarettes and some paracetamols and returned home. Luckily the newsagent had been reluctant to speak to me, too involved in a conversation on his phone. Ordinarily, I would have found this behaviour rude, but in that moment, I was simply grateful for his lack of social grace.

I showered, shaved and moisturised. My skin appeared dull, I looked tired. However, I had to get on, I could not just give up. After a rather large bowl of porridge with just a light drizzle of honey, I took the vase from the dining room to the door, ready. I cleaned and polished the table in preparation for the first ever display that I did not want to take the delivery of. Punctual as ever, I received notification of their arrival and took the previous week's arrangement to the side-gate for the exchange. The new display was heaped with orange Asiatic lilies, orange germini and cerise carnations all set against green chrysanthemum blooms. They were tied with yellow ribbon, decorated with a printed line of lilies. Following a thank you and an acknowledgement of the arrangement received, I returned. I had intended to cancel my order face to face, but I had felt unable. I would send an e-mail. I placed them perfectly, their vivid colours reflected from underneath on the glass surface, above in the twinkle of crystals and across in the mirrors.

They filled the room.

I closed the door.

Sensibly, I considered that I should see you before I ordered the food, how much was I to order anyway? I needed a little time to think before that decision could be made. I made a breakfast tea and tidied around briefly, finally feeling ready, feeling strong enough to see you.

Disclosure and Déjà Vu

"Good morning, Lilly."

I was relieved to see that you were showered. The ugly arm still hidden away, I assumed cleaned. The room was perfect. You were sat at the island, tea in front of you and a half-eaten slice of toast and marmite.

"I trust that you are in a better state of mind today."

"Oh, do you? Why is that?"

"Well, sleep usually refreshes."

Usually, I thought, if one was allowed the luxury.

"I did not sleep well."

"And yet, you spoke of exhaustion?"

"Exhausted yes, too exhausted to sleep."

"A contradiction, so typical of you."

"I am worn out, physically, but my mind, my thoughts are loud, and they are continuous."

"I viewed the news last night."

You instantly looked up.

"Was I on? Did you see them?"

"Yes, Lilly. Think of your family, does that help? They love you, you are lucky."

"Lucky? What the fuck are you talking about? And think of them, what else do you think I do trapped in here?"

"I was merely suggesting that your apathy of yesterday,"

"Apathy? You are a stupid twat. I am frightened, I am fucking unable to find the strength to cope. This claustrophobic room is tearing into me, all my coping strategies are failing. I am losing my mind. I can't breathe, my panic attacks have become frequent again."

You stood and paced.

"I did not know that you suffered from claustrophobia, Lilly. You did not say, and the room is quite large."

"Oh, right, so if I had said on day one, by the way, I'm claustrophobic, please don't lock me up, none of this would have happened? I don't fucking remember being given the chance. It does not matter how big the fucking room is if there is no escape, not even a window."

"Lilly, you have your breathing and counting to keep you calm."

"Learned and practiced methods to cope, but they are not working."

"Have you always been this way?"

"What? So frightened that I'm on the fucking edge? My heart and my head are going to explode."

You sat for a while and your breathing slowed.

133

"No, no I haven't. I have always managed to hold it together because that is what I do, for them, because of them."

"You are never really apart?"

"Not really. Occasionally work reasons or something. The children, are obviously away, but we speak, they are there."

"Work? I thought your holiday let was just across the court yard."

"It is, but that's my project, my partner sometimes has to travel, but never more than a few days at a time."

"Do they not mind your neediness?"

"For fuck's sake. Neediness, it's not something that I enjoy. I don't want to be needy, anyway, they don't really know."

"How can they not know?"

"They know that I worry, I get anxious. It's kind of a joke, but not the rest. I am a good mother, you pass on your strengths not your weaknesses."

"The rest, Lilly? I do not understand."

"Oh God, help me."

You screamed, you paced. Pushing back your hair, smoothing it down again repeatedly, tears were rolling down your red face, your nose was running.

"Lilly, please calm down."

You screamed again, pacing around the entire room, then suddenly to the sink. You splashed cold water onto your face, soaking your bandage and screaming again. Finally, and slowly controlled breathing returned. Inhale, exhale, focused.

Eventually, you lit a cigarette. I noted that you usually only smoked with your wine, but then I had not watched your every move. As you blew the smoke upwards under the extractor fan, brushing quiet tears away, you smiled.

"Oh, Sir, you picked up damaged goods. I bet that's a first hey?"

"Oh, Lilly, trust me, this has been a whirlwind of firsts!"

You continued to stand, wiping your face, trying to calm the flow.

I hesitated,

"Talk to me, Lilly."

"I can't. It doesn't matter."

"Well, forgive me, but it clearly does matter. It is good to talk, I have been told."

"Yes, but I don't know how."

"You do not know how to talk? I disagree."

"Where to start, how to start. I don't want to start."

"I can only suggest that the logical place to start would be at the beginning, Lilly."

"Sir, you have triggered memories and feelings that I do not need or want. I have dealt with it, I had dealt with everything."

"What memories?"

You were quiet. In a hushed voice you spoke,

"Of when I was locked in, a prisoner."

"Oh, Lilly, you are a criminal? Well, that explains your language."

"You are such a knob sometimes. I said locked in not up."

"Prisoner, you said."

"A prisoner yes and a victim too."

You breathed out smoke.

"Domestic violence. You know, that makes it sound safe somehow. Almost cosy, like a household routine, domestic chores. I have always thought that it should just be called violence."

You stubbed out your cigarette. I hesitated,

"You were locked in a room?"

"No, I had the luxury of a whole house."

"I do not understand."

"I was literally locked in, kept behind doors, trapped."

I was confused.

"But how did this happen? Even for you, Lilly, this is illogical. You do not purchase a house and then accept never to leave unless that is your choice."

You appeared annoyed.

"For goodness' sake, these things do not happen overnight. When we first met, obviously it was fine. We would always be out but, looking back now, the signs were there. Alarm bells were ringing, but I was young and lacked self-confidence. I pushed them to the back of my mind."

You were shaking your head, yet you remained calm.

I, however, had a sense of trepidation flowing through me and yet, I was intrigued.

"What signs?"

"Small things at first. Only his plans were ever met, where we went, what we did. I went along with it mostly, he was much older than I was. Over time his friends and family were the only other people in my life."

"Where were your friends?"

"They had stopped coming, they had stopped trying to make arrangements. They were made to feel so unwelcome, so uncomfortable and the arguments that would follow were so upsetting that I stopped trying to see them. I don't think I was conscious to the extent of what was really happening. I just wanted a happy, peaceful life."

"But he hurt you and you stayed with him, why?"

"He hadn't physically hurt me, not then. If it was that simple, first date and a smack in the face, everyone would walk away, everyone would be able to walk away. Over time I had become isolated from all that was not his. His world and family were mine and I didn't question it."

"Go on."

"We decided to have a baby. I was very young and delighted when I became pregnant so very quickly. I was excited, but I was scared. I was vulnerable and completely reliant on him.

"As the months passed, I was quite poorly and only left the house for scheduled appointments at the doctors, always with him by my side. If he had to go away I was taken to his brother's house to stay with his wife. I spent my time concentrating with all the preparations, nursery, pram, baby clothes. I lost myself in a bubble of baby-ness and I convinced myself that everything was good."

"But this was not the case?"

"No, of course not. Not really, but by this point I was somehow lost amongst the reality. I had not realised how nervous I had become, how I would jump whenever he walked in. It was a slow shift from shared conversations to me being told. I had no self-worth, it had slipped behind my ever-growing tummy. I was

135

frightened. No friends, no money of my own, I was young and about to be a mummy."

"Your first son."

You looked up sharply and then quickly adjusted your expression, remembering, I suppose, that I had seen your family. You walked over to the sofa and gathered the throw around your shoulders.

"Yes, my beautiful, perfect baby was born, but it had been a horrific birth and we both stayed in hospital for a week. It was beautiful and magical, even though I was desperate with pain and fear. This amazing little boy was so precious, so perfect, he eclipsed everything."

I saw love written all over your face.

"You took naturally to motherhood."

"Yes, Sir, I really did. I fell instantly in love, obsessional and protective love.

As the days went by, I grew a little stronger and as I cuddled him and fed him, I knew that I just wanted it to be the two of us."

"Did you tell him this?"

"No, no of course not. I couldn't. I wrote it down by my medical charts though. I explained how I was scared and did not want to return home."

"A nurse read your letter? What did she say?"

"I will never know if my letter was read. It was removed, and nothing was ever said. I have concluded over the years that it was probably dismissed as a silly girl's panic, a first-time mum scared to care for her baby alone or perhaps it was simply cleaned away unnoticed. Anyway, the week passed, we were discharged and handed over to him.

"That night he went out to wet the baby's head. When he returned, I was feeding my son and he wanted to hold him. He was drunk, so I said no, he became so angry. I ran in to the nursery, closed the door and moved the cot behind it. I sang continuously and loudly so the shouting couldn't be heard. I did not want my beautiful baby to hear it.

"Eventually, he was quiet. I lay my son in his Moses basket and rested by his side.

"In the morning I came out and went downstairs, he was asleep on the sofa. I was making a cup of tea and running a bath. The bathroom was downstairs in that house, small, not even a shower and it was cold. I remember how cold it was."

You shivered, my mouth was dry. You cleared your throat,

"Suddenly, he was behind me, I turned quickly, and he struck me so hard that I collapsed on the floor. He kicked me, directly in between my legs, just once, but, my God, the pain was unbelievable.

"Don't ever disobey me again," he screamed in my face and then walked away and into the bathroom.

I was shocked, shaken and almost wanted you to stop and yet I allowed you to continue.

"Slowly I moved on to my side. Blood was leaking through my pyjamas and I felt so sick, but I had to get up, to get my baby. He was still asleep when I returned to the nursery, blissfully unaware and innocent.

"Then he came out of the bathroom and upstairs, fresh and dressed and stood in the door way. 'He is sleeping,' I remember announcing. He smiled and replied that he was going to work, and I was to go nowhere. The door would be locked until he came home. I blurted out, stupidly, that the midwife was coming. Back in those days, for the first ten days, mummies and babies were checked. Daily house visits, gone now, due to cut-backs.

"Anyway, my son began to stir and there was a knock at the door, followed by a cheery, 'Hello, only me.' Everything happened at the same time. He cuddled up my baby and went downstairs, followed closely and carefully by me. He proceeded to say how pleased and relieved he was that she was here. I was not coping very well. I had fallen trying to get in the bath, he was so concerned. He was very plausible. I looked at us and the way that she looked at me. He was stood, all clean and bright and I was dishevelled, swollen-faced and in bloodstained pyjamas. My son was examined and found to be perfect, as I already knew, and then on the sofa, in front of him, she examined me. My external stitches had split, but she felt that the internal surgical ones would have held. I was told to take more care of myself. I was a mother now.

"He made her a cup of tea and she watched me as I fed my baby, correcting everything, tut-tutting under her breath as I cried. Implications given that I was very fortunate, a perfect baby, a loving, concerned daddy on hand. Young mothers did not realise how hard having a baby would be. She told me to bathe in a salt water bath daily and to rest when baby rested. To eat properly and that she would return tomorrow. She left and so did he, locking the door behind him. That was it, that was how it all began."

I felt quite sick and shaken.

"Lilly, that is truly horrible. Why did you not tell her the truth?"

"I think I was in shock. Obviously, I was terrified, and she looked at me like I was shit."

You paused,

"I don't know why, but I didn't."

I prompted hopefully,

"But, she returned the next day?"

"Yes, and he was there. I had rushed around, got up so early. Bathed and dried my hair, clean clothes, so determined that she couldn't fault me, judge me."

"But you did tell her?"

"No. We were never alone but I'm not sure if I could have told her anyway."

I found this confusing, unsettling as I watched you.

"So, then what, Lilly?"

"She only came once more. My son had lost a little weight, a couple of ounces and she felt that it was probably my milk, I should top up his feeds with formula.

"I felt that I had failed. It was horrible, and I cried. I was told to pull myself together again. He insisted that he would go and buy everything we needed immediately, anything to help. They left chatting and smiling together."

I watched as you gently rocked staring out across the room.

"You know that old school approach is a thing of the past now, thank God. I am pretty sure attitudes and awareness are quite different now."

"I should hope so. Your baby was alright though?"

Your face instantly softened, and you smiled.

"He was more than alright, and he loved the bottle, the plastic symbol of my failure. I told my son I would never fail him again."

You were crying again.

I had an overriding urge to comfort you.

"Lilly, you did not fail. Many babies have bottles, do they not? How were you?"

"I got better eventually, had a huge black eye for over a week, but no one saw. I bathed in salt water. I loved my son."

You left the sofa, put the kettle on, threw your breakfast remains away and had another cigarette. I grabbed a water from the fridge.

"Did he ever hurt you again, Lilly?"

"Yes, Sir, he did. But never on my face again. Hidden bruises, carefully given. It seemed the taboo had been broken and somehow, he felt it an acceptable way to behave."

"Lilly, why did you not phone the police?"

"With what, Sir? There were no mobile phones back then. I was not allowed a landline. My communication with the outside world was via the TV, a whole four channels. You can't imagine, it can you? It is a whole generation ago."

These words were said quietly, dismissive almost. You were right though, I had no insight into the world you were describing.

"No. I cannot, to have no contact, no internet."

"Those were the days that when you were alone you really were truly alone."

I searched for a logical solution.

"What about neighbours? Did you have any?"

"Yes, I had neighbours. I would scream through the walls, crying for help, but no one came."

"They cannot have heard you."

"Oh, they did. I was told later."

"But, they could not just ignore you."

"Oh, Sir."

You shook your head.

"It was a different time in so many ways. People didn't like to get involved, but, they had apparently, called the police on several occasions."

"So did the police get you out?"

"No, they never came. It was policy then that unless the victim came forward, they didn't respond. There was, possibly still is, a reluctance to get involved, 'It is just a domestic.'"

You held your hands up as you spoke these words.

"Just a domestic, fucking ridiculous. It is violence, but that is the way it was."

"That is ridiculous, that cannot be true."

You laughed but it was dry.

"Oh really? How young you are. Do you know that it has only been in the last thirty years that there have been major changes?

"Violence against women was only recognised as a fucking infringement of human rights in 1993. Marital rape was only recognised as a crime in 1991. It is just not taken seriously enough."

"But there have been changes, there must be help now?"

"Things are better yes. Women's aid and refuge they go back to the '70s. Their work was, and is, amazing it is just not given the status or the finances that it truly needs. The police have specialised units now, specific training given. There are some specialised courts. Laws and policy have been implemented, a greater awareness between, say, medical staff and the police. It is all good news, but it is not enough to combat the hidden violence, it still goes on."

"I suppose there will always be some violent households. It is unrealistic to think otherwise, Lilly."

"Some, some yes sadly, but it's not small scale, you know. Over a million women experience this every year. On average, two women are killed every week, it's outrageous that more isn't done. It is fucking wrong."

You were angry, the tone in your voice was sharp. I obviously knew that you were completely right.

"Yes, yes, Lilly, I agree."

We remained quiet for some time, but I wanted to know, I needed to know what had happened to you and your son.

"So, you remained in the house for how long?"

"Almost a year, a whole year."

"What?" I was stunned, incredulous even. "A year, how could that happen? What did you do?"

You shrugged,

"Weeks turned to months, I guess. I did leave the house for doctors' appointments, baby's vaccinations. Always with him, of course, so I guess no one noticed. He did the shopping."

You caught your breath.

"It is so weird to say all this out loud."

"But what did you do?"

"Quite quickly I created my own little world. Funny how you cope."

"And what was your world?"

"Obviously, it was my son. I lived for him and built up a regime, practically military. Exactly the same routine, day after day and every day.

"I would get up at six, no matter what had happened through the night, no matter how little sleep I may have had. I would make tea and my son's bottle. Then I would wash, change and dress him. Then I would run my bath, his baby chair by my side. I was so quick, partly because it was bloody freezing and partly because I hated the thought of him seeing me in the bath."

"Why did you not simply lock the door?"

"There was no lock, ironically, he had removed it.

By eight we were both ready and ate breakfast. He would be up by then and would always disturb our bubble. I think I tried to pretend he was not there, but it wasn't easy, I really only relaxed when he left for work."

Your voice was steady and almost matter of fact which was quite chilling given the situation you were describing.

"So, Lilly, what did you do all day?"

"I cleaned the house, every nook and cranny of it, every day. Washing, ironing, watched TV and played with my perfect baby. The house was always done by lunch time, then my son would have a sleep. One to two thirty. I would exercise, prepare his tea, sometimes sleep, sometimes write. Then he would be up, changed and happy.

"He was a perfect baby. We played and sung nursery rhymes, I read books to him. Then it was baby's tea time. I would clear away, prepare the bed time bottle, then at five thirty I would prepare his bath. When he was tiny, I would fill the blue baby bath up in front of the fire and he would splash and giggle, all pink and then quickly he would be snuggled up in a fluffy towel. I loved bath times."

You were smiling at this memory, you appeared lost in your thoughts.

"You must have been lonely, Lilly?"

"No, I didn't allow myself to think like that, I had the TV on in the background. I had my son and I don't know, it is strange how you adapt, how you cope, how your mind works."

"How your mind works."

"It is a fragile thing, isn't it? The mind. I suppose, I could not allow myself to drift. I developed a routine so rigid, I realise now, to prevent my thoughts having any time to develop. For a sense of security, for the desperate feeling of some control."

A path with no allowance for deviation. No space for thought. Yes, I understood. I diverted the conversation from this topic.

"You said you would write, what did you write about?"

"I would make up stories and I kept a diary of all the new things my son had done. I wrote letters too."

"To whom?"

"To whoever. I would hide them around the house, the back of cupboards, in the side-board, under my wardrobe."

Illogical actions I noted, but I said nothing.

"Why? What did they say?"

"They would say the truth. It was my voice. I would document everything, explain what was happening, what had happened. I often wondered if they were found, if they were read."

"Did you not speak to him? I presume he came home every day, you ate your evening meal together? You must have spoken?"

"We did not eat together. I ate little bits with my son, I had no real appetite. He would eat out most nights or bring himself a takeaway back or get something out the freezer. He drank. He drank more and more as the months passed. When he would return I would know just how drunk he was by the sound of his arrival, how many times it took for him to get the key in the door, the stumble as he closed it. My heart would race. I think, the anticipation of what might happen was almost as frightening as the violence.

"So, no we did not speak. There was nothing to say. The whole situation was twisted and wrong and he knew it. I have, over the years concluded that he was probably scared too."

"Scared? Of what? How can you feel sorry for him?"

"I don't, I didn't, that is not what I mean. I have just tried to understand. He knew that if that door was unlocked we would go.

"I hated him, I resented him even looking at my son and he knew that too. I made no attempt to hide my disgust and I could not hide my fear. He was not wanted. He was excluded from our world."

"I was somewhat caught off guard."

"Lilly, you are surely not justifying his actions?"

"No, no I spent years trying to understand the situation, but not for him, for myself."

"There is no justification. I did not deserve the things he did, I know that I was not to blame. I have dealt with it, had dealt with it, but all this," you gestured around the room.

"I am nothing like him though, Lilly. I am a good man."

"Who has cut me and locked me in a room, no nothing like him, silly me."

I was shocked and hurt. Obviously, I understood your parallel thinking, but I am not a violent bully. I was not responsible for your past. I needed some space.

"I am going to have my lunch now, Lilly."

You were filling the kettle, you were shaking. I left you.

I attempted to eat some sweet potato soup, but my appetite had waned. I cleared away, your words filled my thoughts, your disclosures were distressing. By way of a distraction I began to select meals for the forthcoming food order. I washed, dried and folded my towels, I sat in my chair and gazed out of the window. Eventually, time was pressing on. I returned to you.

"Good afternoon, Lilly."

"Is it?"

You were sat, coiled up in your usual corner of the sofa. The now empty tea cup on the floor.

"Have you eaten?"

"No."

"You must try a little something. It occurred to me that you could have escaped through a window."

"No, I couldn't. The opening was too small, and it only opened at the top. Even if by some miracle I had squeezed through, I couldn't have carried my baby, I couldn't leave him."

"I did try to smash the kitchen window one afternoon. I cracked the glass and then panicked, even if I had removed all the glass, the opening, I realised would be tight and the window was quite high, the jump down with the baby too dangerous. I gave up. I felt beaten in every sense, in every way."

You had shifted position, bringing your knees up and hugging them to you.

"Did he notice the cracked glass? Did he say anything?"

"Oh yes. The violence had been getting steadily worse, but that night, well he found new depths."

"Tell me."

"He had come home earlier than usual, not as drunk and had seen what I had done. He shouted at me and went to hit me, I ran to my bedroom and he followed, he threw me down across the bed, I screamed, and he held his hand against my mouth and whispered, 'don't wake the baby'. He was very strong. I stared up, frozen, trapped. He pulled my jeans down and then picked up a kitchen knife and he cut me. Not mad stab wounds, carefully and slowly he traced over my little stretch marks, one by one, changing them from silver to red and then he left."

I was listening, but it was hard. You were speaking with such control and yet the way you trembled, clutching your legs so tightly reflected your pain.

"What did you do?"

"Nothing, ridiculous. I did nothing."

"When did he return?"

"Not until the following evening. I think I passed out, I don't really know for how long. I don't remember much after that, not until the morning when I heard my baby cry. Six am, like clockwork and another day began."

"Lilly, I do not know what to say, did you ever fight back?"

"As you can see, Sir, I am not really built for fighting." You held your hands up and smiled.

"I need a drink."

"It is quite early, not even five."

"And?"

"I was merely pointing out."

"I don't really feel social responsibility matters right now Sir. Just have a bloody drink with me."

I watched as you poured a glass. Only one bottle left, I noted and remembered the yet undone food order. This irregularity to my schedule was uncomfortable. I e-mailed Sebastian and Co for enough provisions to see us through the next few days. It was consistent with my original ordering pattern, apart from your wine which had obviously become my new tipple. I apologised for the later than usual order, blaming work commitments and said that I would be away for some time but on my return would re-establish with their excellent service. When I returned to you, drink in hand, I felt a little calmer, you were already pouring your second.

"Hello, Lilly, I am back now please, eat something."

"Are you drinking?"

"Yes."

"Cheers."

"Cheers, Lilly."

You twirled your glass,

"You know, Sir, I couldn't physically fight back, but I did do something. I'm not proud of it, but I have forgiven myself over the years."

"What did you do?"

"After that night, apart from hiding all the knives in the back of cupboards, I took all his frozen ready meals out the freezer and defrosted them, then refroze them."

You were laughing.

"I know it's not funny, but it's the madness I'm laughing at, the futility. It was all I had. He would come in late, drunk and eat one. And in the morning when he was sick and in pain, I would say that he should not drink so much."

"Did he ever find out?"

"No and I did that every day. It just became another part of the day. Cold and calculated, but I justified it and I am ashamed to say that I think I took some pleasure from it."

I smiled as I imagined the satisfaction you must have felt.

"How was your stomach? Did you not need to go to hospital?"

"No, as I said, they were not deep cuts, just deep enough to leave their mark."

"So what happened, Lilly? How did you get out?"

I watched as you twirled the glass in your hands, breathing controlled. I waited.

"It was about a month later and to be honest he was either working, drinking or poorly. The violence had stopped, well, the threat was there, but the actions were not. Things were probably the calmest they had ever been. Now that my baby was coming up to his first birthday, I felt he needed to see other children, to attend a playgroup, so I asked whether we could we find one and go."

"That was brave."

"Or foolish, but whichever, it made him angry. I have often questioned whether his anger was because I asked to do something or was it really because he had realised that at some point, clearly, the situation would have to change."

"Go on."

"Well, he shouted and left. It was a long day, a long evening. Waiting, wondering what he would do, how he would be. That time was frightening, the not knowing was almost worse than the beatings.

"Finally, he did return. I had already gone to bed, it was after midnight. I heard the chaos of the key being dropped, picked up, dropped again. The swearing. I heard every footstep pounding up every stair. I heard him slumping from wall to wall. I heard him rattle the stairgate I had across the nursery door. I had locked it and I always placed a book on top, so if ever he tried to get in there I would always wake up. I would always know. I jumped out of bed and went to my doorway. He couldn't manage the lock and then he saw me. He pushed me back with one hand and it was only then that I noticed the gun."

You stopped for a moment, to drink, to reach for your cigarettes. I realised my glass was empty, I had not even noticed, my mouth so dry.

"I walked backwards, halfway in to the bedroom and he said, 'Stop, stand still.' He walked past me and got into the bed. He told me to take my clothes off, the gun was pointing at me, unsteadily and he was laughing. I removed my pyjamas and tried to fight the urge to scream. I was aware that I was shaking, my whole body convulsing. I had no control. I wet myself, Sir, and he laughed even more. I do not know how long I stood, stripped bare, exposed and humiliated. I do not know if the gun was even loaded, but in that moment, I saw no end. In that moment I almost gave up. Eventually, he passed out. I collapsed quietly coiled on the floor and oh how I prayed. My whole entire soul begged.

"At five am I quietly ran a bath, speedily washed and dressed, made tea, prepared my son's bottle and breakfast and was at his cot's side as he woke. Our daily routine continued. When he got up not a word was said. He left the house. Later, when my son was sleeping, I cleaned my bedroom and searched for the gun, but I didn't find it."

I watched as you finished smoking, I waited patiently for you to continue.

"Early that evening, there was a knock at the door. I looked through the window and it was my brother. I had not seen him since I was first pregnant. I was just attempting to explain I had misplaced my key when he also arrived home."

"But, Lilly, why did you not tell your brother the truth, immediately?"

"My first reaction was automatic, practised, embarrassed and ashamed. However, now he had to open the door. My brother entered and how I held him. He tried to hold a conversation but was very drunk. My son was due to have his bed-time milk and he and my brother were playing. There was no logical reason or excuse he could make to justify asking my brother to leave, not without giving himself away. I guess, like most bullies, they are inadequate cowards, underneath."

You paused again, slightly shuffling along the edge of the work surface.

"Plus, the fact that he was drunk worked in my favour, rational thinking gone. As I warmed the bottle, I said, in front of my brother, that I had misplaced my key

143

so could he leave his in the door, so I could lock it when my brother left. He attempted some comment about baby-brain and tried again to hold conversation. I gave my son his milk and talked to my brother. Well, actually, I listened. Finally realising that he could not join in, embarrassed maybe, most definitely angry at my brother's arrival and aware that he could slip up, I don't know, but he said that he was going to bed. I reminded him again, oh so politely about the key. I held out my hand, he paused but then pushed it into my palm. I smiled and said thank you. The look he gave me, his back towards my brother, was of pure anger. We said goodnight. I let my son stay up, he was loving this new face and I did not want to go upstairs. We heard some crashing around, I knew this was my reminder that I would pay. He came downstairs to the bathroom, his presence felt, but my brother did not leave. Instead he asked me how I was, it was like I had rehearsed the conversation as everything tumbled out, almost as though I was telling a story."

"You told him everything?"

"Well, not quite, not all the details, but enough. I knew that I could trust my brother. He said that we would leave that night. He was my hero."

"Why did you not tell him everything if you trusted him?"

"Oh, there was no way I could even begin to admit everything, not then. I felt ashamed that this was what my life had become. I have only told you a small selection, a snap shot, a year is a long time. Anyway, what would be the point of upsetting my brother more than the situation already had? He knew there was violence, he knew I was scared. When the noises stopped, I packed some things for my son, nappies, bottles and for some reason his porridge and breakfast bowl, bizarre. I crept upstairs and took some clothes from his drawers and his favourite blanket from his cot and crept back in to the living room. We hid the getaway bag under the stairs and continued talking quietly, waiting for the right time. We heard him moving around again, I made us both tea and my brother held his nephew so tightly. Suddenly, he was in the doorway, leaning into the frame for support. I returned to my brother's side. He said to give him the baby, he was asleep and should be in his cot, but my brother said it was fine. 'He is enjoying a cuddle and he's only just fallen asleep anyway. You go, catch up on some sleep, make the most of the break.' All gentle and good humoured. 'Me and my sis have loads of family stuff to catch up with, you would only be bored.' Laughter. He couldn't argue. My brother has an air of authority about him, he is kind but firm. He was not capable to stand unaided, let alone find the words to win. He was so angry though, I knew. It must have been the anger keeping him awake, he would normally have passed out by that time. Anyway, he turned, took a bottle from the kitchen and stormed up the stairs.

"I remember thinking, yes, drink some more and just go to sleep. A deep drunkard's sleep. Our conversations continued in whispered conspiracy after that, I was shaking and manic, every creak or sound made me jump. My fear was visible and contagious, my brother tried to remain calm and focused. It must have been so strange to be thrown in to that house of fear and threat, but he was strong. I knew the time had finally come. If not now, I felt certain that by the next evening I would simply be a statistic. There was no going back. We sat anxiously together, the three of us waiting until we felt certain that he was asleep, then my brother took the bag and I, my son. As we walked through the door, accidently, my brother knocked a milk bottle over. The sound seemed to echo so loudly, we froze. My heart was pounding, the darkness heavy, but nothing. I closed the door and we drove in to the night."

"Where did you go?"

"We went to the police station and that's when I learnt about the neighbour's calls and I was told they had just been waiting for me to come forward. They escorted us away, over the county line."

"Did you press charges against him?"

"It was never requested, never suggested."

"So he got away with everything?"

"Well, yes, but I had my freedom."

"But that is not right, Lilly."

This irony was not lost on me, but then I was not, I am not, like him.

"I know, Sir, but that is just the way it was. Don't look back, don't ever come back, don't contact anyone from the past, just disappear. He died prematurely, by the way, from liver failure."

You poured yet another glass.

"Lilly, please choose something for tea."

"To make you feel better? I have no appetite."

"Lilly, I am not responsible for your past."

"No, Sir, but you are responsible for my future."

Your words caught me off guard, but they were true. I watched you, I could not really imagine what your experience had been like. I could not truly comprehend the fear you must have felt, but the snapshot, as you put it, was deeply disturbing and I knew unjust. I had never intended for you to be there. This was not a situation I had planned or calculated. I was not, nor am I, an evil man. The future. We could both have a future. We both deserved our futures, but how?

I left you. I needed air and time for contemplation. I sat on my balcony until the evening's air penetrated my skin. Until I shook and shivered, teeth chattered. Until it hurt. I had another drink. I made a tray of snacks, I too could not face a full meal. I placed the food, the gin, my glass, by the screen. I booked my ticket, Friday afternoon. Australia here I come. The decision was made.

To the Future

"Hello, Lilly, if you eat something, we can talk about futures."

"Hello, what do you mean?"

"I am concerned, you need to eat."

"About futures?"

"I have booked my ticket, Lilly."

"When for?"

"You must eat before conversation."

I ate, and you selected a couscous pot and you ate. Finally, when you were done,

"When for?"

"Friday."

"What day is today?"

"It is Monday night."

"Are you excited?"

"Yes, yes I am, but I am perplexed in equal measure."

"You will be fine, more than fine, your voyage of discovery will be amazing."

"Was it amazing for you, afterwards?"

"I don't want to talk about the past anymore, Sir, only the future."

"But was it easy?"

"Things are rarely easy, but it is a process, a step at a time, but you can do it."

"Can I?"

"Yes. Well, you have booked your ticket now, so I bloody hope so!" You laughed.

"Seriously, Sir, yes, you can and along your travels you can heal, grieve for your father properly, grieve for your mother, grieve for the mother you never had. Understand your past and find peace with it. Then the future, who knows what it will hold?"

"Who, indeed?"

"You, however, hold my future. When will you let me go?"

"Lilly, surely now it is not so much a question of when, but of how?"

"A key, perhaps?"

"Lilly, there is little point in talk of my voyage if I am stopped before I have even begun."

"Stopped?"

"Lilly, you are a missing woman, the police."

"I have told you, I will say nothing."

"Oh you are exasperating at times. It really is not going to be quite that easy, just to let you walk out my door. I would be found in minutes and I doubt they

146

would listen. They would not understand that I did not mean for any of this to happen, then there is your arm."

"Slow down. Okay if I can't just walk out of here, take me somewhere else. Leave me somewhere else, away from you."

"I do not think we can just pop out for a drive."

"We could, at night. I could hide."

"How do I know that I can trust you?"

"Because I promise, because you can."

"Can I?"

"Yes, Sir, you can, and you must, but how do I know that I can trust you?"

"Trust me? To let you go? I said I would not hurt you, I have said I will let you go. It is the how we are attempting to consider."

"And can I trust that you would not do this again? That there is not going to be another missing woman?"

"Lilly, of course not. I did not want this, this happened, that one moment. I would never, I could never. This was a mistake."

The very thought that you could think me capable, that you might even consider it possible, made my blood run cold. I knew then that we had to resolve our situation, I just felt at a total loss as to how.

"The police will question you though."

"I will say I don't remember anything, that I just came around in a room."

"You cannot speak of this room."

"Well, I will say it was dark. No windows and empty, apart from a mattress on the floor. I could say it was cold and had an old toilet and sink in one corner. That the walls were concrete, like an out-house or lock-up."

"So in this hypothetical world why are you so clean?"

"Mmmm, good point. Okay I will say that there was an old shower as well."

"How were you fed?"

"How about a hatch? That was locked, made of steel, but was opened a couple of times a day and water and basic foods were given."

"My voice though, they will ask about my voice?"

"I never spoke to you."

I remembered my post of 'Lilly loves to talk'. This was so much more complicated than you realised. I so much more involved. If secrets were to be kept between us, truths hidden, every detail would have to be believable, realistic and meticulously thought through. Everything had to be beyond scrutiny.

"Would you really lie to the police though, Lilly?"

"If you give me back my life, I will allow you yours. Do we have a deal?"

"Yes, Lilly, but it needs work. We need a plan."

"Well," you raised your glass, "here's to plans and the future, cheers."

I held my glass to the screen,

"Cheers."

I sat and shook my head. I questioned could this really work? Would you really be complicit in this way? Would you really keep quiet once you were reunited with your family? I felt overwhelmed and yet I could think of no alternative path.

Plans

"Lilly, if I can trust you, then we must think every detail through."

"I have told you, I will say nothing."

"Oh, Lilly, that is simply not enough. You will be questioned; your answers must make sense."

And so, our conspiracy began.

"Okay, so where do we start?"

"How did we meet?"

"I could say you snatched me."

"No, oh, Lilly, Lilly, think. You are illogical, I am not. If I had snatched you, a horrible word may I add, you would know my face, my full description."

"You must have knocked me down then. I remember nothing. Maybe it was an accident and you panicked, but then felt such guilt, which is why you finally let me go. That is almost the truth, isn't it?"

"Yes and that is plausible. Do you remember me though, what I look like?"

"I remember that you were tall and young and angry, but little else to be honest."

"Not that you can disclose that, Lilly, but fine. Fine, so then you woke up and were in a room? A building? Or we could say a caravan?"

"No, no, we couldn't. I could escape from a caravan easily. I would not have stayed. There cannot be windows because I would have smashed them, trust me."

"Apparently, I do. Anyway, so where have you been?"

"A solid room, an out-house. But then, why would there be a bathroom? Mmmm, I've got it, an annexe, it could have felt like I was in part of a building because again it is close to the truth. No windows, possibly a basement?"

"A basement would make it harder to escape from surely? Or to be freed from. You would then have to describe the property, in fact, how do you not see the building when you escape? This is not going to work."

"Yes, yes, it is. I will not know the exact building because it will be dark, and I will be running away, not looking back. It will be rural, obviously. A stone out-building, which has maybe been renovated, that's why there is a bathroom."

"Or a converted garage, no windows, just a side door. Separate from the property though because then you wouldn't have seen it."

"Okay, that makes sense. Some sort of garage, remote, so no one has heard me."

"It is small, you have a bed, a bathroom and some sort of heating."

"Why?"

"Because you would be ill if you had not had heating, it is October, Lilly."

"Fine, fine. There is a bed then, light, an armchair and small shower room in the corner, how is that?"

"An armchair?"

"Yes, and maybe a small unit, with a sink and a kettle. Imagine it has been converted as an additional bedroom."

"Yes, minimal but functional. A wall heater, electric."

"Okay."

"So how were you fed?"

"A cat flap, in the door."

"Oh that is quite good, but the door must be solid."

"It is locked somehow. I can't get my hands through, it only works from the outside."

"And food is given through this?"

"Yes, sandwiches, wrapped in foil, small enough to fit through."

"Wrapped in foil, I like the detail. What about your arm though?"

"Maybe that happened when you knocked me down, maybe you thought me dead and in a state of panic dragged me across the road and that is why it's such a mess?"

"I knocked you down?"

"He knocked me down, but I was unconscious. I do not actually really know, it was just like that when I came around."

"Yes, it is possible, but you spoke together, what will you say with regard to that?"

"Why? Why did we speak?"

"Because you would, when the food came, you would."

I remembered again my postings, how had those images been taken? I had no desire to explain this to you, maybe. I concluded, it did not matter that you were unaware of every detail. You would, at least, be genuine in your shock when you discovered all the facts. Your ignorance would be truthful. I reflected that this may even help you to be believed without too many questions.

"Okay, we spoke. Maybe he was sorry? He had thought that he had killed me and panicked. Maybe he had been drinking and so had not wanted to report it and then simply panicked, putting me in his car and taking me. However, when he discovered that I was alive, he talked to me, fed me and eventually the guilt became so much that he let me escape."

I thought of the location. I had been driving the scenic route home, meandering lanes, my thoughts in turmoil and shock on that day. My car obviously had not been captured on camera. I had not driven through the busy town, so despite the relative close proximity, this could not lead to me. Indeed, the thousands of vehicles from that day could not all have been traced and checked, they could not all have been seen.

"So, Lilly, to summarise, we are saying this was a drunk driver with a delayed conscience?"

"Why not?"

Well, I reasoned, why not? I approved the notion of a conscience, it slotted together with my involvement through social media. My alter ego was not a bad man, he had merely made a bad decision, a mistake.

"Lilly, how will you describe his voice, his accent?"

"Where am I to be found?"

"I have not thought that far yet, Lilly."

"Where am I now?"

"Your location is not relevant. I will give some thought as to where you will be found. I need some time. What shall I do about my house, your room?"

"What about them? You're going away. Just lock the doors, you're good at that."

"Oh, how very funny, Lilly. Yes, obviously I will leave everything securely, but I cannot leave evidence behind, evidence that you were ever here. There can be no trace of you."

"No problem, I will clean."

"You are good at that."

"Oh, how funny you are, Sir. But, seriously, I can clean. I will clean. Do you have a steam cleaner?"

"Of course, why?"

"I could use it on every surface, the sofa, the mattress."

"Yes, that is good. There is so much to consider. I need to think. Lilly, where is your handbag? It needs to be washed, I may have touched it."

You went to the bedside unit, the bottom drawer, you placed the bag in the basket.

"Lilly, I need to think, and you must also think. It is getting late now, and we must be thorough, every detail must be considered with care."

"I will be thorough, there will be no trace of me left, no connection to you."

"Good, good. I am still anxious though. Once settled, once home, you could still speak about me."

"But I won't."

"Why?"

"Because, as I have already told you, my freedom is all I want. I have come so close to the edge in here, I have nearly lost everything, that fear only intensifies my love for my family. They are all I want, all I need. I have not gone through the last thirty years of growing, of understanding, of finding peace and love with my family, to have my beautiful life taken away, not now."

"But that is my very point. If we continue with our plan, you will have your life returned and what is to stop you then?"

"To be honest what would I gain?"

"Revenge."

"The best revenge is to be truly happy. I do not think knowing you were in prison would bring me joy and I do not want to be on the news; people staring at me, courtroom appearances, my life discussed. I just want to go home. It could go on for months, questions after questions, trapped in interview rooms, courtrooms." You shuddered.

"I could not bare that intrusion, that focus on me."

I too, shuddered. You had no idea how famous you already were.

However, I had to put these thoughts to one side. I had to trust that your words were true and your desire to simply be with those you loved was, genuine. I had to trust that your repulsion towards attention would work to my advantage.

"Are you not angry with me?"

"I am sad that you have hurt me, resurrected fears, set me back. I am angry that you have caused my family pain. I hate that I am the reason they will be distressed. I should be there to protect them not to affect them."

"Set you back?"

"Yes, but until I am free, I won't really know how badly."

"Explain."

"Well, will I cope in busy places? In quiet places? With people? On my own? It might take time."

"I really do not understand."

You sighed, your eyes filled a little. You twirled your glass. I waited.

"When I first began living on my own, I was so scared of everything. I had to cope because of my son, but I didn't seek the help I should have done. I did not know how to or how very important it was, to talk and to understand what had happened, so instead I tried to fix myself. Over the years, I have recovered with the love that I have been surrounded by, but there are limits, I have limits. I am damaged."

"What are your limits?"

"I understand that there are situations which I will never be comfortable in. For example, I have never been able to work in an environment where I cannot see an exit at all times."

"The café?"

"Yes, and before that retail. Always close to an exit, fresh air, just in case my fear overwhelmed me. Just so I knew that I could leave if I wanted to.

"I have never told anyone that before, but I have managed. I have found ways secretly to manipulate situations to suit my needs."

"Situations?"

"In life, day to day. I do it without too much thought now, I am the master of avoidance. Not in a selfish way towards others, but in a truly selfish way to protect myself. No one realises, but it is easier now. We have a life that is perfect and a home where everyone wants to visit, I am a better host than guest because I feel safe."

"Are you not cross or disappointed with yourself for being this way?"

"Mmmm, disappointed? Well, in some ways, I wish I could be spontaneous. I wish I could be truly free. Mostly though, I am proud at how far I have come. In the beginning, I couldn't even get in a car. I couldn't walk into a shop if there was only a man present. I could not speak to strangers or be amongst too many people and I most certainly didn't socialise. Time, age and obviously the love I found and the support from my family has helped me to be stronger. To be me."

"But you said that they did not know?"

"They do not realise the full extent to which I am affected. Why should they? Just that I worry, it's the joke, 'oh is mum worrying again' They laugh at my silly reactions and I am glad that they do. I have always known how much I need them. They are my strength, my inspiration to try, my rainbow on the darkest of days, but I would never put that pressure on them. I am not their responsibility Sir, they are mine.

"There is a saying, 'Give them roots and watch them grow, give them wings and watch them fly'."

"Like a butterfly?"

"Don't laugh at me."

"Lilly, I actually understand. Before you, yes, I would have mocked such thoughts, but not now. Not now, Lilly."

And this was so true. I had changed. I felt a compassion towards you, a connection. We remained locked in that moment for quite some time. You appeared to be lost in thought, I simply watched and waited. Eventually, you moved and looked up.

"Don't get me wrong, I know that, like me, they all appreciate a shiny surface and they thrive on routine, but, on the whole, I hope that I have been a good mother, am a good mother, passing on my strengths not my weakness. To others around me, I think I am just seen as a happy person, because I am. I love people. I am just selective, protective, but I can and do talk to anyone now. I was once even described as a social butterfly, which thrilled and touched me in equal measure. That is how I cope, socially. I flit from face to face, chatting for just long enough to show interest, to share a joke, but not too long so as not to allow the focus to turn on me, to get too close. It works. My life is good, Sir, I need it returned."

"Yes, I know. And it will be. It is shocking to me that you are so understanding and settled, content. All this talking, a need to understand, to forgive."

"I do not recall ever using the word forgive, Sir."

"Oh?"

"I have I suppose, as it would be described today, suffered from post-traumatic distress disorder. I have faced many fears and I have won. I have thought, talked through and tried to understand others' actions and my own, but that does not mean that I have forgiven."

Your tone of voice held no malice or obvious bitterness and although spoken quite quietly it was strong and defiant.

"Lilly, will you ever forgive me?"

"I do not know Sir. In all honesty, I do not know. Forgiveness cannot be forced or assumed or demanded."

"So, Lilly, my illogical Lilly. If you do not forgive me, how can I trust you to help me?"

"Because, Sir, I feel you are damaged too."

"I am not like you. I am not damaged. I am not frightened."

"Oh really? Well, I beg to differ. I think, despite your age, that you are still, emotionally, that thirteen-year old boy who felt loss and rejection. Yes, you have become successful, but have you not spent your time hiding behind a computer screen? Never really allowing for human contact, being remote?"

I poured another long drink. Your voice was gentle. I did not feel a judgement in your tone, but I was unsettled. I was quiet, absorbing your words.

"Are you there, Sir?"

"Yes, Lilly, I am here."

"Think about it. Your drive to succeed, to prove you could do it all on your own. Yes, you had the advantage of money and education and choices, but you have created your own bubble too. It was the frightened and angry thirteen-year old who hurt me, not the rational, logical man. That is why I will help you.

"You're a child who needs a second chance."

"Lilly, I am not a child."

"Emotionally, I think you are, but I also feel that you're already stronger, you have begun your recovery. The more you understand of your past the sooner your future.

"Look you had almost built your party room, now you have your ticket, you are going to be fine. So, why would I take that away?"

"Why would you not?"

You held your hands up and poured another glass and stood perfectly still.

"Because I believe that you have the chance to have an amazing life. You have everything ahead to experience and enjoy. To put you in prison would take everything away, you would never recover. Prison would not help you, it would probably kill you. You made a mistake, a really fucking big one, I grant you, but emotionally you were a vulnerable child acting irrationally and without thought. I am a mother and my instincts tell me that you are sorry, and I trust when you say that you are a good man. I will give you the chance to be that, to grow up, but you must promise me that you will seek the help, acknowledge that you are in need, learn and grow. Otherwise, it will be a chance lost and you will be the prisoner, but in your own head and trust me, that is a tricky place to live."

"Lilly, what if I cannot be that man?"

"You can. You are young, and it is who you want to be really isn't it? You are just frightened and before you say it yes, you are frightened, but that is okay. It is okay to be frightened, it is just not okay to allow the fear to hold you back."

"I do want to travel. I have booked that ticket.

Do you, do you truly believe I can do this?"

"Yes, yes, I do. Trust in the foundation your father gave you, your family's love and in yourself."

These were powerful words and I knew them to be true. I sat and realised that you, illogical foul-mouthed and unpredictable you, could see me. You knew me more than anyone who had ever met me. Your maternal thoughts towards me were touching and warm. I so wanted your forgiveness. In that moment, I knew that I would try. I would strive to be the best man that I could be, I would not let you down.

'Oh yes the past can hurt. But you can either run from it or learn from it.' [7]

I watched your unsteady hand pour another drink and I refreshed my glass. You stood, resting your elbows on the island, your head to one side.

"Lilly, you look exhausted."

"Yes, yes I am and quite drunk I think."

"Yes, I too. Perhaps we should say goodnight now?"

"Yes." You lifted your head, just enough to have a drink and then you whispered,

"You know what Sir, the good thing about damaged people is they are strong, stronger than others because they know that they can survive."

"Goodnight, Lilly."

You waved your hand. I left you then and rather unsteadily headed for bed.

Tuesday, October 3
Final Delivery

I awoke feeling refreshed and despite the gin, I felt brand new. Excited, alive. I had practically leapt from my bed and was quickly out for my morning run. It was dry and as the sun rose, just after seven, I felt an energy that seemed to engulf me. I returned and showered, shaved and moisturised. I selected my casual clothes and ate my porridge. My aunt had phoned, I told her of my planned adventures, she was incredibly excited for me, but insisted we were to meet before my departure and so it was arranged. I would leave my car at the house and they would take me to the airport to wave me bon voyage. My godfather had shouted his approval.

Our food order was duly delivered and on unpacking a hand-written note had been included, thanking me for my loyal custom and wishing me well. A complimentary bottle of Fleury Blanc de Noirs champagne had been added. I divided the food and packed your basket, remembering the cigarettes, paracetamol and the candle. I placed these items, alongside your wine and the steam cleaner just outside your door. I tidied round, my routine completed, a breakfast tea made, I came to you.

"Good morning, Lilly."

You were not yet showered and still in the lounge-wear, but you were eating. Toast and marmite and a cup of tea by your side.

"Is it?"

"Yes, yes, it most definitely is. How are you?"

"I'm getting there, second cup of tea underway."

"Good. We must continue to plan today, there is still so much to do and check and think about, Lilly."

"Yes, of course. Just allow me my breakfast, my shower and then we can begin."

"You really are not a morning person, are you?"

"No. I am not, but it is more serious than that, I am feeling quite ill, my arm is just not healing. I feel sick."

"Lilly, not much longer now, I promise."

You did indeed look unwell, but I had to insist.

"Shower when you are ready, I will begin my packing. I will return to you later."

I left the screen on and continued to check on you as I cleaned my office and organised my desk. You had continued sitting for quite some time, breaking small pieces of toast with your fingers and slowly eating. After what felt like an age, you disappeared behind the doors. I added disposable gloves, more antibacterial spray and bleach to your delivery and exchanged the old for the new, swiftly and quietly in the usual way. I retrieved your shopping bag from the garage, along with the washing from your room. I loaded up the machine, then gloves on, I emptied the contents of your handbag out and put that in too. A hot wash selected. I cleaned the house, room by room, closing each door behind me. I knew that I would refresh everything again on Thursday, just before we left. I had decided we would leave on Thursday night. I would leave you at some point on the drive to my family. I would surprise them with my early arrival. We could enjoy breakfast together.

I placed my Rimowa case on my bed and began to pack. As I folded each shirt, each t-shirt, trousers, shorts, my excitement grew. When the main case was packed and placed in readiness, I returned to you. You had unpacked the basket and appeared a little stronger I was relieved to see.

"Hello, Lilly."

"Hello, thank you for the paracetamols. I have already taken two and they are working. What's with the candle?"

"I thought it might help with the smell, it has a fire-side aroma, I thought you would like it."

"I do, have you started your packing?"

"Started? I have completed the main, just the hand luggage to do, well and some toiletries to add. I have been busy."

"You have only given me three meals, so are the plans sorted?"

"We will leave Thursday night."

"We?"

"Yes. I am going to surprise my family with an early arrival on Friday morning. I will leave you en-route to them."

"Where?"

"I am still thinking the location through, Lilly. There is time. It must be right. I have provided you with disposable gloves, save these for the final clean on Thursday. In the mean time I thought it would be advisable for you to begin the steam cleaning."

"I have already started the wet room. After I have slept Wednesday night, you will need to take the bedding, the pillows and duvet to be dry cleaned. The sheets will need to be washed and actually the towels and the throw too."

"Yes indeed, I will book that in. I am going to purchase the extras I still require, I will be back soon, Lilly."

"Okay."

You returned behind the doors. I felt optimistic as we fell into our roles with purpose. When my shopping duties were completed, I re-cleaned the car, polished the leather interior and covered the back seat and foot wells with large black bin liners, carefully arranged and stuck together. I re-cleaned through the garage and the hallway and then the stairs. All the time deliberating as to where to leave you. Not too close to our starting point and yet not too close to my destination. I became a little panicked at the thought of you being discovered before my plans were completely underway. I changed my flight time for an earlier check in. Business class has many perks, money does indeed provide choice.

The day was already drawing in as I dried your washing. I returned to you again. You were sat on the sofa, the book closed by your side.

"Hello, Lilly, have you finished the book?"

"Hello, yes. It was so good. I needed to sit down."

"Are you still feeling unwell?"

"I am tired, my arm feels hot. I will take more pills when I eat. Did you get everything you needed?"

"Yes, thank you. Which meal have you selected for dinner?"

You un-coiled yourself and slowly walked to the fridge.

"Moussaka, that was really good before, maybe that will help me feel better."

"Excellent choice. I will join you, Lilly. Shall we say seven? Then we can continue with our plans."

"Seven, yes, I'll be here."

You smiled, but it was half-hearted. I was a little anxious, I had expected you to be in a far more buoyant mood. The morning's optimism had gone as quickly as it arrived. Now really was not the time for illness I thought.

Final Plans

Seven o'clock arrived so quickly. I had finished my packing. My luggage was already in the car. I had finished the laundry, gloves appropriately worn as I re-packed your handbag. I had taken a moment to go through your things; you had some money, not much, but some and a bank card, I noted. I placed the bag within your shopping bag and in turn placed them in to a new bin liner and put them on the covered rear seat. I had researched my route and felt that I had found a sensible location for your disposal. My dinner and drink prepared, I came to you.

"Good evening, Lilly."

"Good evening."

"How are you? Better I trust?"

"Not better, but no worse. I have taken more pills and re-cleaned my arm, piled on the savlon, look."

You raised your arm, it was quite inflamed and despite the white cream, the redness could be seen.

"Oh, Lilly, you will put me off my dinner."

"For fuck's sake. Really? It needs air now I think. Anyway, what are you having?"

"Moussaka, the same as you. Where is yours?"

"Just about to serve."

I looked and yes there was a warmed plate and cutlery ready, your wine obviously poured.

"I have found the correct location, Lilly."

"Where?"

"Do not concern yourself with that, but his voice could have a Birmingham lilt."

"Okay, noted. What time will we leave?"

"The early hours, the roads will be quiet in the darkness. We are travelling for some time, you will be okay, I hope?"

"I told you, I can cope with cars now. Anyway, I have no choice, and this is a journey I want, you know."

"Yes, yes, naturally. I too, Lilly. Why do you think me child-like Lilly? I am highly regarded in my field you know."

"Oh, Sir, it was not an insult and I said emotionally like a child, not child-like.

"Look you were hurt as a vulnerable child, rejected. You withdrew understandably, you shut your emotions down because it was painful, exposed, there was potential for more pain. It is natural to go into shutdown."

"Shutdown?"

"To attempt to lock your emotions up. Their development halted, frozen at that point in time. You were left with no one to guide you."

"Until you."

"Me? No, you would have got there eventually."

"Really?"

"Yes. The funeral would still have happened, you would have reconnected with your family."

"But, I do not think that I would have thought to question or had the courage to talk."

"I think you would, I was merely your catalyst."

"I am not so sure, Lilly, but you have indeed sped up my life. Do you believe it fixable? That I am fixable?"

"Yes. Understand why you have avoided emotional attachments and then begin the process of re-discovery. People, on the whole, are good, remember that."

"How is your moussaka?"

"It is lovely, I do feel stronger than I did, I needed to eat. Will I be far from my home when you leave me?"

"Not close and yet nor too far, you will be found. I am slightly concerned about the weather, but I will keep following the forecasts. It is going to be a full moon though, the harvest moon apparently."

"What does that mean?"

"Apparently, the moon will appear larger and may appear orange in colour."

"How beautiful. I love the night sky and a full moon at any time is lovely, so this will be special."

"Yes and hopefully mild. I will not be able to provide you with additional clothing or a blanket, Lilly, you do understand that? I know you dislike the cold."

"Ah, yes I do." You looked at your attire,

"I am not really dressed for a night walk it is true, but if I just keep moving then I guess I will be fine."

We finished our meals and you washed up your things.

"Lilly, on Thursday, please use the mini dishwasher on the hottest programme for anything you have used and when you empty the contents do not forget to wear your gloves. Why do you not use it anyway?"

"I will put everything through, just in case and obviously I will wear the gloves. I don't use it now because I have the time to wash up, it is another time filler, I suppose."

You lit up a cigarette when all was done and lit your candle too. I cleared my things also and replenished.

"How is the candle?"

"It is lovely actually, very effective. So, Sir, tell me are you finally going to order your snooker table?"

I smiled. "Yes, when I return, I think I will. I do not know what to do with the bed though or the sofa for that matter."

"Give them away to a charity. They will even collect, and they will have no problem finding a good home for them, they are beautiful."

"Give them away?"

"Yes, you can afford to and anyway, the quicker they are removed, the better. No questions, just collected and quite possibly re-distributed the same day."

"You said that you would leave no trace of you."

"And I won't, but still, why would you want them? The quicker they are gone, the quicker your party room."

"Yes, that is true. Adventures first though."

"Of course."

"What will you do first, Lilly?"

"I will hold my family, kiss them, tell them that I love them. Make sure they understand that I did not choose to leave them. I will make sure they are good, they are happy."

"And then?"

"I will be at home, we will have a huge fire and champagne and music, we can laugh and dance. I will be home."

"And after that, Lilly?"

"I don't care."

"Your yurts, your land? I thought they were your dream?"

"Well, yes, but one dream at a time. I cannot think past just being at home, holding them, seeing their faces. I just wish I could tell them, reassure them."

Even in your poor state of health I was moved by your priorities. Your family and being with them, looking after them, it was, I could see, everything.

"Sir, what if I am not found?"

"Lilly, you will be, you will find your way."

"Promise me? I don't live anywhere near Birmingham."

"Lilly, you will return to your home, I promise. Now we need to think detail. All your rubbish must be disposed of, everything you have touched must go. There is a bin collection on Thursday."

"What time?"

"They usually collect between three and four, why?"

"I was just wondering about my shower."

"I see. You will be able to shower as usual, but then all the products, used or unused, toothbrush, hairbrush, everything must go along with the rubbish. Actually Lilly, please clean everything before it is thrown, remove any hair from the brush and bleach it along with your toothbrush and the cotton pads you use to clean your arm. We must be meticulous and methodical."

"Yes, I know. I will be, there will be no trace of me, I told you. I will find my way home, won't I? It's not a trick is it? Me here, cleaning away all evidence of my own existence for you, for you just to dump me or worse."

"Lilly, I am shocked. I have promised I would not, could not, ever hurt you again. I thought you were the one who spoke of trust?"

You poured another glass, lit up and blew the smoke away. You were shaking, the tears were beginning to come.

I wanted to reassure you.

"Lilly, you will be home soon. You must understand everything has to be exact. I cannot begin my voyage with such unease, such fear of discovery."

"I know, I know, there will be no trace. I am scared, I just want to be home."

"Scared of what?"

"That it might go wrong, what happens if you crash the car?"

"I will not crash the car, I am a good driver."

"Really? Because as I remember that is kind of how we met."

"Now is really not the time for sarcasm, Lilly. I am a very good driver and there will be no real traffic when we are travelling anyway."

"What if I am not found?"

"Lilly, I have already answered that question. Calm down, believe, it will all be over soon."

You nodded and cried, drank and smoked. I remember thinking how much frailer you were looking. Your complexion pale features gaunt. The difference of you at that moment and the you so publicly shown was stark. A world away from the social butterfly.

"Lilly, please stop crying."

You wiped your face, slowly regaining your composure, breathing deeply, controlled.

"What if I'm found by a bad person?"

"Honestly. People, on the whole, are good, remember?"

You were almost child-like, vulnerable. Your reactions and thoughts as always, not what I would have expected.

"Lilly, I am going to leave you in the countryside. The moon will be bright, there will be no one around. All you will have to do is walk until you reach the closest village. It will be safe."

"How will I know which way to go?"

"It will be obvious, follow the path, then the road."

You smiled, and half sang,

"Follow the yellow brick road, follow the yellow brick road."

I smiled, I knew I should have renamed you Dorothy.

"I cannot promise it will be yellow, Lilly. Do you feel reassured now?"

"A little, I guess. It's the not knowing. I don't think I could cope with anything else. I just want to go home, to be safe."

"I appreciate that. I too want the same for you."

It had, I admit, never crossed my mind that you could potentially come to any harm. I had just thought of it all as a process. Drop and go. Your fears unnerved me, but I had to dismiss them. There was enough to think about, details, real details without the room for distraction. Suddenly you began to cry again,

"Lilly, please, regain your composure."

I did snap a little and I made you jump,

"Lilly, breathe, breathe with me."

I began to breathe slowly and steadily, deliberately sounding each inhale and exhale in to your room until finally you joined me. We continued together in this bizarre fashion simultaneously, in sync and constant.

Finally, you were calm.

I, however, was left shaken. It was surely me who should be fearful. I had everything to lose, you only everything to gain. I needed you to be strong and in control, any disruption to the plan, any sudden out bursts or unpredictable behaviour could not be allowed, could not even be entertained. I needed you to focus.

"Lilly, oh, Lilly, just concentrate your mind, just imagine home, nothing else."

"I do, I can't help my thoughts though."

"Well, you must try, you must stop over-thinking."

"It's not that easy, you know."

"Apparently not, but we cannot allow your irrational fears to jeopardise our plans."

"They are not irrational."

"Lilly, enough, enough. I do not want an argument, have a glass of wine."

"Fuck off."

"Well, I feel the usual Lilly has returned, why do you have to swear so much? It is most unnecessary."

"No, it is most necessary, actually."

You poured, I poured. I could sense your defensive attitude. I felt quite exhausted by you.

"Your partner must be a very patient man."

"He is, very and kind. What made you say that?"

"Because your behaviour is exhausting."

"Oh, I'm sorry, but your behaviour hasn't exactly been perfect, has it? I can't help being scared and for your information when I'm scared, I have two reactions, I either cry or I swear. I guess it's fear or fight."

Apart from my initial moments with you I felt that my behaviour had always been thoughtful, generous, even. I was annoyed and irritated with you. Disappointed with your criticism.

"Lilly, I am going now. I will leave you to fight your fear."

I saw your head turn, your mouth began to open, but I switched the screen off. I returned to my room, my chair, my thoughts. Your outpourings and out-bursts caused me great concern. Your erratic behaviour could potentially cause complications. I swivelled and stared in to the night, the moon was indeed brighter than usual, not quite full, but soon. That night could not come quick enough, I mused.

After a period of calm, of undisturbed quiet, I headed to bed. Peaceful sleep my only thought.

Wednesday, October 4
Reflections

I woke refreshed, a much-needed sleep achieved. As I ran that morning, the earth hard beneath my feet, not quite a ground frost, not yet, I imagined heat and sunshine on my skin. I allowed my mind to drift away, to escape the liability of you. I smiled to myself, liability Lilly. I imagined myself exploring new places, discovering new delights, even engaging with new people. I longed to be absorbed in my fresh, uncontaminated new life. This was my beginning. Goodbye to the past and goodbye to you, how I longed for those goodbyes.

As I returned, passing the car, packed and ready, a sense of optimism clung to me and I cherished the sensation. I showered and selected my clothes, gap skinny jeans, a woollen checked shirt and my converse. I stared at my reflection, my eyes were bright, skin glowing, freshened by both the morning's air and the shower. My chosen outfit for tomorrow's getaway hung, crisp and clean, slim-fitting chinos, polo shirt and a zip-through funnel neck jumper. Simple, light grey, brogues, to match the stripe detail on my shirt. Smart casual. Layers. Comfort for travelling.

I ate my breakfast and re-cleaned the unused bedrooms. I knew there would be no need to return to those rooms again. As I opened the dining room door, instantly the sweet, spicy aroma hit me. It was so thick and filled the air. I was overwhelmed, the odour was too much for my senses. I hastily rolled up my shirt and gloves on, the potential risk of stains considered, I removed the flowers, bagged them up and threw them in the bin outside. I regretted ever bringing them in to the house. The unwanted smell took me instantly back to her funeral and the torment I had experienced, endured that day. I cleaned the glass, the lemon spray cutting through the invisible cloud. When I was done, I closed the door and I said goodbye to mother.

I will never like lilies and vowed that they would not be allowed near me again. I sat on the balcony to clear my nostrils and my head. To be taken back so abruptly had startled me, had shaken me, had triggered memories I did not want.

I thought of you. You. I had triggered your unwanted memories, unintentionally of course, but I had. I had locked you inside the room and unlocked your demons to keep you company. I shivered and not for the first time, I wished one able to rewrite the past. I questioned my feelings of annoyance towards you and I considered that perhaps I may have been a little harsh. Patience was indeed a virtue and as our time was drawing to a close I accepted that I must endeavour to maintain a sense of calm, of order, for both our sakes. For both our futures.

Final Post

It was after lunch when I returned to you.

"Good afternoon, Lilly. Did you sleep well?"

"No, not really. I had nightmares but hey, ho."

"Only one more night, Lilly. I have been thinking, even though we shall not be leaving until the early hours, do try not to sleep tomorrow. You should sleep in the car, I could provide you with a sleeping tablet if you would like?"

"I am not taking a sleeping tablet and why should I sleep in the car?"

"Lilly, we are not going for a tootle round chatting to pass the hours. You will be laid on the back seat. I do not want to talk to you whilst I am driving. I will require you to be quiet at all times."

"Why?"

"Lilly, please. Because, obviously, you are not in my car, nor have you ever been. I do not foresee that there will be many others around, but I cannot risk any suggestion that I have company. I thought the offer of a tablet would be mutually beneficial."

"I will be quiet."

"Can you be though? Can, unpredictable you, really be? I am not so sure."

You began to make tea and set about making a cheese sandwich, neatly placing the slithers of cheddar perfectly.

"Lilly, Lilly," I repeated.

"Lilly, we are supposed to be engaging in conversation and now you are ignoring me. Your lack of response rather proves my concerns."

"Rather proves the opposite, I would say."

"This is not a game."

"No, it is not. I think I am more than aware of that. I am not taking any tablets. I intend to be fully conscious, to be fully aware at all times."

"Are you planning to escape, to try and jump out?"

"Don't be ridiculous, what and risk my own life? After all this? No, but I am not going to be abandoned at night, God alone knows fucking where and not have my wits about me."

You sat at the island and broke the sandwich up, eating tiny pieces one at a time, chewing with such purpose. Quietly, you sipped your tea.

"Do you honestly believe that you will be able to lie still? To be quiet? To remain hidden?"

"Yes, silent but conscious at all times. Understand?"

"I understand the theory."

"It will be a reality. No sleeping pills, no more of me not being in control. I will be quiet. I will be still until I can find my way back to them."

163

You threw the remaining chunks of bread into the bin. You washed and dried up the few items around you and returned to your chair. You looked so pale, your arm appeared no better for the air. Your loose jumper and jeans were ill fitting now and crumpled. You had aged so much in such a short space of time.

"I wish I could tell them, I wish I could let them know."

"They will know soon."

"Hopefully, yes."

"Definitely, yes. What shall we have for tonight's dinner? The pizza or the casserole?"

"You have the same meals as me?"

"Yes. Your choice though."

"Casserole then."

"Lovely, shall we say seven?"

"Usual place?"

"Very amusing, Lilly."

And actually, you had made me smile. You were clearly determined to refuse my offer of a tablet, but I sensed an equal determination for the need to feel in control. I understood.

I had not intended to send another post. Not wanting to create any further attention or speculation concerning you, but I knew that when you were home and discovered my involvement, you would see how I had tried. I wanted you to know that I had tried. You would understand that I had fulfilled your wish. I pondered for an extraordinary length of time. Finally, I was satisfied. I uploaded a scene for you, for them. Purple butterflies flying high in to a starry night sky with a leather key fob hanging in the corner, bearing your name. This uncomplicated picture I created for four reasons,

1. Your symbol of faith, to carry on.
2. The night sky, a bold clue as to when you would be reunited.
3. The key fob obviously representing the unlocking of your door.
4. The leather to mark what would be our third anniversary.

It was simple. It was your message for them. It was, I hoped, reassurance.

When my mission was complete, I set about the task of destroying my mac-pro. I would have no use for it again. Not now. Not ever. Obviously, no back-ups were required so to erase all content was simple. Once all was clean, I intended to dismantle and dispose, ensuring nothing could be traced or retrieved.

Dinner

I spent the remaining time before our evening, checking and double-checking our route. The minor roads were all reassuringly camera free. Obviously, I had no intention to use the sat-nav and my phone would be switched off. That journey would only ever exist in my memory. That journey would have no history.

I checked the tyres, water and oil, fuel was good. All was good. I heated up my casserole and poured a gin.

"Good evening, Lilly."

You were sat, organised, waiting.

"Good evening, Sir."

"A fine choice for dinner, may I say?"

"Thank you."

"Lilly, I feel it wise that an early night should be had, you have much to do tomorrow."

"I do."

You looked around your room. I saw that you had already placed some things in the basket by the door.

"It will require several collections tomorrow, to remove everything. We will have to agree to a system for disposal."

"In what way?"

"You must promise to remain behind the sliding doors when asked."

I distinctly remember the way you glanced from door to door. I was desperate to read your mind and I felt anxious. Could I really trust you?

"Lilly, it is the only way."

"It is a way, but yes I will. How will I know how long to remain in there?"

"You can count."

I imagined myself running from the screen, downstairs, key retrieval, unlocking and collecting, closing and relocking.

"Count to two hundred, slowly like you do, that will provide adequate time."

We sat and ate, I, far quicker than you. Indeed, everything you did seemed to have slowed, every action and movement laboured. I was grateful that our departure time allowed so many hours for all that was required. No haste; it was essential, imperative, that you fulfilled your tasks comprehensively. I cleared my plate and tidied up, then returned. You appeared to have lost interest with your dinner and were smoking, candle lit.

"Lilly, did you not like your casserole?"

"Yes, I just can't eat it all. I have made a list for tomorrow, do you want to hear it?"

"A list?"

"Of jobs, so I don't forget anything."

"Go on."

"Remove bed linen and duvet, pillows and throw.

"Shower and then with gloves on, clean, remove all products and towels.

"Empty bin.

"Remove all cupboard items, use the dishwasher.

"Steam clean.

"Empty fridge and clean.

"Reclean surfaces, handles and doors.

"Bleach.

"Well?"

"Yes, that appears to be a start. I appreciate that you are not the strongest, Lilly, but you must move the bed and the sofa in order to clean underneath them."

"Yes, I know."

"And, Lilly, once you have steam cleaned those, you will not be able to use them. To lie down or to sit in your corner."

"I know, they will be damp anyway."

"Quite. I trust you will check the shower trap and bleach thoroughly?"

"Of course, I do know how to clean, Sir."

"Yes, yes you do. Good, we have a busy day ahead."

"The last day."

"Our last day."

You poured a glass, your arm was looking increasingly inflamed and ugly, your hand shook a little. I hoped you would find the strength to carry out your tasks effectively.

"Cheers, Lilly."

"Cheers. I'm looking forward to seeing the moon."

"Lilly, your eyes will be covered for the journey, but yes, your walk will be moon lit."

"How will you cover my eyes?"

"I am still considering some of the finer details for tomorrow, Lilly, but do not concern yourself, you will have much to focus on."

"Yes, I suppose I will."

"Now I am going to leave you. I still have things to do myself and an early night is essential for the both of us."

"I hope I can sleep."

"Lilly, you must, you need to be strong."

"Always, I know. I will try."

"Good. Goodnight, Lilly."

"Goodnight, Sir."

As I left, you were beginning to clear away your unfinished meal, I was optimistic that your routine would help you to remain calm and ensure adequate rest. I replenished my glass and sat in my chair.

The News

I had decided to view the late news. I think I was a little excited, eager to witness your family's faces, hopeful, smiling.

"The case of the missing woman Lillian Brown has yet again taken another disturbing twist. A new post has been uploaded on the eve of what will be the third week since her disappearance. To discuss this matter we can now go live to the police spokeswoman.

"Good evening, what do the police and Lilly's family take from this new image?"

"Good evening, following the new image, Lilly's family have, understandably, decided to remain together at home. They have a police liaison officer with them. As for our work, it remains intensive."

"What interpretation have the police drawn from the new image?"

"We do not believe it to be helpful to speculate, but obviously we are deeply concerned for Lilly's wellbeing and again urge anyone with any information to please come forward."

"There has been much discussion, via social media, that the image could be seen as representing her death. The butterflies, heaven bound, the headstone with her name. Do the investigation team still have faith that Lilly could be alive?"

"Absolutely, and we would like to make it known that this theory is not helpful and is increasingly distressing for Lilly's family and friends. Our investigation is very much on-going."

"Thank you."

Phone numbers. Your photo. I switched off.

Anger does not cover how I felt. I was exasperated by their stupidity again. Why were my actions, so thoughtfully considered, so continually misunderstood? I was annoyed that they could have mistaken your message, your sign, irritated by their lack of thought, their lack of insight. To mistake the fob as a headstone was stupidity itself. My intentions had been honourable. I had tried to help. I had wanted to help. Their shameful corruption of the detail hurt.

I paced, like you. I drank, like you. Yet I still needed an outlet for my frustration. I took my Mac-pro, gloves on, I washed it and then placed it inside a heavy-duty bin bag. I took it to the garage and pounded at it, each drop of the hammer creating a satisfying sound and a release. Eventually, I stopped. I replaced the hammer in its rightful place and put the bag, ready for disposal, in the corner. I returned upstairs, gloves removed. I had a nightcap and gazed at the evening's sky. They were idiots, all of them, but I knew I would show them. I would ultimately prove them all so wrong. All their theories exposed, they did not know me, they did not understand.

Thursday, October 5
Collection

I had, surprisingly, slept well. Perhaps the additional gins had helped, however, I had already decided to forgo my run. All my energies were needed for the journey that lay ahead. I showered, my routine and ablutions adhered too. I drank my espresso, ate my toast. It was a mild, clear day and I felt good. I cleared, cleaned and began to sort through the perishables, leaving just enough to cover lunch and dinner. I took water bottles to the car along with a couple of flapjack bars, just in case an energy boost was required. Then I came to you. You were drinking tea and clearly not that long awake. I was, I must say, surprised by this. I had pictured in my mind that your excitement would have had you happily working your way through the list by now.

"Good morning, Lilly. I see you have not yet begun."

"No, not yet. I couldn't settle last night, everything was going around and round in my head. I'm just going to have this and then my shower."

"The bedding first, before you shower, remember?"

"Yes, yes. Just let me have this, for fuck's sake."

"Oh, Lilly, please not today."

"What?"

"The swearing."

"For goodness' sake that's not really my major concern and I can't really understand why it is yours."

"Well, I would hardly say it is major, just unnecessary."

"Whatever." You flicked your hand up and winced.

"Have you taken your paracetamols?"

"Yes, only got two more, I'm going to have them later. It still hurts though."

"Keeping busy will take your mind off it, Lilly."

You shook your head and finished your tea. I watched as you stripped the bed, folded the covers and placed them on top of the folded duvet by the door. You stacked the pillows and placed the throw on top.

"There, happy now? I'm going for my shower."

You wrapped your arm, I had forgotten this detail to your routine, the care you took when you did this, before you quietly walked through the doors sliding them shut behind you.

Yes, I was happy, this was the beginning of the end. I quickly ran downstairs and made the first collection of the day. I placed all the washing on the hottest cycle and bagged up the duvet, the throw and the pillows. I placed the remains of the Mac into a rucksack and left. The drycleaners provided a reliable and efficient service, I had always used them, so I dropped in the bedding, same day collection arranged. I then proceeded to walk and on passing public bins I placed my gloved hand in to the rucksack taking out a couple of handfuls of the decimated technology and depositing them discreetly. When all was off-loaded, I returned home. When the washing was completed and in the drier, I returned to you.

Much to my relief you were in full swing. I observed that the bathroom contents had all been placed in the basket, along with the lounge-wear, robe and towels. A full bin bag was by their side.

"Hello, Lilly. I am pleased to see that the day's work has begun."

"Yes, of course."

You had your gloves on, busily emptying cupboards and loading the dishwasher with the contents. I noticed your rather haphazard manner for loading and stacking but did not share my observation with you. I was apprehensive that you might explode or change your mind with regard to our plan.

"Lilly, I will collect now, are you ready to count?"

You had switched the dishwasher on and looked around.

"Lilly, are you alright? Have you remembered the rule? Count to two hundred."

"Yes, I know. I was simply checking if there was anything else that you could take, tea towels, there we go."

You folded them and placed them, ready.

"Start counting."

I watched as you obediently slipped behind the doors,

"One, two three, four, five, six…"

And you were gone. I counted too as I ran down the stairs, I trembled slightly as I retrieved the key, seventy-eight, seventy-nine, eighty. I tried to calm my breathing, ninety-two, ninety-three, ninety-four. There were doubts and fears as I went to turn the key. I needed to check you had remained in place. I ran so quickly to view, yes, you had. Back again, one hundred and fifty-one, one hundred and fifty-two, one hundred and fifty-three, unlock. One hundred and sixty-one, one hundred and sixty-two, one hundred and sixty-three, slowly opening the door I grabbed the items. One hundred and eighty-eight, one hundred and eighty-nine, one hundred and ninety, door locked. I collapsed in the hallway. I had just succeeded in what can only really be described as a most unnerving game of roulette, a sinister take on hide and seek. One which I knew I would be forced to repeat. Despite the plans we were making I knew it would be foolish to allow you to see me again. I had no desire to be a fresh memory in your head. I acknowledged to be much more efficient with the time. After some reflection and consideration, I regained my composure. The bin bag was placed safely outside, the next wash on. I dispensed the toiletries into a new bin liner and cleaned the basket. I had to calm, I knew this. I reassured myself that you could have broken the rules, but you had chosen not to. You were following our plan. I gathered up the bag and went to put it outside, the collection would happen soon. I can only surmise that my hands were unsteady or that my gloves had become covered with product because I dropped it. The jumble of tubes and pots of creams tumbled out. I repacked and realised not quite everything had been included, doubts concerning your attention to detail and its absolute importance filled me. I stormed back to the office.

"Lilly, where is your toothbrush and toothpaste? Are you trying to trick me?"

I did shout, and I had done so with no warning. I made you jump, your pale features appeared frozen in shock.

"No, no. You frightened me then, you, fuckwit. I just kept them to use after my tea, it's not a trick, I am working really hard here you know so back off."

"Lilly, I know you are. I am on edge, I am having some doubts."

"Oh no you don't. Don't you dare go back on your fucking word. You promised, you said I could go home."

You slumped down against the unit, knees up, head in your hands.

"I know, I know. You can, and you will. I do want that too."

"Really?"

"Trust me, Lilly, I want to be free of you, of this, of everything."

"So what are your doubts about?"

"That something may go wrong, that you might decide to talk."

"We agreed the story."

"Is it plausible though? The man?"

"It is practically the truth."

"Look at you? Look at your arm? Can you really promise me that once you're home, you will not feel anger towards me? Every time you look at that mess you will not feel the need to hurt me?"

"Trust me, I have learnt to only see what I need to see. As for anger I think my sheer joy and relief to be home will outweigh everything."

"Trust?"

"Trust is all we have, what other choice is there?"

I was quiet. You were right. There really were no other options. I knew I had to remain focused in order to remain calm. In order to remain in control. I went to my bathroom and splashed cold water onto my face, my heart was still racing, my eyes were dilated, my muscles so tense. I ran the water and allowed it to flow over my hands, washing my face again, breathing slowly. Finally, I felt a stillness, a sense of peace, of balance.

I made tea and toast and returned to you. You were unloading and carefully refilling the cupboards, every item in its correct place.

"Lilly, have you had lunch? It is quite late I know for lunch, but…"

"No."

"Please have a piece of toast, a cup of tea, I am."

You finished, closing the last cupboard door, you looked around,

"Yes, you know, I think I will."

"What is next?"

"Steam cleaning is next, bathroom, bed, sofa, walls, floors."

You were reading your list.

"Lilly you must destroy your notebook before throwing it away."

"I will. Are you ready?"

"I have a few matters to sort, but I will be. We will be."

You sat then, with your tea and toast and I with mine. We did not speak, then we both stood to clear, lunch break concluded. I re-gloved and re-gathered the toiletries and took them outside. All would be collected soon. The last remaining rubbish from your room, I had decided, could be placed in a public bin before departure. I re-cleaned the kitchen floor again and sat in my chair awaiting the refuse collection and considering the best, the most effective way, to cover your eyes and lead you out to the car. Just before four, the rumble of the lorry broke my thoughts and when all had been emptied, safely on its way to landfill, I retrieved the bin and wheeled it to the back of the house. Although I, obviously, always bagged up any rubbish and therefore, the bin was clean, I power-washed inside and out. Cleaned, lined up and emptied. I quickly went back to the drycleaners, all items safely sealed and returned. I packed the duvet, throw and pillows away in one of the guest bedrooms. The washing was now in the dryer, everything was in order. I checked in on you and true to your word, you had pushed the bed out and were steam-cleaning underneath and along the walls. Reassured, I returned to my thoughts. Inspired by this perhaps, my confidence boosted and needing every detail in place, I resolved the final dilemma that you had left for me. I would use my buff to place over your eyes, its fleece lining was soft and would leave no mark on your face. It was clean, however, I rewashed it. No trace could be risked, no detail too small to be ignored and added it to the dryer.

Next to find a sturdy stick. Hunter boots and fleece on I walked along my usual running route, kicking through the fallen leaves until finally selecting just the right one. It was almost the perfect size for me to walk with as I strode home, one man enjoying the early evening under the incredible moon. One man with his trusted walking stick that would soon become your guide and our last connection. A stick left in a wood was hardly likely to arouse suspicion, it would not even be noticed, especially by them.

I returned home and left my find in the garage, in place and ready. I freshened up and unloaded the dryer. The buff, placed in a sandwich bag, equally ready. I was prepared. Only a few more hours now. I baked my pizza and came to you.

Final Dinner

"Good evening, Lilly."

You were sat at the island. The bed was back in position, the mattress on its side on top, the sofa was pulled forward, the cleaner in the middle of the room. You looked exhausted, drained even.

"Good evening. Our last evening."

"Our final evening, our last supper, Lilly. How are you?"

"I'm really tired, but I am so restless. Does that make sense?"

"For you, Lilly, yes. Have you eaten?"

"No, but it is in the oven, have you?"

"Just about to start. How is your schedule? There are still hours ahead, please do not rush or compromise on the detail."

"I'm on track, I need a break now and anyway until I have eaten and cleared away, the last jobs are on hold."

"Maintain the order, nothing must be forgotten."

"Nothing will be. I feel apprehensive, unsettled though, doing all of this."

You gestured around the room.

"Why? Surely you should be excited?"

"I am literally removing every trace of me, I hate being told what to do and yet here I am, wiping away my very DNA, removing every hint that I existed here. I don't know if that makes me incredibly stupid or positively sane?"

"Lilly, we agreed. This is the only way, the only way for both of us."

"I know what we said. I know why, but I'm fucking scared."

"I too am apprehensive, but our plan is the only way, for both of us to have the chance for a future."

Your pizza was ready, you slowly cut exact triangles and placed them on the warmed plate in front of you.

"Eat, Lilly, it is good."

You looked up and straight into my gaze, bottom lip trembling, the oh-so-familiar signs of the tears to follow.

"Lilly, no more tears please, think of home. You will share your next meal with your family."

I watched as you slowly regained your composure, well enough to stem the flow.

"You have to stay strong, we are so close to the end now."

I had so hoped that you would be filled with excitement, your smile wide as in your official photo. I had thought you would be happy, but you were so visibly frightened, so fragile.

"Lilly, please eat, even if it is just a little. It really is good. Shall I talk you through the final details? Will that help?"

172

"Yes."

"After dinner, all the remaining rubbish, toothbrush etc. need to be placed by the door. Please ensure that everything is bleached first. I will collect, as before. I will leave you a buff for later, this will act as your blind fold."

"Then what?"

"Then we wait. I will dispose of everything, double check all is done and then I will tell you when it is time. That will be the last time we speak, Lilly. Our communication must then cease. I will knock on the door and you must be standing, eyes covered just behind. I will guide you out and into the car using a stick."

"A stick? How?"

"Yes, a stick, I will hold one end, you the other. Then you will lie in the back of the car and remain hidden whilst I drive. I do not want you to move until you hear the car stop and the door open, then I will guide you, as before, out of the car. I will remove your gloves, but you must promise to remain standing away from me, no turning around. Then I will remove the buff and I will leave you. Lilly, you will then be free to find your way."

"What will you do with the gloves and the buff?"

"I will obviously discard them, the stick I will simply throw at the time. I thought a drain further along my route for the other items."

"How long will I be in the car?"

"The roads will be clear, a few hours, Lilly. Are you worried about being in the car?"

"I am a bit, but I will be fine. I just wondered."

"It is going to work. We will both be free to move on, just in different directions, the correct directions."

You tentatively ate, I had already finished. I felt stimulated, energised and positive. Yes, naturally there was some nervousness, some tension, but this was the new beginning and it was in reach.

"And you are positive that I will be found?"

"Yes, yes, Lilly. You will have to walk for a while, but yes."

"Okay."

You stood and replaced your gloves before lighting a cigarette.

"Am I really going home?"

"Yes, Lilly, you are really going home, and I am starting my voyage. It is real, it is over."

You smiled. I positively grinned.

I watched as you cleared away. The half-eaten pizza placed in the bin, the surfaces cleaned again. I watched as you pushed the heavy sofa back in to position and steam cleaned the floor. I watched as you washed the notebook, your words dissolving into pulp. I watched as you cleaned the now empty fridge. I watched you for hours, busy in your cleaning. Slowly and methodically, working through each task. I wanted to chat, to be light-hearted even, like we had been some evenings. I almost wanted just one more night to feel the confidence you gave me, the freedom to talk, time with my friend even? However, I knew it was best to allow you to be lost in the physical monotony. The routine and repetitive work was at least keeping you calm.

Eventually, you stopped.

"Sir, are you there?"

"Yes, Lilly, I am here."

"I think I'm done."

"I will collect, go behind the doors and count as before."

"One, two, three, four, five, six, seven," and you were gone.

I ran and retrieved, relocked and re-examined the contents of the bag. The smell of bleach was harsh and instant, burning my nostrils, making my head throb, a slight nausea creeping up. I turned for a few moments before checking that all had been included correctly, yes it had. I smiled though just your paper butterfly had remained unwashed. I took it out, the intricate pattern undamaged, the wings so delicate. I confess, a part of me wanted to fold it up and keep it. This, your symbol, your sign. Your illogical behaviour had clearly taken an effect deeper than I had realised. I stood quite still and held the paper in my shaking hands until, thankfully, I came to my senses. I replaced it under the pulp and washed cigarette ends, toothbrush and paste, pizza, empty cleaning sprays, hand-wash. I shook the contents up and disposed of them on my final night walk.

When I returned to you, you had covered one of the chairs with a bin bag and were seated. I viewed the room.

"Lilly."

"Yes, is it time?"

"Not quite. Please will you open every cupboard and let me see?"

You proceeded to demonstrate the fruits of your labour. The drawers, the fridge, the bed-side unit, the bin. All was perfect. All was done.

"Thank you. How do you feel?"

"Ready. Ready and exhausted and frightened and excited and hot."

"And breathe, Lilly."

"Yes, breathe."

You stood and removed the bin bag from the chair.

"Can we go now?"

"I will be by the door very soon. So, Lilly, this is our good bye. When I collect you, we will not speak again."

"Good bye, Sir, and good luck."

"Good bye, Lilly, and thank you."

We remained frozen for a moment together, bound, but in silence. Connected.

I erased the internal recordings, the loop lost. I unravelled and washed the tape, then cut it up and placed everything into a bag. I dressed for the journey and by then the time had come, the final collection. I knocked on your door and gently edged it open, my heart pounding once more. In that split-second scenarios raced through my head, but they were without foundation, as there you were. In front of me, face covered by the buff, the sandwich bag containing the bin bag clasped in your gloved hands. The room was warm and moist and smelt of bleach. I extended the stick to your hand and you held tightly, knuckles white, clutching on. In this way I led you through the door. I locked the door and I led you to the car. I had forgotten how small you were as you cautiously lay down on the backseat, you pulled your knees up and allowed your disfigured arm to rest upon your side. I shut your door and walked quickly to the driving seat, all doors now locked, and our journey began.

Disposal

The drive was, as I had predicted, in so much as the selected route was without diversion and there was, indeed, a total lack of traffic. My reactions were far more heightened than I had expected though. The constant checking and rechecking of the mirrors was almost too distracting. My levels of paranoia were extreme. I thought that I would be able to somehow pretend that I was alone, but although you remained silent, I could smell you. I appreciate that I am particularly sensitive, but there was a putrid odour that hung heavily in the air. The air conditioning did not help and anyway I was conscious not to make you too cold. Obviously, I could not just open the windows. The journey was difficult and felt so long, it could not end quickly enough.

I felt nausea and disgust. I felt fear and I felt true shame.

Three hours and ten minutes and we had reached my selected, secluded destination. I quickly jumped out of the car, stick in hand and took several deep breaths of the fresh clean air. The moon was indeed large and the weather mild. A level head and balance restored, I came to your door and opened it. I carefully placed the stick in your hand and you rather clumsily uncoiled and almost fell out. I waited for you to find your feet and then I removed your shopping bag, your handbag inside, from the plastic bag and placed it onto your shoulder. I removed your gloves and placed them inside the sandwich bag. I closed the door and stood behind you. I threw the stick as far away as I could. Your tiny frame was shaking, there was no time to waste. I removed the buff and placed it too inside the bag. Then I simply drove away, my disposal complete.

I did glance back, as you faded away, just once. Your silhouette was lit by the moon's glow. I do not know why, but I cried. Ridiculously, embarrassingly so, with no self-control or restraint.

An hour later and still travelling along quiet roads, I pulled over at a layby. I deposited the contents of the bags down the drain and put the bags in the bin. I removed the bin liners from the back seat and the footwells and disposed of them too. Finally, I removed my gloves and all the deposits were made.

I continued. You were now completely unconnected to me, physically at least. I arrived at the house just a little before seven. The familiar crunch under the tyres felt reassuring. I unloaded the boot, locked up and cheerily knocked on the door, shouting 'good morning'. My aunt was soon at the door, expressing her surprise at my early arrival, apologising for her dressing gown, for not being suitably dressed. I was suddenly in a jubilant mood, laughing, nothing mattered. I hugged her and we all gathered in the kitchen. An Americano later, a slice of toast and with bursts of excited conversation, I was on my way to the airport. My godfather was on such good form that morning, genuinely over-joyed for me, chuckling and re-living snippets from his own travels. My uncle, giving sound, sensible advice, my aunt insisting I phone regularly. Good byes were said. Hugs were held. Handshakes and back slapping all completed. I left them. All three, in a row of waving hands, as I strode with purpose and poise, a man on a mission, on a voyage of discovery.

The News

I was sat in the lounge, a complimentary glass of champagne in my hand, when I heard the news.

"Breaking news. The missing mother of three, Lillian Brown, has been found. Three weeks after her last known sighting, Lillian Brown was discovered by a passing motorist on a minor road in the rural village of Canwell, just outside Tamworth. Apparently, distressed and needing urgent medical attention, but alive."

The words swirled around in my head, relief and fear in equal measure. A professional looking woman sat close to me, gasped.

"Thank God, I really thought she was dead."

I felt a pressure, an expectation to reply,

"It is, indeed, a wonderful relief."

It was all that I could manage.

"Further information in regard to this unfolding story will follow, as soon as the details become clear, but, to confirm, the missing mother of three, Lillian Brown has been found alive."

So as my travels into the unknown began, my steps in to my new world, the chance to be lost in life; I was secure in the knowledge that you had been found. The futures we both longed for were ours for the taking.

Good Bye

So, Lilly, that is our story. Our journey, dare I say? Our three weeks together, explained. I have questioned myself, I do that now, as to why I have written to you. I am not sure if it is for you, for me or for the both of us. Does this make me stupid? Or positively sane? You told me that to write could be cathartic. I am talking and questioning and learning, Lilly. I am moving forward. I think that you would be proud. I hope that you would be proud. I have even danced in the light of the moon, laughed and made friends. I have thought of you.

The gentleman who found you, described you as hysterical and frightened on the news. He explained to the reporter, that morning, that on his usual commute to the hospital where he worked as a nurse, he had seen what he first thought to be a child at the side of the road. How he had stopped the car and only then realised that it was you. How he had called your name, how you had screamed. Oh, Lilly, I imagine you were swearing too. He apparently had calmed you a little and stayed by your side until the police and an ambulance arrived. I trust your arm has healed and that you can look beyond the scars.

This past year has gone by so very quickly. You have faded into history, forgotten now by social media, but not by me. I will never forget you. I am certain that you must have faced many questions, many requests for interviews. You have clearly declined all attention. You have not jumped on the bandwagon of wannabe celebrity. You have not fuelled the feeds, instead you have become invisible. So quickly, evaporated from the social conscience. Your needs were never publicity-driven or fame-hungry, were they? Your need was only ever to feel safe with the people you love. Lilly, I truly hope that you are happy.

I read this proverb whilst I was writing this,

'Just when the caterpillar thought the world was over, it became a butterfly.'

I thought you might like it.

You have been wise with the fame I enforced on you. Please be wise with the fortune I give.

Goodbye, Lilly. Thank you for trusting in me, for seeing and allowing my potential. For giving me my future.

From Sir.

References

1) *An American Werewolf in London,* 1981. [film]. Directed by John Landis.
2) *Psycho,* 1960. [film]. Directed by Alfred Hitchcock.
3) *Beaches,* 1989. [film]. Directed by Garry Marshall.
4) *Mamma Mia,* 2008. [film]. Directed by Phyllidia Lloyd.
5) *1984,* 1984. [film]. Directed by Michael Radford.
6) *The Wizard of Oz,* 1939. [film]. Directed by Victor Fleming, King Vidor, Mervyn LeRoy, George Cukor, Norman Taurog.
7) *The Lion King,* 1994. [film] Directed by Rob Minkoff, Roger Allers.